OTHER BOOKS
BY JOHN MCNALLY

FICTION

America's Report Card (2006)

The Book of Ralph (2004)

Troublemakers (2000)

ANTHOLOGIES

Who Can Save Us Now?: Brand-New Superheroes and Their Amazing (Short) Stories (coedited with Owen King) (2008)

When I Was a Loser: True Stories of (Barely) Surviving High School (2007)

Bottom of the Ninth: Great Contemporary Baseball Short Stories (2003)

Humor Me: An Anthology of Humor by Writers of Color (2002)

The Student Body: Short Stories About College Students and Professors (2001)

High Infidelity: 24 Great Short Stories About Adultery (1997)

GHOSTS
OF
CHICAGO

by John McNally

jefferson
press

ISBN: 978-0980016437
Library of Congress Catalog Card Number: 2008930321

Book design by David Jones Graphics
Cover design by John McNally
Cover photo by Mary Farmilant

Printed in the United States

Published by Jefferson Press

jefferson
press

P.O. Box 115
Lookout Mountain, TN 37350

CONTENTS

Acknowledgments

STORIES

Notes on the Stories

About the Cover

About the Author

ACKNOWLEDGMENTS

I would like to acknowledge, with gratitude, the editors of the following magazines and anthologies in which some of these stories first appeared: *Columbia: A Journal of Literature and Art* ("Men Who Love Women Who Love Men Who Kill"); *Crazyhorse* ("Love's Latent Defect"); *f magazine* ("The Memoirist"); *Freight Stories* ("Ascension"); *Gargoyle* ("Planetary Danger"); *Make: A Chicago Literary Magazine* ("At the Chateau Marmont, Bungalow 5," "The Goose," "Samsonite," "The Something Something," "Sweetness and the Fridge"); *Passages North* ("Return Policy"); and *Virginia Quarterly Review* ("Contributor's Notes," "Creature Features," "The End is Nothing, the Road is All," "The Immortals," "I See Johnny").

"Creature Features" was reprinted in *Before: Short Stories About Pregnancy From Our Top Writers* (The Overlook Press, 2006); it was also chosen by Stephen King as one of the "100 Other Distinguished Stories" in *Best American Short Stories, 2007.*

"Planetary Danger" was reprinted in *The Best Underground Fiction, Volume One* (Stolen Time Publishing, 2006).

"Remains of the Night" first appeared in *Who Can Save Us Now?: Brand-New Superheroes and Their Amazing (Short) Stories* (Free Press, 2008).

"The Immortals" was a finalist for the 2005 National Magazine Awards.

I would be remiss in not thanking Wake Forest University for awarding me (numerous times) something called the Archie Grant, a much-appreciated funding source for summer research. Special thanks to my friend and colleague, writer Eric G. Wilson, for his support. I would also like to thank Ted Genoways, editor of *Virginia Quarterly Review*, for providing a home for so many of these stories. A huge thanks to David Magee, publisher of Jefferson Press, for giving this book a chance to live on its own. I thank my agent, Jenny Bent, for her fine representation of my work and sound advice.

My wife, Amy Knox Brown, has made each story here infinitely stronger by going over it with a keen editor's eye. She is a hugely talented fiction writer who indulges my wind-baggy first drafts. I take full responsibility for any unnecessary excesses still lingering herein.

*This book is dedicated to the
Fiction Writing Department at Columbia College Chicago,
with gratitude to their faculty, staff, and students for all their
generosity, support, and friendship.*

RETURN POLICY

When Mark Timbers awoke in the middle of the night and opened his front door for some fresh air, he saw through the fog-laden light of the street lamp a dog carrying a cat side-long in its mouth. The cat was dead. The dog, walking toward Mark's house, struggled to keep the cat clenched in its jaws. It was unclear whether or not the dog had killed the cat. It was possible, Mark supposed, that the dog and cat lived together, that the cat had escaped, and that the dog had gone out in search of the lost animal, only to find that it had perished. Even sleepy, barely able to keep his eyes open, Mark didn't consider this to be the most probable scenario. More likely, the dog had found the cat already dead and was bringing it home to its owners as an offering, a bestial expression of gratitude.

In the end, who knew? Life had begun presenting itself to Mark lately as a series of unanswerable questions. Six months ago, his wife of eighteen years had left him, taking only one suitcase full of her belongings. He hadn't heard a word from her since. No messages on their answering machine. No postcards from faraway cities. Nothing. Where did she go? Why did she leave? Other questions bubbled beneath the surface of obvious ones. How long had she wanted to leave? And what was it about him that had inspired her to pack up and go?

The dog stopped in front of Mark's house. The fur on both animals, the live one as well as the dead one, had wilted from the soupy air. Mark wasn't sure of the dog's breed. A Rottweiler with maybe a little German Shepherd mixed in. The dog met Mark's eyes. It arched its neck to get a better grip of the cat, then shook its head several times, growling, as if the cat were a stuffed animal.

Mark shut the door and returned to his bedroom. When he awoke in the morning, he hoped the incident with the dog had been a terrible dream, but an hour later, while drinking coffee and digging through a shoebox full of old receipts, the phone rang. At the sound of the ringer, he spilled coffee on the table.

"Hello?" he said.

"Mark? It's Jimmy. Next door. Hey, you got a cat?"

"No."

"Well, there's a cat on your lawn outside. A dead one."

"Thanks," Mark said. "I'll take care of it."

"Yeah, I wasn't sure if you had one or not. I didn't think so, but I wouldn't have put money on it one way or the other."

"Thanks for calling," Mark said. "I appreciate it."

After hanging up, Mark walked to the living room and opened the front door. The cat's eyes were still open but unfocused. Was this a gift from the dog to Mark? Would Mark understand the gesture if he himself were a dog? Mark, sensing that he was being watched, pivoted abruptly and saw the dog waiting at the corner. It must have been sitting there all night. "What the hell?" Mark whispered. The dog wagged its tail, four slow swipes across the concrete. Satisfied that Mark had returned, the dog stood and turned around, crossing the empty intersection without looking for traffic.

Two months after his wife had left him, Mark Timbers gathered up all their old wedding presents and mailed them back to the friends and family who'd brought them to the church all those years ago. It was a time-consuming chore, but Mark didn't feel in good conscience that he could keep them anymore. Inside each box, he placed a short note: *Sorry but things didn't work out between me and Jennifer. I feel guilty keeping the enclosed. I hope you're still able to get some use out of it. With sincere regret, Mark Timbers.*

Fortunately, Jennifer had kept a detailed list of who had given them what. The Mulcaheys had given them the Sunbeam iron. The Robinsons, the toaster that could accommodate four pieces of bread at once. Gregg Winston, an old college buddy, had purchased bedding from their gift registry. In the unfortunate instance that a gift-giver had died, Mark returned the item to the next of kin. He mailed nearly fifty packages back, and for those who had given money, he sent a check for the amount, plus interest.

He couldn't bring himself to replace any of the things he'd returned, and so his clothes, in need of a good smoothing out, remained wrinkled now. If he wanted toast, he placed the slices of bread on a rack in his oven and used tongs to flip them over. At night, he lay on the mattress without blankets, shivering. In the long history of suffering, Mark really wasn't all that uncomfortable. He'd made no bed of nails for himself. There would be no self-flagellation occurring inside his house. The sacrifices he made were small ones.

On the morning of the dead cat, Mark searched the basement for his shovel. He distinctly remembered it because the handle was too short for his height, and his lower back always pulsed afterward, as if he'd been stabbed with a searing hot spear. He searched all the obvious places. When the shovel failed to materialize, he pulled all the boxes away from the basement wall, but this yielded nothing but ghostly balls of dust and web. There was only one logical answer. His wife, who had taken virtually nothing with her, had taken the shovel. But why?

Outside, Mark dragged the stiff cat by its rear paws around to the back of his house. His next door neighbor, Jimmy, walked from window to window, watching Mark's every move. Jimmy's shades were always up, lights blazing. It was as if the house itself were a living, breathing thing that never slept – a hulking beast of brick and glass that watched Mark's every move.

From what Mark had pieced together, Jimmy had moved to this sleepy college town in the early 1980s but never finished his degree. For twenty years, he'd cobbled together an income from minimum wage work in bars, used record stores, and thrift shops. When he wasn't at work, he stayed home and smoked pot. The town was full of Jimmys, thirty- and forty-something-year-old men who somehow managed, by expending the least amount of energy possible, to remain sheltered and fed. You saw them everywhere, floating through town like shabby superheroes, powerless but oddly indestructible.

After draping a beach towel over the small corpse, Mark stood up and waved at Jimmy. Momentarily frozen in that timeless gesture of a man trying to light a joint – head tilted, eyes almost shut – Jimmy raised his lighter-clutching hand and returned the wave.

Before noon, Mark finally found the receipt he'd spent weeks looking for. It was for a piece of artwork that Mark had given Jennifer for their wedding, an impractically large reproduction of Georges Seurat's famous painting, "A Sunday Afternoon on the Island of La Grande Jatte." Mark had always thought it was too big for any of their walls, but Jennifer loved it and wouldn't hear of taking it down. She had spent one college summer working at the Art Institute in Chicago, where the original was on display, and had wanted a reproduction of it ever since. And so Mark had purchased one at Lockhart's, the last remaining locally-owned department store in town. He'd gone to the mall that day to buy hiking boots but came home with the Seurat instead. Mark's brothers hung it in their living room while he and Jennifer were away on their honeymoon.

But it sat on his floor now, facing the wall – reprimanded.

Mark tucked the receipt in his wallet. He lifted the Seurat and carried it to his pick-up truck. He hoisted it over the truck's side, wincing when it clanged against the bed.

Driving to the mall, Mark considered the possibility of making do without a shovel. Maybe he could use his hands to dig a hole for the cat. Or maybe he could scoop dirt out with the large no-stick pot he used for boiling water. But no: he would be able to go only so deep with those options. He probably wouldn't even be able to dig a shallow grave with his hands. Why had his wife taken, of all things, the shovel?

"Goddamn her," he said. He hit the steering wheel with his palm. "What's she trying to do to me?"

The mall's parking garage was already filling up. It was Saturday, almost time for lunch. Mark dragged the Seurat over the truck's side. He balanced it on the ground before hoisting it up and carrying it toward the mall's entrance. The damned thing was so large he couldn't see where he was walking, and twice he was nearly plowed down by drivers taking the parking garage's corners too fast. When he scraped the door of a parked Mercedes with the sharp corner of the frame, he muttered, "Shit," but kept walking, fearing the extent of the gouge. At the mall entrance, he hit the wheelchair access button and waited for both doors to mechanically open.

Taped to Lockhart's windows were several "Going out of Business!" signs. Other signs announced, "Up to 80% Off!" and "The Ultimate Liquidation Sale!" The part of the store that took returns looked ransacked. Piles of ticketed bras lounged on the counter next to a gutted box for a DVD player. Empty hangers bloomed from shopping bags, and a mannequin, looking more alien than human without clothes, stood guard in the corner, staring at Mark as though silently challenging him.

A woman eating French fries from a grease-stained sack glanced up but said nothing as Mark approached. Her nametag identified her as Justine. She looked about Mark's age, give or take a few years.

"I need to return this," Mark said.

Justine reached into her sack and pulled out a few more fries. She put them in her mouth and chewed slowly. "Don't mind me," she said. "I mean, what're they gonna do? Fire me?" She rolled her eyes. She looked down at the Seurat. "Hey, I like that one. What's it called again?"

"'A Sunday Afternoon at...'"

"That's right, that's right," Justine said.

Mark produced the receipt. Justine picked up a returned halter top and wiped her hands, then took the receipt. She studied it a moment before squinting and holding it closer to her face. "You bought this *when*?"

"Eighteen years ago," Mark said.

"And now you want to return it," she said flatly.

Mark nodded.

Justine laughed. "You're kidding, right? This is a joke?"

"No joke."

Justine took a deep breath. "I was afraid of that," she said. "Like most stores, we have a return policy." She pointed to theirs. It hung behind her – an enormous hand-painted sign. "It's even a generous one, as you'll see. But, sir, we can't take back something you've had for eighteen years."

"This is an extraordinary circumstance," Mark said.

"Mister," Justine said. She gave Mark a tight-lipped smile, nodding. She even shut her eyes. She sighed. "I'll be honest," she said, opening her eyes. "We're closing our doors next week. I'm losing my job. I've *worked* here for eighteen years. I probably *sold* this freaking thing to you."

"May I speak to a manager?"

"A manager," Justine repeated. "Sure. Why the hell not? I'll go get her." Justine left the counter. She took the bag of French fries with her.

Mark waited over fifteen minutes. When it was clear that no one was coming, he retrieved his receipt and lugged the

Seurat back through the store. He looked around for someone exhibiting even the remotest shred of authority, but the new rule of law in the store's remaining days appeared to be anarchy.

The mall was full of running children, mothers with strollers, and sullen teenagers who wouldn't think of moving out of Mark's way. Mark collided with a stationary couple he couldn't see and then banged into an old man who was inexplicably walking backwards from the food court.

As soon as he stepped into the parking garage, someone called out to him. "Hey! You with the painting!"

Mark spun awkwardly around. It was Justine. She was sitting against a wall with the crumpled French fry sack cupped in her palms.

"The manager never came," Mark said.

Justine nodded. "Yeah; I know. You don't have a cigarette, do you?"

"I don't smoke. Sorry."

"What's your name?"

"Mark."

"Well, I was thinking, Mark. I'll just buy the damned thing from you. What do you say?"

Mark set the frame down. His arms were starting to kill him. "I don't know," he said. "The point is to return it."

"Don't take this question personally, okay, but have you quit taking your medication?" Justine tossed the crumpled sack toward a wastebasket but missed it by a good yard. "Oops. Hey, listen. I'll give you my number. Mull it over. Chew on it. All right? But don't think we're gonna take that back and give you a refund. You're deluding yourself if you think *that'll* happen." She reached into her pocket, pulled out a napkin, and said, "Got a pen?"

Mark, knowing he didn't have a pen, patted himself down. He shrugged and sighed, miming futility. He was about to leave when Justine touched the side of her head and then removed a pen from behind her ear.

"I knew I had one somewhere," she said and smiled.

Mark took a detour on his way home. At least once a day, he made a point of crossing the intersection of Oak and Illinois. He wanted to view it in every possible weather condition: rain; dry and gray; snowy; or, like today, clear and sunny. He wanted to see every possible angle of shadow, every blind spot, every conceivable arrangement of pedestrian and auto. He expected, he supposed, for that day eight years ago to recreate itself, for the same configuration of cars and child to appear. Maybe then Mark would finally be able to understand what precisely had happened.

It had been raining that particular day, rain that would later cause local meteorologists to warn of flash flooding, and Paul Timbers, Mark's son, was wearing a yellow rain slicker with the hood up to keep from getting wet. He was nine. He collected stamps and made everyone he knew scissor theirs off envelopes. His favorite was an old ten cent "First Man on the Moon" stamp that featured the drawing of an astronaut climbing down the ladder of his lunar capsule. In the background loomed Earth.

On the far south side of town lived a man named Terrance Ipsley, who worked at the Tru-Value on Market Street. He was forty-four years old and had never been pulled over for a moving violation. He was on his way to work that morning when he ran the stop sign at the corner of Oak and Illinois and hit Paul, knocking him clear off the road. Eyewitnesses, mostly other children walking to school, claimed that Paul was still alive after the accident, but he was not alive by the time either Mark or Jennifer could get to St. Luke's. With so much bleeding in the brain, there wasn't much the doctors could do. The brain continued to swell, and Paul died.

That was eight years ago. Jennifer, who had to be se-
dated for the weeks that followed, eventually carried on as
though nothing had happened. She wouldn't talk about Paul;
she wouldn't go to his grave or acknowledge his birthday; she
wouldn't revisit the site of the accident. Mark, on the other
hand, couldn't stay away. Hadn't they told Paul to look both
ways? Had they not stressed the importance of safety? How
could his death not be the result of Mark's failure as a parent?
Mark could no longer remember when it became a daily part
of his routine, but not long after Paul's death he began driving
out of his way to cross that intersection. Some days he wasn't
even planning to go there, and yet there he would be, like a
somnambulist behind the wheel, a man being pulled by forces
beyond his control, driving up Oak while slowly approaching
Illinois. Terrance's story never added up. Here was a man who
took the exact same route to work every day. Surely he would
remember, if by instinct alone, to stop at the intersection. And
yet, on that particular day, he didn't stop. Why?

Back home, Mark parked the truck and carried the Seurat inside. Just as the frame touched the floor, the phone rang.
It was Jimmy, his neighbor.

"Dude. You want to come over? Watch TV or something?"

"No thanks, Jimmy."

"I've got cable. Whatever you want to watch. You make
the call."

"I appreciate it, but I'm pretty much in for the night."

"All right, man." There was a pause. Then: "Hey. How's
that cat?"

"Still dead."

"Bummer," Jimmy said and hung up.

Mark showered for the second time that day. He'd
worked up a mean sweat carrying the Seurat back and forth,

and he thought he could smell vestiges of the food court on his clothes. Still clinging to the shower wall was one of Jennifer's hairs. It was long and squiggly, and looked, from a certain angle, like the feeble attempt of a child writing cursive for the first time. When Mark initially discovered it months ago, he had aimed the shower head directly at it, but the hair wouldn't budge. He wanted to believe that a supernatural force kept it there, but it was probably just soap scum. Mark could have eased his nail under the hair and pried it free, but he feared, having done that, that he wouldn't be able to dispose of it. And then what?

After his shower, Mark called Justine.

"Do you still want to buy the print?" he asked.

"Where do you live?"

Mark gave her his address. "Bring a shovel," he said, "if you've got one."

"Oh," she said. "It's *that* kind of party. All right then. I'll add 'shovel' to my list."

Justine arrived sooner than Mark expected. She, too, drove a pick-up truck, but hers was smaller and older. A long, diagonal crack ran across the windshield, and she was missing a headlight. She had changed into jeans and a T-shirt. She must have had pins in her hair earlier because it was wild now, even slightly exotic. She took a shovel from the front seat and lifted it into the air at the sight of Mark like some kind of medieval warrior greeting. Clutched in her other hand was a bottle of wine.

"Lockhart's told me not to come back. Apparently, they have enough people to wrap up their goddamned going-out-of-business sale."

"You're unemployed then," Mark said, walking toward her.

"I'm liberated," she said. "*Tomorrow* I'm unemployed."

She handed Mark the shovel. "What are we digging up?"

"We're not digging anything up," he said. "We're burying a dead cat."

"Where is it?" she asked.

They walked around to the back of the house. Mark could see Jimmy hoisting himself off his sofa, where he'd apparently been watching TV, and then following them from window to window. When they reached the cat, Jimmy lit a joint.

"What's its name?" Justine asked.

Mark stuck the tip of the spade into his lawn then forced it deeper into the ground with his foot. "I don't know," he said.

Justine said, "You don't look the cat type."

"I'm not." Sweat had already broken out across Mark's forehead, and his shirt, normally loose, was starting to cling to him. He paused shoveling and asked, "What're you going to do about work?"

"Good question," she said. "Last check is in two weeks. Rent's due in three." She smiled. "Got any leads?"

Mark shook his head.

"What do *you* do?" she asked.

"I work in Admissions at the university."

"Good for you," she said. Mark had expected sarcasm, but she sounded sincere, maybe even a little impressed.

Mark was about to explain what it was he did when Jimmy started knocking on his window. He held up a finger, urging them to hold on. A moment later, Jimmy was standing among them, holding a flashlight.

"It's getting dark," Jimmy said. He tucked the flashlight under his arm and re-lit his joint. He passed it to Justine, who took a hit.

"Here," Justine said, nudging Mark.

Mark shook his head. "Thanks, but I'm fine."

"Just take a fucking hit," Justine said, and Jimmy smiled.

Mark pinched the joint away from Justine and took a hit.

He hadn't smoked pot since college, and the first wisp to touch his lungs felt like battery acid. He leaned against the shovel and coughed until his eardrums hurt.

Jimmy said, "Don't drop it, dude."

Justine crouched next to the cat and stroked its stiff fur. She said, "To cure illness in a family, wash the patient and throw the water over a cat. Then drive the cat out of doors, and it will take the illness with it."

Jimmy said, "Whoa! Where the hell did that come from?"

"It's a superstition," Justine said. "You want to hear another one?"

"No," Jimmy said, laughing. "You're freaking me out! Is she freaking you out, Mark?" He took another hit from the joint and, in a strained voice still full of smoke, said, "She's freaking *me* out!"

Inside Mark's house, Jimmy and Justine sat on the floor and flipped through Mark's old record albums. The cat was buried. Justine had even gone so far as to assemble a grave marker out of stones and chipped glass she collected up and down the street. After going inside Mark's house, the three of them smoked another joint and finished off Justine's wine.

"I can't believe you still own *albums*," Jimmy said. "You're so '70s. I love it!"

"Look," Justine said, holding one up. "The Jackson Five. Can we play this one?"

Mark nodded then excused himself. The way the house had been built, he had to walk through his pitch-black bedroom to reach the bathroom. He sat on the edge of the tub and put his head in his hands. He was going to be sick, he thought. Smoking pot! Drinking wine! What the hell was he thinking? He looked up and saw the squiggly strand of hair on the shower stall. With a little imagination, it almost looked like the word 'overall.' But what would that word mean in this context? Was the message the first word of a summation? But summing up what? His marriage? His life?

When the nausea finally passed, he returned to his bedroom and clicked on a small reading lamp. He kept a phonebook in the bed-side table's drawer, same as a motel. He searched the white pages until he found him: *Ipsley, Terrance*. The phonebook was an objective document. It did not say *killed child* next to Terrance's name. But who knew what the other people listed in this book had done? This single page probably represented the full spectrum of earthly woes, from marital transgressions to torture. Mark picked up the receiver and dialed Terrance's number. The phone rang three times.

A man said, "Yellow."

"*Hello*?" Mark asked as if to clarify the greeting.

No one said anything. The volume on the man's TV, which was playing some indiscernible sporting event, finally lowered.

"Terrance, please," Mark said.

"You got 'im."

"This is Mark."

"Mark? Mark *who*?"

"Mark Timbers."

"Mark Timbers?" There was a pause. "Do I know you?" There was another, longer pause. Then, "Oh God. Yeah; yeah. Mark Timbers."

"Do you have a minute?"

"Sure, sure," Terrance said. "I'm glad you called, actually."

"Good," Mark said. "This is okay then?"

"Absolutely," Terrance said. "You have no idea how many times I was going to call you, but then I'd chicken out. It'll be nine years in March, right? March the tenth. Nine years," Terrance said, sighing. "Where does the time go, Mark? Nine years. Good Lord."

◎

It was after midnight before Mark and Terrance finished their call. They had talked for so long that Mark had sobered up. The phone call had been the right thing to do, but he was drained now – drained to the point of nearly-paralytic exhaustion. He needed a glass of ice water, a few aspirin, maybe even a bite to eat, but when he forced himself to walk the few feet it took to reach the living room and saw Justine and Jimmy making out, he decided to call it a night. He crawled back onto his mattress and curled into a ball to keep warm.

At two thirty in the morning, he opened his eyes. It was the same time he had gotten up the night before and witnessed the dog carrying the dead cat in its mouth. Why had he been awake in the first place? Why had he needed fresh air? Would the dog have continued walking if Mark hadn't gone to his door and looked outside?

Mark didn't open his eyes again until morning, and he did so only because he could hear people outside talking. He wasn't certain, but he thought he heard someone say his name.

In the living room, Justine and Jimmy were crouched together and peering out the front window. Jimmy turned back to Mark. "You've got to see this, dude."

"What is it?" Mark asked.

"I don't know, but they're looking for *you*."

Mark took one step then paused. There was something about where he was standing in relation to Justine and Jimmy that reminded him of his conversation with Terrance. There was a couple, Terrance had said, standing off to the side of the intersection. The rain was coming down so hard that the images he saw were indistinct, fuzzy. "Splashes of color" was how he described it. He saw this couple, and for a second, through the blur of rain, he intuited something about the way they were standing, and he was certain one of them was about to do harm to the other. It was a flash through his brain, maybe not even a fully-formed thought, more of an impulse, really. He had taken his foot off the gas and begun riding the brake in order to get a better look.

Mark, walking toward his front door, tried putting himself into his son's mind, seeing the scene through his eyes now – a nine-year-old boy crossing the intersection, walking to school. Maybe he was thinking about his friends and what they would be doing later that day. Maybe he was thinking about a homework assignment he had failed to complete. Maybe he was thinking about his stamps – the astronaut putting the first footprint on the moon. The hood on his slicker would have been up, tunneling his view. As Mark Timbers walked in the general direction of the surrogate couple, Justine and Jimmy, he saw how it all could have happened: the slicker's hood creating a cocoon for Paul; Terrance, who'd argued with his wife the night before, distracted by the wrong thing.

Mark opened the front door. Outside, on his lawn, stood several people he vaguely recognized but couldn't place. Each was holding something different – a toaster, a set of silverware, an iron, goblets. There were at least a few dozen people; their cars were angled up and down the street. Mark stepped outside for a better look. "Oh my God," he said. These men and women, they had all been guests at his wedding, and now they were here holding the gifts that Mark had worked so hard to return.

Mitchell said, "You okay, buddy?"

Roscoe Robinson said, "I called Larry to see if he'd heard from you, and then Larry called Pam."

"You had us worried," Mitchell added.

Pamela Garrett, who had been the maid of honor, walked up the front steps and kissed Mark on the cheek. She was holding a sterling silver serving tray. "It's cold out here," she whispered into his ear. "You should invite us inside."

"Absolutely," he said, and then he called out, "Come on

in! Please! Come in and make yourself at home!"

One by one, Mark greeted his old friends, shaking their hands or hugging them. Ginger Selman, whom Mark had not seen since the wedding, brought a shopping bag full of bagels and cream cheese. Harry Lindquist carried in two thermoses full of coffee. Before going inside and joining them, Mark saw a flicker of movement out the corner of his eye. It was Jimmy and Justine; they were inside Jimmy's house now. They must have sneaked out Mark's back door, stepping over the cat's still-fresh grave. Mark wanted to wave them over – he wanted them to meet everyone – but neither one noticed him. Justine sat on Jimmy's couch and stretched her arms out, draping them around the shoulders of two imaginary friends, while Jimmy walked from window to window, pulling down the shades, as if the house were finally – mercifully – closing its eyes.

THE GOOSE

(Frazier Thomas, 1918-1985)

You host a kid's TV show. The premise is simple: A goose talks to you. The goose, whose head is filled with some-one's hand, thinks he's the King of the United States. He wears a gold crown. His beak, long and yellow, clacks and clacks, but there are no words, there are never any words. The goose whispers to a rabbit who then whispers to you. You mollify the goose by pretending that you're his prime minister. You wear a royal jacket with official-looking pins and such. You're a team, you and the goose. But his eyes, they look like dots of licorice, and you can't help thinking that he's always staring at you. Even when the hand is slipped out of his head and the goose is lying prone, the eyes look pleadingly in your direc-tion: *Don't leave*, the eyes say.

You take the Addison Street bus home. You don't have to; you're a celebrity, after all. Kids see you but don't believe it's really you. You sit behind the driver. In winter, in Chicago, there are days it's so cold that your face, that thin layer of skin, feels as though it's searing itself to your skull. You can almost feel the two fusing together, skin and bone. Other passengers – even the middle-aged, even the infirm – steal glances as they walk past you, the plume of air from their mouths still vis-ible: *Is it really him?* You look out the window. You think that you see his eyes through the snow, two black dots, but no: It's just an optical illusion, a trick of the eye that always happens when it's snowing like this, when the snow melts as soon as it

touches the window, and when it drips down the glass in er-
ratic, zig-zaggy streaks.

The goose waits each morning for the arm that gives him
body, the hand that fills his head. Then he waits for you, his
trusty compatriot. The second you walk onto the set, the goose
starts to clack. There's so much he wants to tell you, so much
that's happened since the last time he saw you. The goose talks
to the rabbit, the rabbit whispers to you, and you play to the
camera and to the kids at home, telling them what the goose
has told the rabbit. There are cartoons, too. *The Mighty Hercules. Bucky and Pepito.* This is your down-time, this is when you
and the goose finally get to relax. From where you sit, in front
of a set that looks like the balcony of a miniature castle, you
can't see the arm slipping out of the goose. All you ever see is
the goose going slack, its heavy head with its sheet-metal beak
tilting, as if the downy neck has been broken, the goose dead.
But the eyes, pitch-black, never close. Or is it that they never
open?

You have another show, too. It airs once a week. Sundays.
You introduce movies based on books, classics for the family.
It's just you sitting in a fake library. It's quiet. No clacking, no
whispering. No rabbit to interpret. No castle. Just books. And
a ship in a bottle. But on the wall is a portrait of the goose. It's
only a silly painting, you tell yourself. But still: You feel him
behind you. You sometimes stumble over words and have to
tape the segment again. People who work with you call you a
perfectionist, but is that really it? What is a perfectionist, really, but a nervous man who's afraid of making mistakes?

You're the one who edits the movies, those family classics, so that they can fit conveniently into the time-slot. This
is work you enjoy. There are times you think this is what you
were meant to do. You're good at it: trimming away the footage, piecing together a film so that it still makes sense, the heart
of the story intact. You work alone until late at night, and then
you take the Addison Street bus home. The bus driver knows

who you are, but he never calls special attention to you. He nods or says hello, but he doesn't ask you about your work, and he never asks for an autograph for his kids, though you know he has three: two boys and a girl.

The truth is, you never look entirely at ease in front of the camera. You're overweight and self-conscious about it. Each year, you gain a little more weight, and each year, you need a new suit-jacket, new slacks. You have a double-chin, and it eventually begins to sag. Here you are, a fifty-something year old man, surrounded by puppets, and you think, *This is my life, it's not so bad.* You know, in fact, that it could be worse. You see all those men and women who get on the bus, the ones who, yawning billowy streams of breath, work nine-to-five factory jobs, or who, kneeling before strangers, help fit them with too-stiff shoes fresh out of the box. *It's not so bad,* you tell yourself, and you see the way they look at you – with envy, as though looking at a man who has everything he has ever wanted. So, then, why do you ride the bus?

Eventually, though, things change. You are lured to another show – the *clown* show – and though it's more popular than anything you've ever done, more popular than any show of its kind anywhere, you understand right away that it's not a good fit for you. There's a live audience; most of the show is adlibbed. Worst of all, the goose is forced to take a backseat to the clowns. Occasionally, the castle set is rolled out, the goose comes alive, the beak clacks, but it's not the same. Where's the nuance? Where's the silence? Whispering doesn't work when there's a studio full of kids waiting for the famous clowns, the thrown pie, the sprayed bottle of seltzer. You'll shoulder on, of course; you have no choice, really. But you miss talking to that damned goose. And he to you.

The end comes in a hallway, at work. You collapse. Later, a janitor finds you. An ambulance is called, you are rushed to the hospital, but too much blood has already whispered through your brain. Two days later, you die.

The goose is deposed now, in exile behind glass in a museum. Some of the older men and women still recognize him, but the kids don't. *I used to be King of the United States,* he wants to tell them, but what would they care? They *don't* care. It's absurd to them: a deluded goose, a hand-puppet. They knock on the glass. The younger ones – and sometimes ones who aren't so young – press their mouths up against the glass and blow. A few even lick it. And so the goose waits. He no longer needs the arm, the hand. Something – he's not sure what – holds him up, but his beak won't move. He waits for you to come and get him. He wants to know where you are, to know when you're coming back, but when people who know these answers find themselves around the goose, they are silent. No one tells him anything anymore. No one ever mentions your name. No one has the heart.

CREATURE FEATURES

In April of 1971, my parents sat me down at the dining room table and delivered the horrifying news: I would no longer be the only child in the family.

I said nothing. Rain pounded our windows, and our lights blinked off and on. When lightning zapped a nearby tree, I jumped a good inch off my chair. It was the first serious thunderstorm of the year.

Mom did all the talking. According to her, she was already four months along. Dad, who normally did all the talking, pulled a napkin free of its holder and dabbed at the sheen of sweat across his upper lip. He looked from one corner of the ceiling to the other, as if anticipating a leak to start any second. He was a roofer; a leak was something he could fix.

"So?" my mother asked. "What do you think, Timmy?"

"Huh!" I said, nodding. I was eight years old. The only things I cared about were monsters. Movie monsters, to be precise. I wouldn't talk to anyone unless they had something to say about monsters. If the word *monster* didn't come up within the first few seconds of a conversation, I quit listening. Monsters was the only acceptable topic – the only topic, in fact, worthy of my undivided attention. When my father brought home a schnauzer from the pound, I named him Dr. Jekyll. When he brought home a parrot in a cage, I named him Quasi-

modo. Whenever Mrs. V., our neighbor, knocked on our door,
I'd open it slowly and, in a thick Eastern European accent, say,
"I bid you welcome." Weekends, when my father took me to
the dusty Twin Drive-In flea market, I spent hours flipping
through boxes of musty monster magazines with titles like
Castle of Frankenstein, Mad Monsters, and *Fantastic Monsters of
the Films.* I searched for the magazines that cost a nickel, since
those were the only ones I could afford.

My mother wasn't talking about monsters, so I felt no
obligation to listen to what she was saying.

"I have to admit," she said, "you're taking the news aw-
fully well."

I nodded. I smiled. I imagined biting her neck, turning
into a bat, and flying out our kitchen window.

We lived in a two-bedroom apartment in Chicago. Most
nights I fell asleep on the couch with the TV still on. Freight
trains chugged behind our building all day long, and the Stevenson Expressway hovered above our third-floor window.
My parents complained about the noise, but I didn't notice.
It was like living in a valley except that there were no valleys
in Chicago. There were only overpasses and underpasses. We
lived under an overpass. I could climb up to the expressway
and motion for the semi drivers to honk their horns, or I could
stand by the railroad tracks that ran below and yell for the
conductor to throw chalk. Why train conductors carried chalk
with them I didn't know, but occasionally a huge chunk would
come sailing toward me, and I would then spend my afternoon
drawing peace signs on every Dumpster in my neighborhood.
What more could I ask for?

The highlight of my week, however, was Saturday night
at ten-thirty when "Creature Features" aired on channel nine.
"Creature Features" was like any other station's late-night

movie show, except that it starred a monster. Since our tiny black-and-white TV had pretty bad reception, I would start fiddling with the antennas a full half-hour beforehand, twisting them back and forth, then toward me and away. In desperation, I sometimes wrapped a sheet of aluminum foil around them. Eventually the snowy images cleared and recognizable objects came into focus. With my parents sound asleep, I turned out the lights, settled into the couch, and, keeping the volume low, waited for "Creature Features" to begin.

In truth, "Creature Features" wasn't much of a show. There was no host; there weren't any contests. Except for the opening sequence – a series of short clips featuring all of my favorite monsters, including Dracula, who bared his teeth, and the Wolf Man, who loped angrily through a layer of waist-high fog – there wasn't anything more to "Creature Features" than the monster movie itself. But a movie with a monster in it was enough for me.

The monsters reminded me of certain groups of kids at school. There would always be the popular ones – the Frankensteins, the Wolf Men, the Draculas of the playground – and then, off in the corner, the less popular ones – your Creatures from the Black Lagoon, your Mummies, your Invisible Men. I loved all the monsters, but my hope was always to spend time with the popular ones, and so my heart sunk, if only momentarily, whenever the Mummy came on, much as it sunk each time Raymond Gertz, with his sagging pants and bad breath, joined me on the blacktop to see why I hadn't come over to his house lately. I liked Raymond – he was okay – but he was no Dracula.

I usually fell asleep right around the time the monster started running amuck. By morning, the TV would be turned off, my father'd be smoking a cigarette at the dining room table, and my mom would be in the kitchen making pancakes and bacon. The apartment was laid out in such a way that I could see from one room to the next without having to budge. There was Mom, there was Dad, and here I was on the couch: the complete family unit.

On this particular Saturday night, while my father prepared himself for bed (preparations that included, among other things, plucking long hairs that had appeared suddenly from the cave of a nostril) my mother plopped down next to me on the couch. She ruffled my hair and pulled me close to her. I had been trying to read a monster magazine in preparation for "Creature Features," but I couldn't concentrate with all of Mom's squeezing and touching.

"When the baby arrives," she said, "you two are going to have to share a room. You realize that, don't you?"

"What baby?" I asked.

Mom sighed. "*You* know what baby," she said. "We talked about it the other day. Remember?"

I shrugged. I folded open my magazine, creased it down the middle, and held it out for my mother to look at. "Iron-on monsters!" I said, pointing to the advertisement.

My mother wouldn't even glance down. "You don't need iron-on monsters," she said.

I read the description aloud, as if I hadn't heard her. "*Any two monsters, one dollar.*"

"You don't need iron-on monsters," she repeated.

I shut the magazine. I got up and put a leash on Dr. Jekyll. "Come on, boy," I said. "Let's go for a walk."

Dr. Jekyll sniffed the same spot outside but wouldn't do anything. "Do something," I begged. "*Please.*" I was the only one who ever defended Dr. Jekyll. Whenever he messed in the house, I blamed it on his alter-ego: Mr. Hyde.

The last time Dr. Jekyll made a mess, Mom and I stood outside the sad circle of pee on the rug and stared down at it.

"That wasn't Dr. Jekyll," I said. "Mr. Hyde did that."

Mom shook her head. "Dr. Jekyll. Mr. Hyde. It doesn't make a difference to me. I'm going to ring his little neck the next time he messes inside."

I gave the leash a gentle tug now and said, "Why won't you do anything?"

Mrs. V., who was retired and lived across the hall from us, wobbled over with her cane. She was blind, but she always knew where I was. According to her, I talked too much. "I can hear you through my walls," she'd told me once. "You never stop talking."

Today, Mrs. V. said, "How's that dog of yours?"

"He's okay," I said. "He won't pee, though."

"How's your mom?" she asked.

"Mom?" I said. "She pees all the time."

Mrs. V. pursed her lips. She didn't like me, but I didn't like her, either, so it didn't really bother me that she didn't like me. She said, "I hear you're going to have a baby brother or a baby sister soon."

"Really?" I said. "I haven't heard that."

Mrs. V. stared in my general direction for a good fifteen seconds before turning and caning her way back toward the apartment building. I finally gave up on Dr. Jekyll and led him back upstairs. I didn't want to miss the opening to "Creature Features." Mom and Dad were already asleep; their light was out, and the door was shut. I gave Dr. Jekyll a corn chip.

Tonight's movie was one of my favorites, *The Wolf Man*. It was the story of Larry Talbot who, after years away from home, returns to Europe and falls in love with a girl, only to be bitten by a werewolf and then, once he turns into a werewolf himself, is beaten to death by his father.

One thing I loved about monster movies was how different everything in them was from my life. I lived in an apartment building with my mom and dad; Larry Talbot lived in a castle with his father. When the lights went out, my parents lit a few squatty candles; the Talbots owned fancy candelabras. When my neighbors were angry, they swore at each other and made threats before slamming their doors shut; in monster movies, when people were angry, everyone gathered in the town square, and then they hunted down whatever they were mad at, using guns, dogs, and torches. *The Wolf Man* had all of this and more – spooked horses in the fog; fortune-telling gypsies; walking canes with silver wolf-head handles.

If you watched enough monster movies, you started noticing how one movie interlocked with another. Lon Chaney, Jr.'s father was Lon Chaney, who played Quasimodo in *The Hunchback of Notre Dame*. Lon Chaney, Jr. played Larry Talbot, who turns into the Wolf Man. Claude Rains, who played Lon Chaney, Jr.'s father in *The Wolf Man*, also played the Invisible Man. Bela Lugosi, who played Bela the Gypsy in *The Wolf Man*, was the original Dracula. From where I stood, the monster community looked like one big happy family.

When Larry Talbot's father started talking about the legend of the werewolf being nothing more than a myth about the nature of good and evil in every man's soul, I pulled the blanket up to my chin. Dr. Jekyll hopped onto the couch with me, curling up and pressing himself against my belly, and together we watched mere men turn into wolves. "Look," I said, nudging Dr. Jekyll when Larry Talbot changed into the Wolf Man. "That's one of your relatives," I said. "What do you think about that?"

I opened my eyes. I sat up and looked around. "What was *that?*" I asked, blinking. A loud thud, in the vicinity of my head, had woken me.

"I got these at a garage sale yesterday," Dad said. "Left them in my trunk overnight. Almost forgot about them." He pointed with his cigarette to a stack of four medical encyclopedias that smelled like they'd been fished out of Lake Michigan.

Mold dotted their spines. "Fifty cents," he said. "Not bad."

I blinked some more, trying to focus. "Thanks," I said. I was afraid to ask – I didn't want to hurt his feelings – but I decided to ask anyway. "What are they *for?*"

"In case you wanted to, you know, read about what your mother's going through. It's all there under 'p.' Or maybe it's under 'b.' I'm not sure. I didn't look."

"'P,'" I said.

"Or 'b,'" he added. "You know. For *birth.*"

"Where's Mom?" I asked. "What's for breakfast?"

"I took your mother out this morning. A treat." When he saw that my feelings were hurt, he added, "We didn't want to wake you." He turned away from the intensity of my glaring. He said, "I dropped her off at Mary Rudolph's."

The Rudolphs lived around the corner. I was in love with Eileen Rudolph, who was two years older than me and epileptic. She liked monsters, too.

After Dad left, I searched the apartment for a pair of gloves so I could open one of the books without actually having to touch it, but all I found were big, puffy winter gloves. I put them on, anyway. Turning pages with such huge gloves proved nearly impossible. Instead of finding the entry for *pregnancy*, I ended up at *psoriasis*. "A common immune-mediated chronic skin disease," it said, "that comes in different forms and varying levels of severity." On a glossy page next to the definition was a color photo of a woman's face with red patchy spots all over it.

"Ugh!" I said and shut the book.

Later, bored, I picked up one of my monster magazines and examined, at great length, the face of Lon Chaney as Quasimodo in *The Hunchback of Notre Dame.* One eye was white and kind of bulged out. His cheeks were abnormally puffy. Dirty, crooked teeth erupted from his down-turned mouth. Quasimodo, I concluded, probably had psoriasis, but by the look of things, psoriasis was the least of his problems.

I held the photo up to the bird cage and said to the parrot inside, "Look. This is who you're named after. What do you think?"

When my mother came home from the grocery store, she wrinkled her nose at the encyclopedias and said, "P. U.! What garbage can did you find those in?"

"Dad bought them for fifty cents," I said. "Not bad," I added.

Mom rested her twined fingers over her belly. "Is there anything about pregnancy in there?" she asked, smiling.

I shrugged. I opened the book to the photo of the woman with psoriasis. "You don't have *this*, do you?"

She shook her head.

I shut the book and pulled a monster magazine from my back pocket. I showed her some of the other things I could order from the back pages, but it didn't matter what I showed her – "Monster Notebook Binders," "Punch-out Monster Masks," or the "Frankenstein Target Game" – she always came to the same conclusion: I didn't need it.

"Okie doke," I said. I put the leash on Dr. Jekyll. "Come on, boy. Let's go outside."

Eileen Randolph was the only girl I knew who faithfully watched "Creature Features." When I biked over to her house Sunday night to ask her what she thought about *The Wolf Man*, she raised her hands up like paws, bared her teeth, and growled at me.

"So you liked it?" I asked.

She growled again, exposing her wolf-man-like underbite, and nodded.

"Me, too," I said.

When she finally transformed back into herself, she looked like she was going to cry. "It was so sad at the end, though," she said.

"I guess," I said. "But he *was* a monster, you know. You can't let monsters run loose."

"Maybe not," Eileen said. And then she did the very thing I'd hoped she wouldn't do: she stared intensely into my eyes. Whenever she did this, I had to look away. I didn't want to tell her that I was in love with her, but I was. She wore her hair really long, like Susan Dey in *The Partridge Family*, and she wore necklaces strung with candy. Sometimes when I was talking to her, she'd lift the string of candy up to her mouth and take a bite. It killed me every time.

"When's your Mom due?" she asked.

"Due?" I said. "Due how?"

"When's she having her baby?"

"What baby?" I asked.

Eileen punched my arm. She was strong for a girl, and whenever she punched me, I ended up with a dark bruise the next day. "*You* know what baby," she said.

"If I knew," I said, "I'd tell you, but I don't, so I can't."

"When are we going to kiss?" she asked. Kissing was Eileen's new favorite subject. Before that, it had been God. Before that, frogs. She'd been putting a lot of pressure on me lately to kiss her, but so far I had managed to wiggle out of it. She whispered into my ear, "I'm epileptic. I could die any minute, so we should kiss."

Whenever Eileen started mixing kissing and dying together, I clammed up. Some days I would start picking at a scab on my knee or elbow, or I'd simply change the subject and talk about monsters she might not have heard of, like Nosferatu or Mothra, but today I decided to take action. I straddled my bike and started pedaling as fast as I could.

"Where are you going?" Eileen yelled after me.

"Away from you!" I yelled back without turning around.

◎

Weeks went by before I finally broke down and opened the encyclopedia to the part about pregnancy. The first section began with three see-through pages. What you saw, with all three pages together, was an illustration of a pregnant woman wearing a blue maternity blouse and white pants. She looked like a grown-up and pregnant Jane from the *Dick and Jane* books at school, but when I peeled back the first see-through page, Jane was totally naked.

"Wow!" I said. Her belly was gigantic, and her belly button was poking way out. I wanted to keep looking but didn't want to get caught staring at a naked pregnant woman, even one in an encyclopedia, so I quickly turned to the final see-through page, which showed the inside of her belly, where a sleepy, drunk-looking baby floated around.

My heart continued to thump hard. I wiped the sweat from my palms onto my thighs. A few pages later I found a black-and-white photo that looked like a scene from the scariest monster movie ever: a small but slimy melon was popping out of the top of someone's bushy, split-open head. I brought the book close to my eyes, then held it away, hoping everything would come into focus. When I still couldn't make any sense out of it, I read the caption: "A newborn baby passing through the mother's vaginal canal." I screamed and threw the book.

Mom rushed into the living room. "What happened? Did Dr. Jekyll bite you?" At the mention of his name, Dr. Jekyll's tail started thumping.

"No! I'm fine." I tried catching my breath.

"If you're fine, why did you scream?"

"I didn't scream," I said.

She narrowed her eyes. "You're an odd one. Do you know that?" Then she looked beyond me, out the window behind my head. "Look at the moon, Timmy," she said, pointing. "It's so huge."

The moon, like an old movie, was always in black-and-white. I cleared my throat. "Even a man who is pure in heart and says his prayers by night may become a wolf when the wolfbane blooms and the autumn moon is bright." This was what everyone had told Larry Talbot in *The Wolf Man* before he turned into a wolf himself.

Mom stared at me for so long, I worried that a pentagram – the mark of the werewolf – had appeared on my forehead, but then she leaned toward me and kissed my cheek. "Nighty night," she said.

"Night," I replied.

The following Saturday, my father took me to the drive-in's flea market. The sellers, who parked their vehicles next to cast-iron poles that held the heavy speakers, displayed goods on either fold-out card tables or blankets spread over the gravel. My father liked to get there early to haggle before the noon crowd showed up. Noon crowds, according to my father, were the worst. "They're not shoppers," he said. "They're browsers. All they do is get in your way."

Week after week, I was stunned by the junk that people had the nerve to put out to sell: dolls missing heads, tools fuzzy with rust, an Etch-a-Sketch without knobs.

"If you see that Dr. Spock book," my father said today, "let me know. Your mother loved that book when she was pregnant with you, but I don't know what happened to it. I might have thrown it out."

I'd had no idea that Mom was a *Star Trek* fan. I was the only one who ever turned it on to watch. "*Mr.* Spock," I said for clarification.

"*Mr.* Spock. *Dr.* Spock. Whatever. Just don't spend more than a nickel on it."

Later, while digging through a deep box, I found a sci-fi magazine with Leonard Nimoy on the cover. I held it up and showed it to my dad.

"Look!" I said. "Mr. Spock!"

Dad nodded; he wasn't impressed.

"You don't want it?" I asked.

"Why would I want it?"

"For Mom," I said.

Dad shook his head, and I tossed it back into the box.

When we got home and I saw Mom, I raised my hand and gave her the *Star Trek* greeting. "Live long and prosper," I said.

Mom smiled. "What a sweet thing to say," she said. "I hope you live long and prosper, too, honey."

The bigger my mother grew, the less desire I had to crack open the medical encyclopedia and find out what was going to happen next. The less I knew, the better. The photo of the kid with the slimy head popping out of his mother had made me want to believe that nothing like that was going to happen to anyone – *ever*. But there were worse thoughts. I tried pushing them out of my brain, but the scariest of them – that *I* had once been that slimy-headed kid – kept returning. And once I started thinking about myself as the slimy-headed kid in the photo, a thousand more questions followed: How was it possible that I had once been *inside my mother?* How had I managed to breathe while squeezing myself out? Why couldn't I remember any of it?

It was all too disturbing to think about, and every time a new question popped into my head, I'd start walking for blocks and blocks, zombie-like, wondering how everything had gone so wrong so fast. I had always been a good boy, the sort of boy that women in grocery stores commented upon, and at a very young age, three or four, I knew how to feign shyness, how to duck my head at compliments, how to look at my shoes, how to twist my feet ever so slightly inward and tap the tips together, a kind of Morse Code that women – mothers, especially – intuited as gestures of a modest boy. "Oh, *look* at him," they would say, and I would clutch the bottom hem of my mother's blouse and, wide-eyed, give it an almost imperceptible tug, further cementing public opinion that I was such a *cute little boy*.

But those days were gone.

When Jerry Stroka showed me the final card of his *Partridge Family* trading card collection – the much-coveted "Road to Albuquerque"– I ripped it in half and gave it back to him. I expected Jerry to punch me, but he didn't. He broke into tears, his face as raw and open as a sliced tomato, and he took off running.

When Joey Rizzo showed me his can of Silly String, I took it from him, shook the can for a good half-minute, the way my father shook cans of spray paint, and then I sprayed Joey's face. When I was done, Joey looked like someone had thrown a huge plate of foam spaghetti at his head.

"I'm blind!" he yelled, clawing at his face. "I can't see!"

What I did, I did without emotion. I felt no malice toward these boys; I felt no jealousy or rage. The sad truth was, I felt nothing – nothing at all. Something inside me was happening. I was becoming a different boy, and there was nothing I could do about it.

"Timothy O'Reilly," Mom said before I could shut the door. "Guess who just called me."

I looked down at my mother's belly and then back up at her. I shrugged. Mrs. V. was smoking a cigarette at our dining room table. She said, "I better skedaddle," but she couldn't resist smiling, thrilled at the prospect of my getting punished.

For Mrs. V., who was blind, each day must have been like a monster movie turned inside-out in that *everyone* was the Invisible Man. She smashed out her cigarette and then walked toward the door, hitting me with her cane. If Eileen wasn't busy giving me bruises, Mrs. V. picked up the slack. Tomorrow I would have a new one, purple and puffy, on my shin.

With Mrs. V. gone, Mom said, "Do you have any idea why Joey Rizzo's mother might call me?"

I walked the rest of the way inside and shut the door. I took off my coat. I hung it on our wobbly coat rack. I understood now how Dad felt when he came home from a long day at work only to find himself interrogated about one thing or another the second he opened the door. In all fairness to Mom, she didn't interrogate Dad very often, and she always had a good reason when she did. Even so, my heart went out to my father.

"What's gotten into you lately?" Mom asked. "You used to be such a good little boy. I'm not even sure I recognize you anymore. Do you have anything to say for yourself?" She waited for an answer. "*Nothing?*" she asked.

I growled, just enough to let her know that I was in no mood, before heading for my bedroom and shutting the door between us.

When summer came to an end, so did my trips to the flea market.

"It's the same old stuff, week after week," Dad said.

"What about garage sales?"

"Wrong time of year."

"Are there any good flea markets in Michigan?" I asked.

My father gave me one of his are-you-out-of-your-gourd looks. "You got a wad of bills burning a hole in your pocket or what?"

Instead of driving me around to look for old monster magazines, my father went out by himself, returning later with things for my mother, like Italian beef sandwiches, which she craved all the time now, or boxes of cookies he bought at the factory outlet store, where he was putting on a new roof. The cookies were cheaper because they were damaged, but Mom claimed that she preferred crumbs, anyway. I kept wanting to ask Dad, *What about me? What about the things I want?* but I knew I'd sound like a big baby.

"Since when do you like crumbs?" I asked Mom after Dad left the room.

"Shhhh," Mom said. "You'll hurt his feelings."

One night during "Creature Features," our telephone rang. I was watching *The Creature Walks Among Us*, in which a team of doctors decide that the Creature from the Black Lagoon (a.k.a. Gill Man) would be happier if he could walk around like the rest of us, so they try fixing up his looks by cutting, sewing, burning, and scraping him. I sat on the edge of the couch, leaning toward the TV. I was appalled at all the different kinds of torture the doctors were putting the Creature through, but I was kind of enjoying it, too. When the phone rang, I nearly wet my pants.

My father bolted from the bedroom, yelling, "What's that noise?"

I pointed to the phone.

Dad stared at it, as if it were a smoking meteorite, before looking at the clock on the wall and then picking up. "Yeah?... Yeah?...*What?*...We'll be right over." Dad hung up. "That was Bill Rudolph. Eileen's having seizures. They're taking her to the hospital, and he wants us to watch the kids." I stood to get ready, but Dad motioned for me to stay put. "Just watch your movie," he said.

"But it's *Eileen*," I said.

"We'll call you if there's a problem," Dad said. "Otherwise, we'll see you in the morning."

It took my parents no time to get ready. Mom slipped back on the clothes she had worn earlier that day, while Dad put on a thick coat, winter gloves, and a knit cap. When he left the apartment, though, he was still wearing his pajama bottoms.

I got up and fiddled with the TV antennas. Despite all the advancements in modern medicine, Gill Man was still having a difficult time adapting to life among humans. At the sight of all the injustices Gill Man suffered, my upper lip started to tremble, and my vision got blurry. Poor guy, I thought. Poor fella. I knew exactly how he felt. I *was* Gill Man.

When my parents returned to our apartment early the next morning, I figured Eileen must have been okay. Mom walked over to the couch, but I kept my eyes shut and forced my teeth to chatter.

"Look how cold he is," Mom said.

"He's fine," Dad said.

Mom rested her palm on my forehead. "He's *warm*. Maybe he's got the flu."

"Just throw a bunch of blankets over him," Dad said. "I'm going to bed."

Mom piled several blankets over my trembling body. "There there," she said and kissed my head.

By the time school started up in the fall, word had spread about what I'd done to Jerry Stroka and Joey Rizzo, and my old friends kept a safe distance from me, fearful that I might grab hold of someone's exposed underwear and rip the elastic band free, or that I might remove my left-handed scissors from a pocket and quickly cut a patch of hair from an innocent kid's head. Overnight, I had become a boy capable of anything.

Meanwhile, my mother's stomach grew to ungainly proportions. When she walked, she tilted from side to side. She sometimes stopped whatever she was doing to let out a long sigh. *"Whew,"* she'd say and then take a deep breath before carrying on. She spoke more often to the kid inside her than to me. "You must be sleeping on my kidney, kiddo," she'd say. Or, "Your *brother* didn't even kick this much."

One afternoon, while my mother napped on the couch, I tiptoed up to her and had a few words with her belly.

"The bedroom's all mine," I said. "Find your own damned place to live." I stared at my mother's stomach, hoping my words were penetrating. I leaned closer and said, "I like monsters. If you don't like monsters, don't even talk to me, okay?" I waited a few seconds before adding, "Are we clear on things?"

Mom opened her eyes. It reminded me of a scene from *Dracula*: You think Dracula's asleep in his coffin, but then he opens his eyes and your heart clenches like a fist. "Who are you talking to?" she asked.

"Quasimodo," I said. I reached over and stuck my finger inside the bird cage, but he bit me, thinking my finger was a cracker.

"Oh," Mom said. "Do you think you could whisper then?"

Okay, I mouthed. I zipped my mouth shut. I put the leash on Dr. Jekyll. "Shhh," I whispered. "Don't bark."

The baby was due on September 8, 1971. I wasn't sure how they knew the exact date, but they did.

One day in late August, while Mom sat at the dining

room table writing down possible names for the baby, I suggested naming it Boris after Boris Karloff, who played the Frankenstein monster, if it was a boy; or Elsa after Elsa Lanchester, who played the monster's disappointed bride, if it was a girl.

"I'm not naming the baby after a *monster*, for Pete's sake," Mom said. The pencil slipped from her hand and fell to the floor. When she leaned sideways to pick it up, she looked like she was going to fall over. Her stomach was that big. I reached down, picked up the pencil, and handed it back to her.

"Those aren't *monsters*," I clarified. "They're the names of actors who *played* monsters."

"Boris," Mom said and snorted. "What kind of name *is* that, anyway?"

The due date – September the eighth – came and went. So did September the ninth. On Saturday the eleventh, I biked over to Eileen's to ask her if she was going to watch *Frankenstein* on "Creature Features" later that night. Neither of us had ever seen the original *Frankenstein*. We'd seen *Bride of Frankenstein*, *Son of Frankenstein*, *The Ghost of Frankenstein*, *Frankenstein Meets the Wolf Man*, *House of Frankenstein*, and our favorite, *Abbott and Costello Meet Frankenstein*. How was it possible we'd seen all of these but not the most famous monster movie of all time?

We were sitting on a pile of logs behind the tool shed in her back yard. Her mother had made us a pitcher of Tang, and we each had a tall glass.

"I hear he drowns a cute little girl," Eileen said.

"Who?" I said. "Frankenstein's monster?"

"Who else."

"I can't wait," I said.

Eileen set her glass of Tang on the ground. She took my glass and set it next to hers. And then Eileen did the one thing I kept hoping she would never do: she leaned in and kissed me. Her lips actually touched my lips. I expected it to be worse than it was. Surprisingly, it wasn't too bad. She was chewing a wad of Bazooka Joe, and since I chewed Bazooka Joe all the time, her mouth tasted a lot like my own mouth, only better – better because it *wasn't* my mouth.

"Do you know how to French kiss?" she asked.

"Do *what?*" I said.

Instead of answering, she showed me. It was shortly after this that I might have blacked out. I didn't actually black out, but I lost all track of time, the way Larry Talbot, after he turns into the Wolf Man and kills innocent villagers, wakes up the next morning, confused, only to discover paw prints on the carpet and then dirt on his feet, leaving him with one logical conclusion: He *is* the Wolf Man!

When Eileen slipped her hand up under my T-shirt, touching my bare skin, I told her I needed to go.

"Why? Don't you like this?"

"It's okay," I said. "But I don't want to miss *Frankenstein.*"

"You'd rather watch *Frankenstein* than kiss me?" she asked.

It was a crazy question; I almost didn't answer. I gave her one of my father's are-you-out-of-your-gourd looks. A whine crept into my voice when I said, "But it's *Frank-en-stein.*"

"I see," Eileen said. She stood up and brushed herself off. I could tell by the bounce in her step as she walked toward her house that she was mad.

"Now, don't be like that," I said. My words were eerily familiar, but it was only after Eileen had stopped abruptly, the way my mother would have stopped, that I realized the words I spoke belonged to my father. It was something he said at least once a week.

"Like what?" Eileen said. When she turned around, I saw that she was crying. "Like *this?* I could die tomorrow. I *could,*" she insisted, "and what do you care?" She waited for me to answer, but I didn't know what to say. I felt weak, like I'd been punched. It was starting to drizzle. I wanted to go home. But then Eileen delivered the final blow. "I don't even *like* monsters," she said.

"You *what?*" I said. Eileen was already opening her screen door to go inside. "You lied!" I yelled once the door shut. For good measure, I added, "How could you not like monsters? What's wrong with you?" The porch light flipped off, leaving me in the dark. "Eileen?" I called out, but no one answered. I looked closely for her shadow against the shut curtains, but when I didn't see anything that looked like her, I got on my bike and headed for home.

The rain came down in heavy sheets, and the roads were especially slick. I was so wet by the time I reached the apartment, my pants and shirt clung to my skin. Every time I peeled my shirt away from me, it slowly suctioned itself back to my flesh. My shirt was like a living thing, the way the Blob was a living thing: it wasn't human and it wasn't animal, but it was going to eat me alive if I wasn't careful. Even after I changed my clothes, rain continued to roll from my hair and down my face.

A note was taped over the TV screen. I was afraid it was there to let me know the TV was broken, but it was a note about Mom.

WENT TO HOSPITAL.
NEW BABY ON THE WAY.
COULDN'T WAIT FOR YOU.
DAD

I looked down at Dr. Jekyll. "Did you know about this?" I asked. He cocked his head, then wagged his tail. For Dr. Jekyll, every question was the same: *Do you want a treat?* I gave him a Cheez-It.

Rain hammered our windows, and I could hear a steady plop somewhere inside the apartment. I marched from room to room until I found the problem: rain was dripping from the kitchen ceiling. I set a sauce pan down to catch the drip.

Quasimodo squawked, and I said, "Easy, boy, it's only water," but then I saw that rain was dripping into his cage. When I picked up the cage to move it, Quasimodo squawked again. "You're welcome," I said.

By the time I turned on the TV and settled onto the couch, "Creature Features" was already starting. I covered my entire self with blankets, except for my eyes and the top of my head. At last, I was going to see the greatest monster movie of all time – *Frankenstein*! What a lot of people didn't realize was that Frankenstein wasn't the name of the monster. Frankenstein was the last name of the scientist who created him. It had crossed my mind that if I ever created a monster, people might start calling it O'Reilly. The very name O'Reilly would cause women to scream and men to gather their weapons.

Quasimodo squawked some more – an angry squawk this time. The rain had followed him, still dripping into his cage. "I'm going to miss the *movie*," I whined. I threw off my blankets and quickly moved the bird cage again.

As Dr. Frankenstein and his hunchbacked assistant, Fritz, started digging up the freshly buried corpse, rain poured in from new places in our ceiling. During the first commercial break, I found more pans and cups to place strategically around the apartment. If Dad was here, he would have known what to do.

"Dr. Jekyll," I said. "Do you know how to swim?"

His tail wagged. *Yes*, he was saying. *I'd love a treat.*

Eileen's lips still felt like they were touching my lips. It was like being kissed by the Invisible Man. Even the smell of Bazooka Joe lingered. What if she was telling the truth? What if she *was* going to die any day now? I was almost too upset to concentrate on the movie, but I watched it anyway, lying across the couch with Dr. Jekyll curled up next to me. I decided that I would memorize everything in the movie so that I could tell Eileen about it tomorrow: the way Dr. Frankenstein's laboratory was in a watchtower, the way Fritz climbed down a long rope from the top of the tower, the way the monster was strapped to a table, still dead. And then there was the laboratory itself with all its flywheels, chains, and glass bubbles. I would buy Eileen a box of chocolate. I would give her some of my favorite monster magazines. I knew she was lying, of course; her knowledge of monsters was too great for her *not* to like them.

It was storming in *Frankenstein,* a storm as bad as the one outside. At the height of the storm, Dr. Frankenstein cranked a flywheel, and the table upon which the monster lay rose to the very top of the watchtower. My hands were sweating. Rain hit the top of my head, one thick plunk after another. Electricity struck the bolts sticking out of the monster's neck and then Dr. Frankenstein lowered the monster back to ground level.

The telephone rang, and I clutched my chest. This was the most famous part of the most famous monster movie of all time, and I wasn't going to miss it for anything. The phone rang two more times before it stopped.

I had to squint through the rain to see the lightning on TV. Dr. Jekyll whined and looked up at me, and Quasimodo squawked. There was a knock at our door. "Go away!" I yelled, but then came another knock. I groaned and stood. I looked out the peephole. It was Mrs. V.

"What?" I yelled through the door.

"Your father is trying to call you!" she yelled back.

"So?"

"Your mother had a baby girl!"

"That's great!" I said. "Is that all?"

"What are you doing in there? Why won't you open the door?"

"None of your business," I said.

"You're an evil little boy," she said. "Did you know that?"

"I'm not a boy," I said. "I'm a monster."

At this, Mrs. V. backed slowly away from the door. She looked like a movie being run in reverse. My heart was pounding. *My mother had a baby,* I thought. *I've got a sister now.*

I pulled my eye from the peephole. "Wow," I said. "A sister." When I reached the couch, I watched the monster raise his hand all by himself.

"Look," Dr. Frankenstein said. "It's moving. It's alive."

"Look!" I said to Dr. Jekyll. "It's moving."

"It's alive!" Dr. Frankenstein bellowed. "It's alive! It's moving!"

Dr. Frankenstein looked so happy. I imagined my mother and the new slimy baby. I imagined my father towering over them, smiling like Dr. Frankenstein. I walked to the window and opened it wide. I was already soaking wet, and Dr. Jekyll was crawling under the couch for shelter. I poked my head out the window and yelled, "It's alive! It's alive!" Sheets of rain smacked my face. Dr. Frankenstein continued to yell: "It's alive! In the name of God, now I know what it feels like to *be* God!" "It's alive!" I yelled again. I was shivering, but I didn't mind. I was happy. I was happy for Mom; I was happy for Dad; I was happy that I had a plan to win back Eileen. I was even happy for the slimy baby I hadn't yet met.

Mrs. Willis, who lived below us, opened her window and looked out to see who was making all the noise. Mr. Sleezak, who lived next door, opened his window, too, and poked his head outside. A family running through the rain to their car paused to peer up at me. Behind me the TV sizzled and popped a few times, and then something inside it exploded. A glass tube, I suspected. From under the couch, Dr. Jekyll barked.

"In the name of God!" I shouted.

Tomorrow, I would knock on Eileen's door and when she answered I would take her in my arms. I would whisper into her ear that she wasn't going to die. Not anytime soon, at least. And not before we'd kissed some more.

"What's *wrong* with that kid?" Mr. Sleezak asked Mrs. Willis.

"I don't know," Mrs. Willis said, "but I always suspected he wasn't right in the head."

I held my hands out into the rain, as if to catch a falling baby, and yelled, "It's *alive!* It's *alive!*"

I SEE JOHNNY

(Romper Room – Chicago, 1954-1975)

It's December, 1967: the summer of love is over.

Miss Betsy saw footage of it on the evening news – long-haired California boys and girls, naked or nearly naked, smoking grass and wearing pounds of beads. But the summer of love never touched down in Chicago, and it certainly isn't going to come here now while Miss Betsy stands on the windswept El platform, waiting for the train that seems to get later and later each morning. Her knit cap reaches her eyebrows, and a scarf covers her mouth and dripping nose. Her coral-colored coat goes all the way down to her ankles, and she wears the collar up like a vampire. The cold is so concentrated it's easy to pretend that the skin is burning instead of freezing, and Miss Betsy sometimes passes the time imagining that she's standing stock-still in the middle of a house fire while flames lick her flesh.

Miss Betsy is the host of a local children's show. The show's purpose is to teach kids appropriate behavior, nice manners, and good hygiene. Kids recognize her on sight. So do mothers. Most men, however, have no idea who she is. The show has had other hosts over the years – Miss Patty, Miss Trixie, Miss Wanda – but Miss Betsy has endured the longest. The key to her success, she believes, is that she flirts with the camera. She smiles and winks, and often she gives sidelong glances from a distance while helping the children with one of their projects. The show's producer hasn't told her to stop, so she pushes it a little more each time – but just a bit, never too much. Most likely, the kids who watch her on TV interpret her flirting as a conspiratorial nod, as if she's saying to them, *I'm not your mother, so follow me to the ends of the earth and we'll have loads of fun together!*

In her dressing room, before the show, Miss Betsy sheds layers of wet winter clothes and puts on a pink polyester dress. Claire, the make-up girl, comes in and fixes her hair. When Miss Betsy was growing up in Beloit, Wisconsin, landing prominent roles in high school productions of *The Man Who Came to Dinner* and *Harvey*, she imagined herself becoming the next Katherine Hepburn. She took classes from a vocal coach so that she could learn how to enunciate better. *E. Nun. See. Ate.* She could often be found wandering the side-streets of Beloit, a mathematics textbook balanced on top of her head, practicing sentences like "Stephanie sat six sick simians on the sidewalk" or "What wayward whale waited in Waikiki water while we wiggled?" When little kids stopped her to ask what she was doing, she would keep walking, eyes focused straight ahead, all the while motioning with her fingers for them to scoot. She was going places, and no one was going to stop her – that is, until she met Johnny.

Johnny was three years older than she was but a good two inches shorter. Grease clung to the edges of his finger-nails, his mouth tasted like cigarettes, and he used phrases that sounded like swear words but were actually things he'd made up, like "mother spelunker" or "God slam it!" Johnny usually had an arm slung over Miss Betsy's shoulder, pulling her snug against him, but when they made love she got the eerie feeling that he was picturing someone else beneath him, maybe one of the pin-ups from *Wink* or *Beauty Parade* or *Titter*. She knew he owned those kinds of magazines; one day when he went across the street to buy a pack of Lucky Strikes, she looked through a box of old comic books featuring superheroes with names like Steel Sterling and Black Terror, and there at the bottom she found a stack of barely dressed women, one after the other, raven-haired beauties wearing black bikinis, sexy redheads in polka-dots. And so while making love, Miss Betsy would think, *Look at me, look at me,* but when Johnny's eyes finally came back into focus, he often seemed surprised to find her there. That was 1951; Miss Betsy was sixteen. She told herself that she wasn't in love with Johnny, and she certainly didn't envision any kind of future for the two of them together, but neither of these facts mitigated the unexpected malaise that took hold of her when he enlisted in the Army and left for Korea.

One afternoon, while taking a nap, Miss Betsy thought she felt the hot tip of a bayonet slip into her belly and spread her guts around, and when she woke up and saw the bed stained with clots of blood, she screamed, so certain was she that someone had sneaked into her room and stabbed her. It was, she learned later, a miscarriage for a pregnancy she never knew about, the clots a baby that was already dead before she had known something inside her had been alive.

When Johnny was killed during the Chinese Counter-offensive – shot, she learned later, through the head – she'd just as soon been told that she herself had only three more months to live. No one could console her. She cried so hard for so many days that she reached a point where she simply couldn't cry anymore, as if her body'd had a quota of tears and she'd used it up.

Dolores, Miss Betsy's mother, never liked Johnny, which, in turn, gave her license to pretend that nothing at all had happened to him in Korea. She had her own life to worry about. A once-devout Catholic, she'd recently become fascinated by other belief systems, reading musty books and sweat-wrinkled pamphlets on religions Miss Betsy had heard of, like Hinduism and Judaism, but also at least one pocket-sized paperback about paganism and another that featured nothing but a pentagram on its cover. Dolores must have understood the dangers of reading them in a town the size of Beloit because she kept them squirreled away in their mud room, hidden behind a pair of mukluks and a box of stiff winter gloves. What if people started thinking she was a heathen? Or worse – a Satan worshipper? Dolores had social obligations in town. For starters, she belonged to the Junior League of Beloit and often hosted luncheons for the other women, serving her famous chicken and tongue sandwiches. When her turn came to host again, only three days after news of Johnny's death, she didn't sway from her initial plans.

With all the false good cheer she could muster, Dolores said, "They're easy to make!" Miss Betsy had walked into the kitchen for a glass of milk and two aspirin; she had no idea what Dolores was talking about. Dolores, who must have sensed Miss Betsy's confusion, pointed to her meal-in-progress. "You take a pint of boiled tongue and chicken," she said, "you mince it, and then you put it in the fridge to cool. Once it cools, you add a half-cup of melted butter to it, an egg yolk, a little black pepper, a few shakes of Worcestershire sauce, you mix it all up and – *voilà!* – you're done. Just spread it over buttered bread before the guests arrive."

Miss Betsy's father, a dour man ten years Dolores' senior, came home each day from the small savings and loan where he served as V.P., filled his thermos to the brim with either Singapore Slings or Gin Rickeys, and then headed down into the chilly bowels of their basement to tinker with a Hoosier cabinet he'd bought from an Amish man in Shipshewana, Indiana. Miss Betsy wasn't sure that her father even knew she'd been dating Johnny, let alone that he was dead. Not just dead, she reminded herself, but *killed*. Her father moved through their house like a man in purgatory, trapped between life and afterlife, and utterly unsure how he ended up where he did.

All of that was sixteen years ago now – half a lifetime ago.

"Jesus," Miss Betsy says.

"What?" asks Claire, the make-up girl. "Something

wrong?" Their eyes meet in the mirror. Claire looks like she was out most of the night, sleeping somewhere other than where she lived, coming to work wearing whatever she'd had on the night before.

"It's nothing," Miss Betsy says.

Later, during the show's taping, Miss Betsy holds up the Magic Mirror to her own face. The Magic Mirror is a hand-held mirror frame that's missing glass so that Miss Betsy can look through it and into the TV camera, pretending to see the kids watching her show from home.

"I see Bobby," she says, "I see Annie. I see Joey. I see Crystal."

Each week Miss Betsy receives a bag of mail from kids asking her to say their names, and after each taping Miss Betsy becomes increasingly aware that she's disappointing far more kids than she's pleasing. But what can she do? To make matters worse, she never sees Johnny. All the little boys named Johnny who watch her show must wonder why she never sees them, but even now, after all this time, she can't say his name without tears welling up or her voice catching: grief's surprise appearance.

After today's taping, Claire sidles up next to Miss Betsy and says, "Want to go to a party tonight?"

Miss Betsy smiles, as if to say, *No, that's not my scene*, but Claire writes down the address and hands it to her, anyway.

"All my friends want to meet Miss Betsy," she says.

"How old are your friends?" Miss Betsy asks. "Five?" She doesn't mean to sound so nasty, but as soon as she hears the disdain in her voice, she hates herself for it.

"You never know," Claire says. "You might even have fun." Claire's words would have stung except that Claire reaches out and touches Miss Betsy's arm, then squeezes it.

That night, Miss Betsy takes a cab to the address. She

isn't sure what possesses her – she *isn't* the sort who goes to parties – but she can't stop thinking about Claire. Who is Claire, and why did she invite Miss Betsy to a party? A part of her – the mean-spirited part – thinks it has to do with her celebrity, that the invitation was a bet Claire made with some friends: *Get the TV host to come to our party, and we'll give you ten bucks.* But Miss Betsy knows that the sin of pride is making her think such things. This, at least, is what her mother would have told her.

"The only reason people become actors," Dolores once hypothesized, "is because they think too highly of themselves. They think everyone's always looking at them. Normal people don't live like that. Normal people have the opposite aspiration."

"Which is?"

"To be invisible."

Miss Betsy tried explaining to Dolores that some people went into acting because it was an *art*, a form of *expression*, but Dolores wouldn't have any of it. And the longer Miss Betsy stays on television, the more she suspects Dolores is right. It *isn't* about art. It's about how many people watch you. The more people who watch you, the better you're doing.

"How am I doing?" she'd asked her producer recently, and when he answered, "More people are watching each week," Miss Betsy tried not to reveal the histrionic pleasure she felt at this news.

The cab delivers Miss Betsy to a dark street full of old, run-down brownstones. It's a part of the city Miss Betsy has never been. She hears in the distance a bottle break and someone yell or something howl – human or animal, she can't tell. The cab leaves, and Miss Betsy squints to find the address that matches what Claire wrote down for her. When she steps closer, she hears the pulse of music coming from inside, and then a burst of laughter. Miss Betsy climbs the steps, holding onto the rail for support. She shouldn't have worn heels, not with ice still lingering beneath fresh snow, but it's too late now.

"E. Nun. See. Ate," Miss Betsy says softly, clearing her mouth's moist cobwebs while exercising her tongue. "E. Nun. See. Ate," she says again and then knocks on the door. Claire opens it.

"Holy shit," Claire says. "You actually came!"

"I can leave," Miss Betsy says, but Claire has grabbed her by the arm and is tugging her indoors, reeling her in.

"Why would you leave?" Claire says. "You're here now."

"Could you do me a favor?" Miss Betsy asks, and she's about to ask Claire not to make a big deal about her appearance, but Claire is already yelling for everyone to hush.

"Listen up, everyone," she says. "This is my friend, Miss Betsy! I want everyone to be kind to her, okay?"

"Thank you," Miss Betsy mouths.

"I'm glad you're here," Claire says. "*Mi casa, su casa.* Except that this isn't my house." She shrugs then leaves, following a bearded man wearing a turtleneck into the bathroom.

No one talks to Miss Betsy for the first half-hour. She pours herself a glass of wine and nibbles on some crackers. She hasn't seen Claire or the bearded man emerge from the bathroom yet. Is there another exit? Why, of all places, are they in the *bathroom* together?

"I know you," a woman says. She's wearing a polka-dotted dress and fake eyelashes.

Miss Betsy smiles.

"You're that lady," the woman adds.

"I guess I am," Miss Betsy says.

"My name's Peggy. You want to get high?"

Miss Betsy follows Peggy into a room where coats are piled on a bed. The only light in the room comes from a fish tank. The room is full of wavy shadows, and it's easy to imagine that they themselves are underwater. Peggy sits on the coats as if they aren't even there. She lights a joint and passes it to Miss Betsy.

"I haven't done this before," Miss Betsy says.

Peggy smiles. "The thing to remember is to hold it in your lungs as long as you can. Okay?"

Miss Betsy does as she's told, but then she starts coughing. "Oh God," she says between coughs.

"You'll get used to it," Peggy says. "Don't worry."

Later, after they leave the underwater room and Peggy has disappeared with someone else into another part of the house, the bearded man with the turtleneck approaches Miss Betsy and introduces himself as Worthington.

"Terrible name I know," he says. "I'm told you're the famous Miss Betsy. I don't own a TV, I'm sorry to say. I love your shoes," he says. "How high are those heels?" He laughs and says, "I'm asking you how *high* your *heels* are." When Miss Betsy says nothing, he says, "How *high*? Get it?" He shakes his head and says, "Claire wants me to share my mushrooms with you. You ever do shrooms? Yes? No? Well, what you do is smash them up and mix it with tea. You can eat them, too, but they taste like shit and sometimes get caught at the back of your throat. They're drier than hell and leave a kind of metallic taste in your mouth, but you won't notice it once you start peaking. Here," he says. "Watch."

Worthington pours them each a cup of tea and then crumbles an equal amount of mushrooms into each cup.

"There," he says. "Bottoms up!"

Miss Betsy, who feels dizzy listening to Worthington, sips her tea.

"No, no, no," Worthington yells. "You gotta *down* it."

Miss Betsy drinks faster. She wants to ask Worthington what he and Claire did together in the bathroom, but she can't stop staring into Worthington's beard. It's tangled, and there are crumbs stuck around the rim of his mouth. Doesn't he know that she hosts a show about, among other things, proper hygiene? She forces the tea down in three long gulps.

"Enjoy the ride," Worthington says. He touches her face

with the back of his hand before leaving her alone.

Two hours later, Miss Betsy has locked herself inside the bathroom and is sitting on the edge of the tub, staring at a single square of tile on the floor. *Inside this one square of tile,* she thinks, *are the answers to the universe.* She is certain that she can feel all the veins in her body, the blood rushing through them, the nerve endings reaching out toward the tile square, the way plants are drawn to the sun. Why has she not known about this bathroom until now? Why has it been kept a secret?

"She's probably tripping her ass off right now," someone outside the bathroom door says. Miss Betsy hears the knocking – again. Whoever is outside the door has been knocking for a while now. Miss Betsy *wants* to get up and open the door – she really does – but she is paralyzed. The tile won't let her move.

"In a minute," she says, and her voice sounds funny, like something that can bend in unexpected directions, something a person could see, maybe even taste. She reaches into her purse and pulls out her Magic Mirror. She carries the mirror around with her because kids are always stopping her when she goes out in public, and they want her to say their names. Upon such occasions, she'll pull out the Magic Mirror and look through it, into the face of the child, and then she'll say whatever name the parent has whispered into her ear – but tonight, here in this bathroom, she sees Johnny. He is as he was when she last saw him, a smooth-faced boy with grease under his fingernails and smoke pouring from his parted mouth. His eyes are pale and distant. "Johnny," Miss Betsy whispers, but he can't see her or hear her, and when he finishes his cigarette, flipping it out of view, he disappears inside his own last puff of smoke.

They are inseparable, Miss Betsy and Claire. For the next month, the routine doesn't waver: Claire leads the way; Miss

Betsy follows.

"Where to?" Miss Betsy asks.

"I know about a party in Lincoln Park," Claire says. Or, "I heard about these two guys in Bucktown who have some great shit." Or, "My place." Miss Betsy sometimes falls asleep on Claire's sofa. Claire sleeps naked in her bed, a thin bedsheet sometimes pulled as high as her waist but sometimes not. The last two times, she and Claire have gone to work together, sharing a cab and splitting the fare.

Claire, who uses only eyeliner and sometimes doesn't wear a brassiere when she goes out for the night, is the sort of girl Miss Betsy wishes she could have been but, given who her parents were, could never have been. But maybe she shouldn't blame it all on her parents. Growing up in Beloit, Wisconsin, probably played some role in making Miss Betsy who she is today: a woman unafraid to milk a cow or confess to a priest but apprehensive about undressing in front of strangers. You'd think that where she grew up – a city whose land was once owned by a French fur trader who had two Indian wives – would still have been possessed by some residual wildness, but all the vestiges of more carefree days probably evaporated after Caleb Blodgett, a proper New England Yankee, came to town, bought the fur trader's land, and summoned his New England Yankee friends to come join him.

Claire, on the other hand, most definitely isn't from Beloit. Miss Betsy gets the feeling that there isn't anything Claire wouldn't do. Climb a water tower. Pose for *Playboy*. Shoplift. The hair on Miss Betsy's arms stands on end just thinking about her.

Miss Betsy is starting to see the effects of too many late nights. Her upper lip twitches for no reason. Her hands shake. The skin under her eyes is dark and creased. Claire gives her a different kind of pill before each show to help her perk up. Lately, Miss Betsy still smells like smoke when she steps onto the set. Her clothes are wrinkled. The show's ratings have never been higher, though, so the producer doesn't reprimand her. Today, however, she doesn't feel right after taking Claire's pill, and when the time arrives on the show to look into the Magic Mirror, she sees people she shouldn't be seeing.

"I see Zhang," she says, "I see Hu, I see Bei."

During the commercial break, the producer motions her over. He's an ailing man of sixty with gout that causes him to limp.

"When you do the mirror bit," he says, "stick to seeing Jane and Timmy. We don't want to scare anyone at home, now do we?" Before Miss Betsy can explain that she doesn't feel herself, the producer limps away.

Miss Betsy works at the same television station as Bozo and Ringmaster Ned, as Frazier Thomas and Garfield Goose, as Ray Rayner and Cuddley Dudley. She'd gone out on a couple of dates with one of the puppeteers, but she didn't like the way he kept touching her spine, as if searching for a slot to insert his hand. All of them, including the stuffed orange dog, enjoy a celebrity status that Miss Betsy doesn't have and will probably never have, and although there are times that she feels twinges of jealousy when she passes Ned or Frazier in the hallway, it's nothing compared to the feelings that overcome her when she sees the host of *Treetop House*. In truth, Miss Betsy shouldn't feel anything but sympathy for the poor woman. *Treetop House* is always in jeopardy – it's already been canceled once – so there's no real fear of *Treetop*'s host bumping off Miss Betsy, whose ratings are solid. No, the deep-seated anger comes from the fact that they're both chasing the same demographic: preschoolers. *Treetop House* is like a distant cousin who lives in a small town, a girl who will meet neither the quantity nor the quality of men that Miss Betsy will meet, and yet when the cousin *does* come for a visit, the men pay more attention to her than to Miss Betsy because she's prettier and younger. Because she's *different*.

"Have you ever watched *Treetop House*?" Miss Betsy asks Claire one night.

"*Treetop House*?" Claire says. "How old do I look?" She laughs. "I'm young, but I'm not *that* young."

Claire lives is a studio apartment in Lakeview. She fixes cocktails in her small kitchen while Miss Betsy sits on the edge of Claire's bed.

"What was that pill you gave me this morning? Before the show?"

"Oh *that*," Claire says. "Why? Didn't it do the trick?"

After bringing Miss Betsy her drink, Claire lights a joint. Once half the joint has been smoked, Claire licks her forefinger and thumb and then pinches the lit tip, extinguishing it. With uncharacteristic fastidiousness, as if the cigarette were fragile and rare, she sets it down in the kidney-shaped ashtray on the bedside table.

"What are those for?" Miss Betsy points to a short stack of empty liquor boxes.

"I'm collecting them for a friend," Claire says.

Miss Betsy can't help noticing that next to the ashtray is a paperback copy of John Hersey's *Hiroshima* that hasn't been moved since Miss Betsy began coming over. The atomic mushroom cloud on its cover is coated with an ever-thickening layer of dust, and it's getting more and more difficult to tell the difference between explosion and filth. Miss Betsy is staring at the mushroom cloud when she feels Claire's hand on the thigh of her crossed leg. The hand slowly snakes up her skirt, running all the way up her stockings. Miss Betsy wants to resist and not resist, but as soon as the warmth that's pulsating near Claire's hand begins to radiate, Miss Betsy uncrosses her legs and lets Claire touch her.

Later, as Miss Betsy starts drifting to sleep, she tells Claire first about Johnny and then about the miscarriage. For the first time, Miss Betsy admits that she wouldn't mind having children one day.

"Me, too," Claire says. "A whole roomful of them!" Claire presses her palm against Miss Betsy's belly. "Do you want me to get you pregnant?" She whispers this into Miss Betsy's ear but then she starts to laugh, pulling Miss Betsy to her, pinning her to the bed with one of her legs.

Before drifting to sleep, Miss Betsy whispers, "I love you," and Claire, after a moment of silence, whispers, "I see you, too."

The next day, Miss Betsy has a raging headache, the kind of headache that sends shockwaves from her brain to her eyes. With each heart beat, her vision momentarily blurs. Before leaving the dressing room, Claire takes hold of Miss Betsy's face and puts her lips to Miss Betsy's mouth, working her tongue inside with more purpose than passion. Claire keeps her eyes open, too, staring intensely into Miss Betsy's own eyes. When Claire finally backs up, letting her hands drip down Miss Betsy's face, she smiles and says, "Feel better?"

On the set, Miss Betsy's patience with the children is short. She can't stop thinking about what she and Claire did last night. Was it a sin? What would parents whose children watch the show think? During a commercial, when a boy named Edgar yanks on her skirt, she tells him to go away.

"Go on," she says. "Shoo."

In her dressing room afterward, alone, she peers into her Magic Mirror, hoping for a glimpse of Johnny but seeing only carpet beneath her feet. She squints and concentrates but with no luck. There's some mud she tracked in, and there's a hair resting atop the carpet fibers, either hers or Claire's.

Claire. The summer of love may have passed Miss Betsy by, but the winter of love has arrived full-force. Miss Betsy thinks she's in love with Claire, and she suspects that Claire's in love with her, too. Why all this time spent together? Why did what happen last night happen? When Miss Claire looks at herself in the mirror and thinks about being with Claire, her pupils dilate. This, according to her mother, is how you can tell if you're in love. *Jesus*, Miss Betsy thinks, staring into her own darkening eyes.

Even though Miss Betsy showered this morning, soaping herself from head to toe, Claire is still all over her. She's under Miss Betsy's fingernails; she's on the roof of Miss Betsy's mouth; she clings to Miss Betsy's tongue. You can wash and wash and wash, she wants to tell the kids, but you can't wash away your lover so easily. Even if you soap and brush and scrub every last part of yourself, the lover's presence still lingers. Is it merely psychological, or does some kind of molecular combustion take place, fusing your lover's skin cells to your own? All that Miss Betsy knows for sure is that she craves Claire. She craves her and wants to hold her again – right here, right now.

Miss Betsy opens the dressing room door and looks out. The raspy-voiced clown from the circus show walks by, cuts his eyes toward her, and raises his absurdly painted eyebrows, as if to say, *What the hell are we doing here?* He has a red bulb for a nose and orange hair, and he wears white gloves that go all the way up to his elbows. She sometimes sees him in full clown regalia standing out back, sneaking a smoke. At the other end of the hallway is the security guard – a crewcutted fellow named Gleason.

"Have you seen Claire?" Miss Betsy asks.

Gleason smiles. Miss Betsy has never asked him a question before. It's usually a nod in the morning and nod on her way home, but the way he's looking at her now, her question must have been interpreted as something salacious, a connection between herself and Claire that goes beyond the professional. Is the look on her face that desperate? Gleason's eyes are like two fat spiders crawling up her legs. Miss Betsy is surprised to find that she's not as repulsed as she thought she'd be.

"Cute girl?" Gleason finally asks.

"The young one," Miss Betsy says, not wanting to expose her true feelings. "She does make-up."

"Yeah, yeah. She left a while ago. Said she wasn't feeling all that good. Late night, she said."

Miss Betsy nods and is about to retreat back into her room when Gleason clears his throat.

"That mirror?" he says. "You know – the one you look into?"

"Yes?"

"Why don't you ever see me?" he asks. When Miss Betsy doesn't say anything, Gleason laughs and says, "Hey, I'm kidding. You should lighten up. You're still young. Have some fun."

"I do have fun," Miss Betsy says before shutting the door and turning the lock.

◎

It's Friday, and no word from Claire. The weekend goes by and – nothing. Claire doesn't come to work on Monday, and when Miss Betsy goes over to Claire's apartment after taping her show, someone else is already moving in.

"Where's Claire?" Miss Betsy asks two men carrying in box springs.

"Claire who?" one of the men asks, and the other man shrugs.

Miss Betsy wants to cup her palms to the side of her head and scream. She'd read somewhere that in times of stress women reach for their heads while men cross their arms. Her own experience tells her that this is true, but *why* is it true? When she learned that Johnny had died in Korea, she'd cupped her hands over her mouth then grabbed fistfuls of her own hair. When she saw the clots of blood on her bed after taking a nap, she'd reached up and covered both nose and mouth with her hands. What in the long history of women caused them to raise their arms and expose their hearts while men tightened into themselves, as if returning to the womb?

The TV station hires a new make-up artist later that week. Her name is Hazel. She's at least sixty, and her own make-up is off by a fraction of an inch, the way a translucent mask may appear if not suctioned perfectly to one's face. She looks blurry. Out of focus. When Hazel darkens Miss Betsy's eyebrows, she gives them an upside-down "V" shape that makes each eye seem as though it has its own roof. The upside-down "V"s makes Miss Betsy look sinister, not at all the right impression for the host of a children's television show, and yet Miss Betsy doesn't want to hurt Hazel's feelings. Hazel is married and has three kids, all grown now and married with their own kids. *The Breeders*, Miss Betsy thinks bitterly, and whenever Hazel confides in her about this or that family squabble, Miss Betsy thinks, *This is how it happens, this endless cycle of human reproduction, no one stopping to wonder if it's a good thing for the planet, all this extra shit and piss, the exponential increase of worries and grief and nightmares, and the toll it takes on everyone else?*

Nights, Miss Betsy goes to every party she hears about, hoping to find Claire, but the parties are full of people she's never met. Even so, the parties' hosts are pleased when she shows up. She's a celebrity, after all. A *kind* of celebrity, at least. A conversation piece. And she has to admit that she's starting to like the attention. Why not? She's earned the right to enjoy the fringe benefits of fame, hasn't she?

"You're Claire's friend, aren't you?" a woman with a bee-hive hairdo asks Miss Betsy at one of the parties, nodding and smiling as if she knows something personal about the two of them, but when pressed, the woman walks away, saying, "No reason, I was just asking." As the weeks wear on, more and more people, both men and women, seem to know that Miss Betsy knows Claire, and Miss Betsy starts suspecting that

Claire's bragging about their night together, telling people where, for instance, the prim TV host put her tongue or what she sounds like when she moans – the sorts of intimate details that would prompt strangers to want to find out if it's true.

At first all Miss Betsy does is drink wine at the parties, but as the weeks dissolve into months, she begins accepting whatever people offer her – a toke, a hit, a snort. Some nights she falls asleep on a stranger's couch, curling into a ball and pining for Claire; other nights, she hooks up with someone at the party, following him or her, sometimes both, into a room or, failing the convenience of privacy, remaining out in the open. Her flesh is malleable. She puts up no fight, offers no resistance. The body is of no consequence, she tells herself. It's the soul that matters.

One Friday in February, Miss Betsy takes a cab to a party on the west side. It's in an apartment next to a long-abandoned warehouse. Dozens of the warehouse's window panes have been shattered, and Miss Betsy thinks she hears the building itself emit a sound, but then she realizes, after it sweeps over her, that it's just the wind moaning. The driver pulls away, and she is the only living thing on the street. Everything else is made out of concrete or glass or asphalt or brick. Even so, Miss Betsy can't help thinking she's being watched. Somewhere in the dark, perhaps from inside a gutted building, there are eyes trained on her.

I don't hear a party, Miss Betsy thinks, but then she imagines Claire taking her by the hand and leading her up to the apartment. Lately, she has begun imagining Claire beside her everywhere she goes. At first, it was a playful thing to do – conjuring up this woman who has disappeared – but now she has a difficult time not imagining Claire with her, even though she is angry at Claire, furious at Claire, for casually telling everyone intimate details about the two of them. Despite this, she summoned the imaginary Claire to bed with her last night, and this morning they took a shower together, Miss Betsy remaining under the spray until the water turned cold and the landlady knocked on her door, wondering if she was okay.

At the apartment's bank of buzzers, Miss Betsy hears people talking, music playing. The filament inside the lightbulb above her quivers. The fire escape – an ancient ladder attached to the side of the building – rattles.

"E. Nun. See. Ate."

"Who is it?" a voice asks after she presses a button, and when Miss Betsy tells him, he says that he doesn't know anyone by that name.

Miss Betsy puts her mouth closer to the speaker. "I'm a friend of Gabrielle's." This isn't exactly true. She met Gabrielle last week at another party she had crashed with only the barest thread of a connection. They're barely acquaintances, let alone friends.

The door buzzes, Miss Betsy puts her shoulder into it, and up she goes, three flights of stairs. Upon entering the apartment, a man with shaggy hair asks Miss Betsy to open her mouth. She obeys, the way she would for communion, and he gently sets something on her tongue. This is the body of Christ, Miss Betsy thinks.

"Let it dissolve," says the man.

"What is it?" she asks.

"'What is it?'" the man repeats and laughs. "You're in for a treat, sister."

On her way across the room, a woman wearing a shiny silver dress says, "Hey, I know you. You're that lady," and Miss Betsy smiles. The woman, who's slumped so far down in her butterfly chair that her legs jut out like a limp marionette's, says, "My kids love you."

"Tell them I see them each time I look into the Magic Mirror."

The woman says, "They're down the hall, if you really want to see them. I'd come with you, but I can't move. I think this shit's finally starting to kick in. Or maybe not. I keep thinking I'm feeling this giant warm wave wash over me, but then I think, no, no, it's not here yet. Their names are Vickie and Johnny."

Miss Betsy nods. Johnny, she thinks, and her heart feels momentarily clamped off from the rest of her body – an organ without a host.

The woman says, "They're no taller than dogs standing on their hind legs. Is that a weird thing to say? Maybe it is kicking in."

"What size dogs?" a man sitting in the circle asks, and the woman bursts out laughing.

"Oh my God," she says. "I didn't even think of that."

Miss Betsy excuses herself while others in the circle start to laugh, even though it's clear that they don't know why they're laughing. Miss Betsy sits down next to a man who's studying the back of his hand. He holds it up to the light, turning it one way and then the other, as if the hand is see-through. Miss Betsy watches but doesn't say anything.

Unlike the woman in the silver dress, Miss Betsy has no doubt when the acid kicks in. Things she's looking at leave trails when she turns her head. Parts of the room start to melt. Most telling, however, is that she can tell what everyone in the room is thinking; she can read their minds. You have no secrets, she thinks. I know everything. She is aware, too, that everyone in the room is looking at her, even though their eyes are seemingly focused elsewhere. They're stealing glances; they're wondering why she's here among them.

"Excuse me," she says and stands, taking her purse with her, thinking, I don't trust you people.

The woman in the silver dress says, "Such nice manners," and everyone laughs.

Miss Betsy walks down the hall but imagines she's on a moving walkway. She even makes the humming noise to accompany her journey. At the end of the hall, she looks around. Why did she think the restroom was here? The first door she opens is for a closet. Inside is a fake Christmas tree and boxes of lights and ornaments. When Miss Betsy realizes that the tree is still growing, she slams shut the door. Should she tell someone that there's a living tree inside the closet?

She opens another door. This time it is the bathroom, and Claire is already in there with Worthington – Claire facing the wall, her long skirt hiked up, while Worthington pushes himself into her from behind, his pants puddled on the floor. The way his beard is trimmed and his hair is sticking up, he looks conspicuously like the devil. This is no hallucination.

"Are you okay?" Miss Betsy asks Claire.

Worthington laughs. Claire says, "Do you want to join us?"

Miss Betsy knows, in this moment, what death must feel like: the last breath taken, the last drop of blood drained, the coffin sealed. There's nothing but a hole in the Earth waiting for her. She shuts the door.

To escape, she opens yet another door but finds two children inside: Vickie and Johnny. When she sees Johnny, she realizes that he is actually *her* Johnny, except that he is only four years old now.

"Miss Betsy!" Johnny yells, and the little girl named Vickie smiles. She cups her hands over her mouth then inexplicably starts chewing on her fingers.

"Don't eat them," Miss Betsy cautions the little girl, but it's Johnny that she looks at when she speaks. Oh, what a darling little boy he had been! What a terribly sad but beautiful face!

"Let's play a game," Miss Betsy announces, and she leads Vickie to the closet and makes her stand inside. "I want you to wait in here, okay? Wait in here, and Miss Betsy will be right back with a giant ice cream cone for you. The biggest ice cream cone ever!" She pats the girl on the head then shuts the door. She pushes a chest-of-drawers on rollers in front of the door. Taking Johnny by the hand, Miss Betsy leads him down the hallway, past the bathroom of broken hearts, past the woman who claims to be Johnny's mother but who's too busy chattering away about a mythical race of half-rodents-half-men to notice them. They leave through the front door.

"Where are you taking me?" Johnny asks as they head downstairs.

"Shhhhh," Miss Betsy says. "No questions. You're my little Johnny. That's all you need to know."

They step outside, into a tidal wave of wind.

"I'm cold," Johnny says.

"You're fine," Miss Betsy says, pulling Johnny into the street. Miss Betsy hesitates, trying to remember the general direction of her own apartment. It's miles away, she realizes, but maybe someone will see them, a woman and a boy walking in the freezing cold, and offer them a ride. She can see the wind coming toward her. It looks like water, and for a moment, as it passes over them, the two are completely submerged and floating down the street – or so it seems. Choking from the water-wind, coughing and blinking, Miss Betsy staggers backwards.

"I want my mommy," Johnny says. His voice is a tire whining against asphalt, a strip of burning rubber. *She's a druggie*, Miss Betsy wants to say, *probably a junkie. She's unfit for motherhood.* Instead of explaining this to the boy, she pulls him by the hand, ignoring his pleas. They walk several more blocks. *I wonder how tall the tree in the closet has grown*, Miss Betsy wonders. *I wonder if Vickie is still waiting for her ice cream cone. I wonder if Worthington's prick is still inside Claire.*

She stops walking and grabs Johnny by the shoulders. "Why did you die in *Korea*?" she asks him. "Why did you leave me with blood all over my goddamned *bed*? Half of that blood was *yours*." She's shaking Johnny now, hard, and Johnny's crying. "You're a son of a bitch, do you know that? You're why I'm here right now. Do you hear me? It's all your fault! Every last thing."

Miss Betsy sees in the distance several men and women running toward her. They, too, are without coats, and she thinks at first that they are being chased. But no: they are all people from the party. And no one else is behind them. They are heading for Miss Betsy, swarming toward her. Before Miss Betsy can turn and run, she is tackled to the ground, the air knocked out of her.

She hears someone saying over and over, "My baby, my baby," and she hears Johnny saying, "She hurt me." A man on top of Miss Betsy, staring down at her, says, "Are you crazy, lady? Are you nuts?"

Miss Betsy sees Worthington and yells a warning to everyone with him: "You are the children of your father, the Devil, and you want to follow your father's desires." She'd heard a priest say this once in church many years ago, and now it's come back to her, as clear as the pocky face of the man on top of her.

"She's having a bad trip," someone says, and someone else says, "Let's take her back and calm her down."

A knot blooms at the back of her head; her face is too raw to touch. "When he tells a lie," she continues, glaring at Claire, "he is only doing what is natural to him, because he is a liar and the father of all lies!" She lets two men she doesn't know help her while Johnny and his mother keep a safe distance ahead.

A few weeks later, Miss Betsy loses her job. The producer, whose gout has all but incapacitated him, tells her that she has become too unpredictable. "But worse," he says, "is that you don't look all that...how shall I put this...*hygienic* anymore. We need someone more...what's the best word...*clean*."

Miss Betsy refuses to respond to any of the producer's accusations, and after a few days of not speaking at all, she realizes that there is no need for speech. Why talk? The only things to talk about are trivial and insignificant, so why bother?

Miss Betsy expects a lull in the show, but when she turns on her TV the next morning, she sees that the new host is Claire. Alone in her room, she thinks, *Miss Claire?* Her heart clenches, fist-like. Her face is so hot she needs a cool wash cloth to put on her forehead.

She quits going to parties. She stops dropping acid and smoking grass, but there is always gin around to take the edges off and smooth life's corners.

Her father dies one Saturday afternoon after heading into the basement to tinker with the Hoosier cabinet he bought when Miss Betsy was still a teenager. According to Dolores, the last thing he asked, before heading downstairs, was if eggnog really had eggs in it.

"Imagine," Dolores says at the funeral, "living with a man for forty years who doesn't know if eggnog really has eggs in it." Dolores takes a deep breath and holds it a moment. She looks as though she might start weeping. "I turned my back on him," she says. "I refused to answer." Dolores, who's unaware that Miss Betsy no longer speaks, shakes her head. "I should have answered his questions, but I'm just so tired, dear. So tired."

One night, on her way to the corner liquor store, a man with a gun steps out from a darkened alley and demands Miss Betsy hand over her purse.

Miss Betsy shakes her head. *I can't,* she thinks.

The man reaches out and yanks the purse strap so hard that Miss Betsy falls to one knee. He jerks it free of her arm, then turns back into the alley and takes off running. Miss Betsy, on her hands and knees, begins weeping. Her face, slick from nervous sweat and tears, feels as though it's leaking, and for a moment she fears she's been shot, even though she knows that the gun wasn't fired. She opens her mouth to scream, but nothing comes out.

At night, in the pitch-black, she sits bolt upright, certain someone is inside her apartment. It could be the thief who now knows her address, but maybe it's someone from one of those parties, a person to whom she gave her personal information when she shouldn't have. She flips on the light, hoping to scare whoever it is, but no one's here. She checks every room, every lock, every window – all is secure. When she gets back into bed and turns off the bed-side light, returning to darkness, she feels it again: two eyes. But she realizes now that no one's inside her apartment. Someone somewhere has pulled the Magic Mirror from Miss Betsy's stolen purse and is staring at her through its empty oval. She should find it a comfort – someone, at least, is watching her – but she doesn't want to be watched anymore. Like talking, nothing good has come from it.

Miss Betsy drives back home to Beloit the next morning, abandoning her Chicago apartment and leaving her belongings behind.

"So, what are you going to do with yourself up here?" Dolores asks. "Do you want to stay here for a while?"

Miss Betsy nods.

"You got a cold or something?" Dolores asks. "You got laryngitis?"

Miss Betsy writes on a pad of paper, *I quit talking*.

Her mother reads the message, thinks about it, and then starts weeping. After a week in the house, Dolores demands that Miss Betsy speak.

"I won't eat today unless you talk to me!" Dolores says. "I'll starve myself to death!"

Miss Betsy doesn't speak, and Dolores eventually makes

herself a tuna sandwich.

The next morning, Dolores is weeping again at the kitchen table. "My own daughter is a mute," she says when she notices Miss Betsy walking into the room.

I'm sorry, Miss Betsy writes, but Dolores crumples the sheet up and tosses it aside. "Oh sure, oh sure," she says. "You're sorry. But what about *me?*" she asks. "How do you think *I* feel?"

After a few weeks, Dolores gives up her theatrics and the two women fall into a routine, a rhythm of life Miss Betsy remembers clearly from childhood. When she hears Dolores' car keys jingle, she puts on her long wool coat, carefully buttoning it up. She trails behind her mother and listens to the woman's tirades about this or that while she herself remains silent. Today, in the car, Dolores returns to her favorite subject: Miss Betsy not talking.

"Why won't you talk, dear?" she asks. "It's not right, you not talking. Why won't you talk to *me?* What have I ever done to you?"

Dolores pulls into the parking lot of the last remaining butcher shop in Beloit. Dolores has been coming here for over thirty years, but soon she'll probably have to go to the supermarket. Supermarkets are the wave of the future – or so everyone says. But the only future that concerns Dolores is tomorrow. Tomorrow is the Junior League luncheon, and it's Dolores' turn to host.

Miss Betsy follows Dolores, who heads straight for the counter to take a plastic number off its hook. While they wait, Dolores studies the meat.

"I pray for you to talk again," Dolores says. "I pray every night, Betsy, but I'm not sure what else I can do."

Miss Betsy shakes her head. *Not here* is what she tries to communicate.

"Number fourteen?" the butcher asks, and Dolores steps up. She orders a pound of chicken breasts, pointing to the ones that she wants, but when it comes to the tongue, she wants the butcher to hand it to her for further inspection. The butcher tears a sheet of wax paper, picks out a plump one, and hands it over the counter to Dolores.

Miss Betsy's mother is as inexplicable to her as a perfect stranger. The butcher and Miss Betsy make eye contact, and there's a moment when Miss Betsy believes that they are thinking the same thing: *This woman is a handful, isn't she?* The tongue is grey and knobby, an unsightly piece of flesh. Dolores is squeezing and sniffing it. She is making a spectacle of herself, and people have stopped what they're doing to stare at her. The butcher, visibly tired and stained with the blood of silenced animals, smiles at Miss Betsy and Miss Betsy smiles back, while Dolores holds the thick slab above her head. Moving her lips, speaking to herself, Dolores peers hopefully up at the dead tongue, as if offering it to the Gods.

THE
IMMORTALS

In Chicago, while taking the El from Wrigley Field to Evanston, Rudy O'Hara was certain he recognized the woman sitting across the train's aisle, but he couldn't place her. He wanted to lean forward and say, *We know each other, don't we?* but years ago in New York he had asked a woman on a train if they knew each other, and when she looked up at Rudy, she screamed, made whooping sounds, then started blubbering. She was crazy, of course, a lunatic, probably homeless, but Rudy hadn't realized any of this until it was too late. The other passengers glowered at Rudy. An employee from the train arrived to see what the problem was. Only then did Rudy notice the contents of her two shopping bags. Packing peanuts. Hundreds, possibly thousands, of packing peanuts.

Rudy was certain, however, that he *did* know this woman, that she was someone he had known years ago. Someone's mother, perhaps? Someone's older sister? He felt on the brink of recall, but he needed a spark to bring it all back, a name, a place. Each time she looked up and caught him staring, he averted his eyes. Twice, he caught *her* staring. At the stop before Howard – the end of the line where Rudy would need to change trains – the woman abruptly stood and exited. Rudy's heart clenched at the thought of her gone, the mystery unsolved. But once on the platform, the woman stopped walking. Squinting, she peered in at Rudy. Rudy leaned forward. The woman tilted her head, then mouthed his name: *Rudy?* Rudy nodded. And then it came to him: It was his ex-wife. It was Leila Jacobs.

Oh my God, Rudy thought. He hadn't seen Leila in fifteen years. He'd spent the two years after their marriage had gone sour telling his story to anyone who would listen, mulling over every detail of their break-up. He bored his friends to tears by laboriously sifting through the relationship's minutia. He scared total strangers by appearing as an obsessed ex-husband unable to discern the appropriate detail from the inappropriate. "She was terrific in bed," he had told one older couple who, having stopped at their local bar for two glasses of port to celebrate their forty-third wedding anniversary, made the mistake of sitting near Rudy. "No, no, not just terrific," Rudy said. "*Un-fucking-believable*, if you want to know the truth. Kinky stuff." And then, to their horror, he told them.

He had temporarily become another person. An insufferable person, he later realized. And yet telling the story so many times helped to exorcise the entire episode. Repetition diluted its emotional impact. The more he told it, the less real it felt. In time, he was able to hover above the story when he told it, and it began to sound to his own ears like a description of somebody else's life – the curious tale of some poor schmuck's sharp descent after his wife dumps him. But there was always the faint hope that in telling the story he'd stumble across the very thing that had alluded him: the precise moment things started to go wrong. If he could pinpoint that moment, if he could reach into the story's viscera and remove the black spot for others to see, he might be able to undo the damage.

Fifteen years later, Rudy understood full well that there was no specific moment, that there were no definite answers to what had happened. He and Leila had been in their early twenties – two kids, really. But something about seeing her after all these years triggered an irrational desire. He wanted to ask her what had gone wrong. He wanted her to point to a moment and say, "There!"

It was snowing and windy, and everyone on the platform shielded themselves against the elements. Through smeared Plexiglas, through blowing snow, Leila appeared ghost-like staring into the warm train and mouthing Rudy's name. He wanted to speak to her, he wanted to ask her those all-important questions, but it was too late. The train's doors suctioned shut, and the train rocketed north.

Rudy and Leila had met as undergraduates at Illinois State University. They first saw each other from across the shaggy expanse of their friend's carpet while listening, along with a dozen other college students, to the ins and outs of Artemis International – how much money there was to be made, how to shimmy up the corporate ladder, how incredibly easy it would all be. And it *did* seem easy. Artemis International, specializing in household cleaners, was the last successful door-to-door operation in the country, and their friend Larry Borkowski was the regional rep.

During a cigarette break, Rudy stepped up next to Leila, who was dipping herself a cup of spiked punch. He introduced himself, and she introduced herself.

"So what do you think?" he asked.

"I heard there was going to be some good pot here," she said. "WHERE'S THE POT?" she yelled, then smiled. Rudy, startled by the outburst, looked around, but no one else paid her any mind. She was wearing a tie-dyed cotton dress and flip-flops. A paperback was tucked under her arm. "From what I hear," she said in a stage whisper, "this company is a pyramid scheme."

"Oh yeah? Well, I heard it was a cult," Rudy said, also in a stage whisper. "I heard they recruit devil worshippers."

"Really?" she said. "Maybe after the break we can sacrifice a freshman. Who shall it be?" She surveyed the room, her eyes hooded.

Larry nodded at the paperback under her arm. "How's the book?"

"Huh?" Leila looked down as if someone had slid the book in place without her knowing it. "Oh. *This.* You'd like it. It's ancient Arabian erotica."

"Arabian erotica?" He laughed. "What makes you think *I'd* like it?"

Leila took a step closer. She said, "You're flirting with me, aren't you?" When Rudy didn't answer, she said, "It's about sex. Here. Take a peek." Before he could protest, she'd given the book to him and returned to her place on the carpet.

The book was titled *The Perfumed Garden,* translated by Sir Richard F. Burton. *The actor?* he wondered. Surely not. Rudy sat down and opened to a chapter titled "Names Given to the Sexual Organs of Women." It consisted of a list of nicknames, and although the names themselves were rather silly, such as "the swelling one," "the crusher," and "the hedgehog," each name was accompanied by a startlingly graphic description. Rudy looked up at Leila. She was sitting cross-legged on the floor and peering up at Larry Borkowski, who was demonstrating his product's ability to remove mustard stains from a satin blouse. What kind of girl carried around a book like this? Rudy read a few more pages. It was, he hated to admit, gripping. A real page-turner. Who'd have thought there were so many varieties for a single body part? And who'd have thought to give them names? It was like that old folklore about Eskimos having a hundred different words for snow. By the end of Larry's demonstration, Rudy had learned the fine differences between "the glutton," "the fugitive," and "the humpbacked," but he was now mildly depressed by his own fumbling and limited experience with women and, more pointedly, his inattention.

He found Leila outside afterward. She was smoking a cigarette. After each intake, she leaned her head all the way back and blew a stream of smoke straight up into the air. Rudy watched the smoke dissipate into a mushroom cloud above her head, and he wanted to say something clever, like, "You must be thinking about Hiroshima," but he didn't.

She took her book and said, "What did I tell you?" And there was something about the way she looked at that precise moment, the way smoke spread above her, the way crickets moved languorously around them as if sensing cooler weather on the way, something about the graphic descriptions he'd read in a book now tucked under her damp, warm arm – there was something so desperate and sad about all of it that encouraged him to reach out and touch her bare elbow. He did it – he touched her – and she said, "I knew you'd like it."

They moved in together one month later. They divvied up the city to canvas. They hosted their first Artemis get-together, serving cheap wine in boxes. Leila broke out her stash of pot, rolled several joints, and passed them around on silver trays, like hors d'oeuvres. One night, after everyone had gone home, Leila put a scratchy show tune on the turntable. *Brigadoon*. While lip-synching one of the songs and offering a dramatic interpretation, she slowly removed her clothes, transforming a Broadway musical into whorehouse burlesque, until all that she was wearing was a pair of Rudy's old tube socks. Rudy sat on the couch and watched, amazed at the fortunate turn his life had taken.

They married less than a year after that first night at Larry's. Their friends gave them enough money for a trip to the Florida Keys. Artemis headquarters sent them five hundred dollars' worth of cleaning supplies. Rudy was so happy he could barely concentrate on what people were saying to him. What more could he possibly have asked for?

◎

One year after he'd seen Leila on the train, Rudy returned to Chicago for the annual Artemis conference, where
he, as senior vice-president, delivered the keynote address.
Artemis had survived a tough year of downsizing, slim prof-
its, and devalued stock. It was Rudy's job tonight to rally its
regional reps, who, in turn, would reenergize its workforce. At
one point, while on a roll, Rudy ditched his notes. He leaned
forward, nearly touching the microphone with his mouth.

"ARTEMIS," he said, and his voice, deeper and louder,
sounded eerily God-like in the auditorium. "Who *was* Artemis? Let me tell you, my friends. Artemis was the daughter
of Zeus. She was one of the immortals. No one has to tell you
about the tough times we've been through lately, especially in
the media. The *media!*" Rudy, huffing, shook his head. "Well,
listen up, folks. Artemis International, like its namesake, is im-
mortal, too. And I'm here tonight to tell you that we're here to
stay. That's right. We. Are. Here. To. *Stay.*"

For this, Rudy received a standing ovation.

After the speech, Rudy headed straight for the hotel bar
and ordered a vodka gimlet. He needed to unwind. He finished
his first drink quickly, then nursed a second one. He was about
to spin the Japanese lantern hanging above his head when a
woman sidled up to the bar and said, "I loved your speech."
She was wearing a dark business suit, and her red hair was
piled up behind her head, twirled like a cinnamon roll.

Three hours later, they were both drunk. Her name was
Jennifer, and she worked for a chapter of Artemis in Florida.
She was a talker, freely doling out company gossip, one story
of impropriety or weakness after another – employees who'd
embezzled from Artemis, those who'd had breakdowns, men
and women who'd cheated on one Artemis employee with another. Rudy was finding it difficult to focus on anything Jennifer was saying, all the names, their various problems, the way

one person was connected to another person. It was like listening to someone dissect a Calculus problem. But then Jennifer told him a story about a woman from Tampa, and because of the hushed tone in her voice, a reserve that hadn't previously been exhibited, Rudy paid closer attention.

"I met her last year," Jennifer said. "A friend of a friend. Or maybe a friend of a friend of a friend. She worked for Artemis in the '80s. That's how we got to talking. And then a few months ago I saw a newspaper article about her in the *Tampa Trib*."

Rudy felt Jennifer's thigh pressing against his. "What about her?" he asked.

"She was decapitated."

"Decapitated?"

Jennifer said, "Oh, what was her name? I showed the article to some of our Tampa reps, but no one remembered her. I thought maybe you might since you're higher up the food chain. But now I can't remember her name."

"*Decapitated?*" Rudy asked again. He moved his leg.

"She and her husband were on a boat in Tampa Bay, and she fell off. Apparently, the blades on the motor sliced her head off."

"Jesus."

Jennifer's eyes widened, coming into focus for the first time in an hour. "I *know!*" she said. Her eyes went back out of focus, and she sucked up the last of her margarita through her straw.

Rudy and Jennifer rode the elevator up to Rudy's room. While Jennifer used the bathroom, Rudy swept his bed clean of pamphlets, receipts, and still-damp towels. He tossed his suit-bag across the room. It slammed against the air-conditioner and landed upside-down, its pouches blooming knots of socks. Jennifer emerged from the bathroom, completely naked except for her gold bracelets and dozens of charms. She rattled when she walked, as if she were made of nuts and bolts.

In bed, she yanked on Rudy's belt, trying to loosen it, then worked on his shirt buttons. Rudy kicked off his shoes and, using his big toes as hooks, peeled off his own socks. He was on top of her, moaning, when she whispered into his ear, "*Leila Jacobs.*"

Rudy arched back. "What did you say?"

"Leila Jacobs," she said. "It just came to me. That's the woman I was telling you about."

"Which woman?" Rudy asked.

"The one who got decapitated."

"Leila Jacobs?" Rudy rolled off Jennifer. "Oh, Jesus. Leila Jacobs? Are you sure?" he asked. He was trying to make sense of what he was being told, but the jagged pieces of information weren't fitting together. Leila? Dead? Impossible! He had seen her only a year ago, on the train. And wouldn't someone have told him? Not that they'd had any mutual friends, not since college. But still... When your ex-wife dies – when she is *decapitated* – wouldn't someone do the legwork to find you?

"What's the matter?" Jennifer said. "Did I say the wrong thing?"

But Rudy could barely hear her. She might as well have been asking questions from the far end of a tunnel. *Leila*, Rudy thought. *My poor Leila.* He wanted to break down in tears – it's what he thought he *should* do – but he couldn't conjure a clear image of her, except for the one on the train and then, moments later, on the platform. But even those images were blurry, like a double-exposed photograph. And the scary thing was, if Leila hadn't mouthed Rudy's name that day, he wouldn't have known what she looked like at all.

One year after the wedding, Leila came home from a night of door-to-door sales, sighed loudly, and dropped her bags in the middle of the kitchen. Rudy was making macaroni and cheese. He was prying open the miniature can of cheese when Leila announced that she was bored.

"Want to go to a movie?" Rudy asked.

Leila shook her head. "That's not going to do it, boss. Nope. I'm bored with this Artemis crap. I don't have time to study anymore. But I'm bored with school, too."

"Bored with Artemis? What do you mean?"

"I hate knocking on strangers' doors. You never know what kind of hairy ape'll answer. And their kids – *ugh*. This kid tonight had peanut butter all over his face, and the parents stood there like it was normal. *My* mother would have told me to go wipe my face. Not these parents. God forbid." Leila shivered at the thought. "And these parties we throw. They were fun at first. It was something, you know, *different*. But the people who come. I mean, you stand up and start talking about how much money they're going to make, and they get all glassy-eyed. Have you ever seen the look they give you? No wonder people think it's a cult."

Rudy said, "What are you talking about? What's wrong with the look they give me?"

"It's a pipe-dream," Leila said. "It's a scam, and they can't see it. They buy every last word you say."

The muscles in Rudy's neck tightened. "A *pipe-dream*? A *scam*? You don't really *believe* that, do you?"

"Hold on," Leila said. "You don't really think we're going to be *millionaires* one day, do you? Don't tell me you're like the rest of them." She plopped onto the sofa. She stared at Rudy a good long while, then leaned her head all the way back and said, "Oh, boy."

One month later she filed for divorce.

A week before their divorce was final, they met for the last time at a Chi-Chi's. Neutral territory. A restaurant neither of them had ever been before. Rudy had arrived first. After the waitress delivered Leila to their booth, Rudy demanded to know what she had done with their photo albums.

"I took them," she said.

"You *took* them? You're the one who doesn't want to be married, in case you forgot."

"It'll be easier on you in the long run."

"How so?"

Leila, absently stirring salsa with a chip, took a deep breath. She said, "Years from now you'll try to remember what I looked like and you won't remember. And guess what? You won't have any photos to remind you. It'll be like I never existed."

"Oh," Rudy said. He considered this. "And that's a *good* thing?"

Leila nodded. "Trust me."

Her reason for taking the photos had sounded preposterous, but with each passing year Rudy had a more difficult time remembering her. At first, her features shifted ever so slightly. Eventually, her face had begun to melt. In its final stage, she simply faded. By the time Rudy saw her on the train, that whole two-year period of his life – meeting, marrying, and then divorcing her – had seemed like something he'd invented. After the divorce, Leila moved far away and Rudy never saw her again – not until the day on the train.

After the Chicago conference, Rudy returned to his home in Bethesda, Maryland, and arranged for an indefinite leave of absence from Artemis. At the end of the week, he took a flight out of Reagan National, arriving a few short hours later in Tampa. Even after years of airplane travel, Rudy still savored the disorientation that accompanied flying. When he'd left D.C., it was overcast, drizzling, and from the airport terminal, you could barely see the Capitol's dome. The only evidence of the Washington Monument's existence was the pulse of light at its tip, the obelisk's steady heartbeat. Otherwise, Rudy couldn't see much of anything across the murky Potomac. A few hours later, Rudy stepped into brain-piercing sunlight and rows of ludicrously lush flora. Lizards scattered at the sight of him. It was as though, having left behind the moonscape of D.C., he had landed not in another city but on another planet. His clothes were too dark, too drab; his skin, bleached of color. Everyone at the airport in Tampa wore bright colors, peach or mauve or banana-yellow. Some wore stylish straw hats. If he ever wore a straw hat in D.C., he'd likely get mistaken for a vagrant. At the very least, people would point and laugh. But not here in Tampa.

Rudy had brought his sample kit with him – a boxy suitcase about the length and width of a briefcase but much wider. Inside was a variety of cleaning supplies, plus pamphlets and order forms. It had been years since he'd actually been in the field, working door-to-door. He'd spent the greater part of his career in management. He wasn't a millionaire, as he'd been promised all those years ago at Larry Borkowski's house, but he did all right. Low six figures per annum. Not bad for the son of an electrician. He had no complaints.

At the hotel, Rudy generously tipped the bellboy for carrying up his luggage. He collapsed onto the bed and idly flipped through the dozens of cable stations, finding nothing. The air conditioner was on high, turning everything ice-cold, including the pillowcases. Rudy pulled the comforter to his chin. Every time he'd tried sleeping since Chicago, the word *decapitated* came tapping. *Decapitated. Decapitated.* What did it look like? What were the logistics? Had Leila thought of him in those final seconds? He knew the answer – of *course* she hadn't thought of him – but he couldn't help entertaining the notion that the final image that came to her, the person she thought of, was him. *Decapitated.* "Jesus," Rudy said.

Back home, Rudy would fall asleep for only five or ten minutes at a stretch before waking up in a cool sweat, but here, mid-afternoon in Tampa, city of Leila's presumed demise,

Rudy fell sound asleep. He woke up once in the middle of the night to cartoon music coming from the TV, but then he didn't wake up again until the maid keyed into his room the next morning. Rudy, blinking at her, couldn't for a moment remember where he was, so he smiled at the maid, waving away her apologies, as if nothing in the world could possibly ruin his day. "No, no," he said. "It's okay. Everything's okay." There was a lilt to his voice, and in that waking moment of bewilderment, he must have sounded to the maid like a man on his first honeymoon.

No one answered when Rudy rang the bell, so he carried his heavy sample kit back to his car, loosened his tie, and waited. He'd forgotten how much work it was to carry supplies door-to-door, even though he had walked no farther than from his car. It was over one hundred degrees, and he was wearing a suit. He'd have taken off the jacket except that his shirt was now ringed with large damp stains under his arms.

Last week, Rudy had searched Tampa newspapers online until he found the small article about Leila. There were no photos. The article itself was short, inconsequential. Rudy vacillated between believing it was indeed her and writing it off as a coincidence. What, after all, had Leila been doing in Tampa? How long had she been living there? And when had she re-married? He certainly hadn't heard about any of this. Not that he'd heard anything about Leila over the years. After reading the article a dozen times, Rudy remained skeptical. The information in the newspaper seemed remote. There was no mention of *him*, for instance. The only man named was Robert Haines.

Robert "Bobby" Haines. 46 years old. Tampa Bay native. Owner of a chain of bagel stores. Leila Jacobs' husband. They had been married for ten years, and Bobby had been the only other person on the boat when Leila fell overboard. There was, according to the police, no evidence of foul play. The medical examiner had ruled her death an accident.

Part of Rudy's motives for flying to Tampa was to confirm Leila's death. If it was indeed her, he'd find out. If he never went to Tampa, her death would never seem, well, real. But there was another motive as well, a motive Rudy hated to admit even as it nagged him. He wanted to know why Leila had left him. He wasn't sure why he still cared after all these years. He *shouldn't* have cared. And yet here he was, sitting in a rental car and waiting for Bobby Haines to return home.

Bobby lived on Tampa Bay in a home that must have been worth a few million dollars – possibly more. Stucco with orange clay tiles covering the roof, the house was a monster, at least six thousand square feet. If Bobby's house had been as nice as Rudy's or slightly nicer, he might have been jealous; but this house was so far out of his own league he could only be impressed. After four hours of waiting, Rudy was about to give up, afraid neighbors were going to call the police, but then the garage door started to crawl open. A forest-green Jaguar turned onto the driveway and zipped into the garage. The door hesitated a beat, then scrolled back down.

Rudy gave Bobby a good twenty minutes to get settled in. Then he walked up to the house, sample kit banging against his knee, and rang the man's bell. He was about to press the button again when he heard the unclicking of several locks. A heavy wooden door opened, but the outer door with wrought-iron bars remained between them.

"Good afternoon, sir!" Rudy called out. "My name's Mike, and I'm from Artemis International. Are you familiar with Artemis' line of world-famous cleaning products?"

Bobby opened the wrought-iron door. What struck Rudy was how much Bobby was the antithesis of himself. Bobby had an athlete's build, thick jet-black hair, perfect teeth, blue eyes. Rudy had a paunch, his reddish-blond hair was starting to thin, he'd never gotten his teeth fixed, and his eyes were the color of dish water.

"Did you say Artemis?" Bobby asked.

"Yes, sir. Artemis International. What you get with Artemis is industrial strength for a price that's lower than your average household cleaner. We have a proven forty year track record, sir. *Consumer Reports* consistently ranks our products as the very best in the categories of quality *and* cost."

Bobby opened the door wider. He moved aside and said, "Come on in."

The air-conditioning, potent as a drug, reminded him of a theory he'd heard about Vegas, that the casinos blew cold air out onto the sidewalks to lure the sweating masses inside, and then pumped extra oxygen into the casino itself to keep them there. Who could resist?

Rudy pulled a handkerchief from his pocket and dabbed away the sweat. Was the floor in the foyer marble? *Jesus.* There couldn't have been a greater divide between the house he now stood in and the student ghetto where he and Leila had lived. Bobby's place had solid oak bookcases; Rudy's, plastic milk crates. Bobby's walls had original artwork; Rudy's, a poster of Che Guevara alongside a velvet "Dogs Playing Poker." To Rudy's credit, he knew that the real title of his velvet painting was "A Friend in Need," that it was from a series of such paintings with dogs, and that the series parodied the work of a 17th century artist, but none of this negated the fact that, fifteen years later, he still owned "Dogs Playing Poker." It hung in his basement, across from a foosball table.

"Let's go over here," Bobby said, motioning to an overstuffed couch. "What can I get you to drink? You want a beer?"

"A beer? Sure. A beer sounds great."

Photos lined the fireplace mantel. Rudy wanted to examine them, but Bobby returned seconds later with two bottles of imported beer. A parrot took up most of the label. In the background sailed a pirate ship. Given what had happened to

Leila, Rudy would have thought the sight of any kind of boat, real or fictitious, would have been too much to bear. Clearly, he was wrong.

"Artemis," Bobby said. "That's funny." He wagged his head.

Rudy took a long swig, waiting.

"I knew someone who worked for Artemis," Bobby said. "Not in Florida. She worked for them in Illinois. Years ago. Before I knew her."

"Really?" As he raised the beer again to his mouth, Rudy noticed the thumping pulse in his own wrist. His breath had become so shallow, he could barely swallow the beer.

"A long time ago," Bobby said. He didn't say who, and Rudy wasn't going to push him. "I'm in the bagel business," Bobby said, changing the subject.

"Good business," Rudy said. "Twenty years ago, no one could have told you what a bagel looked like. Now it's a dietary staple. I don't know who got the marketing ball rolling on that one, but they did a great job."

"Another beer?" Bobby asked.

Rudy examined his bottle. It was still half-full. "Sure," he said.

Bobby headed for the kitchen, but then Rudy heard a door open and shut, followed by the muffled purr of a fan. The bathroom. Rudy walked to the fireplace, took down a framed photo from the mantel, and examined it. It was Leila all right. Though she looked at some angles like the Leila he once knew, at other angles she looked nothing like Leila at all. She could have been Leila's older sister, or her cousin.

The photo had been taken on a windy day. The scarf on Leila's head gravitated to the right, and Leila had one eye partially closed. She was giving the photographer one of her trademark looks, a look Rudy had forgotten – Leila, clearly pleased and smiling but trying not to reveal the smile, a teasing, tight-lipped look of mock-anger.

A toilet flushed, and Rudy carried the photo, frame and all, back to his sample kit. He slipped it inside and clicked the lid's hasps.

Bobby had changed into shorts and a Polo shirt. "Oh yeah – those beers. Almost forgot." He disappeared again. Rudy drained the bottle.

They drank the next two rounds without saying much of anything, then Bobby said, "Let's get the hell out of here. This place is driving me nuts. Ever been to Beach Bums?"

"Nope."

"It's a roadhouse," Bobby said. "Only locals. No tourists. You up for it?"

"Sure."

"Good," Bobby said. "You'll love it."

They took Bobby's Jag. Rudy set his sample kit on the floorboard, braced between his legs. Bobby wheeled the air conditioner's knob to HIGH. Even though the sun had gone down, it was still as deathly hot outside as it had been at two in the afternoon. How did people live like this? Was there ever any relief?

"Artemis," Bobby said, tapping the steering wheel with his forefinger. He was doing at least a hundred. "Artemis, Artemis. Who *was* Artemis? Someone from Shakespeare?"

"She was Apollo's brother."

"Apollo? Apollo who? Oh, wait. *Apollo.* You mean Apollo *Apollo. That* Apollo?"

"Yep," Rudy said. "From mythology."

"Ah," Bobby said. "So what's her deal? Was she the one with snakes all in her hair?"

"You're thinking of Medusa."

"That's right! So which one's Artemis?"

"Artemis was goddess of the animals!" Rudy said, as if

he were standing behind a podium. "Queen of the hunters!"

"Really? Goddess of the animals? Queen of the hunters? How can she be both?"

Rudy shrugged. He hadn't considered this discrepancy before. Now that he thought about it, all he knew about Artemis was what the company had put in its brochures and what a few mythology geeks had told him in passing at conferences. Perhaps he should have done a little more research. He should have gone to the library and checked out a book.

"I don't know," Rudy admitted. "She's one of the immortals."

"One of the immortals. Ha! I like that." Bobby turned on the radio. He kept his finger on scan. When he couldn't find anything that suited him, he turned it off. They started crossing a bridge that connected Tampa with St. Pete, a bridge so long that at a certain point in the night's darkness, Rudy began to imagine the slab of highway connected to nothing. He pictured them on a large concrete raft, floating aimlessly on water.

"This is wild," Rudy said.

"What?"

"This bridge. It just keeps going."

"You're not from around here?"

"Nope. D.C."

"They sent you all the way from D.C. to sell a few boxes of laundry soap? That's a little strange, don't you think?"

"We're getting a better feel for the market down here," Rudy said.

"Oh. Well, then you probably don't know about the bridge that collapsed," Bobby said, "the one that connected St. Pete to Bradenton. 1980, I think it was. The Sunshine Skyway Bridge. Fishermen miles away could hear the bridge breaking. They heard people screaming. One fisherman told me he thought it was the end of the world. He said he sat in his boat and waited for the nuclear blast, or whatever the hell it was going to be, to wash over him. Can you imagine?"

"Jesus," Rudy said. "The end of the world."

Bobby reached over, slapped Rudy's thigh, and said, "Welcome to Florida, friend."

Bobby took the first exit off the bridge, then, after some time on the main road, wheeled into a jungle-dense stretch of road at the end of which was Beach Bums. Constructed out of unpainted plywood and with open walls on either side for the wind to sweep through, Beach Bums looked like a long-abandoned hideaway, the kind of place bank robbers might have holed up inside while on the lam. Rudy took his sample kit with him, setting it down next to a barstool.

"Look who's here!" the bartender said. "The old *crowbar* himself!" The bartender was tall and sun-burnt. His hair and beard were gray stubble. He shook Rudy's hand and introduced himself as Phineas. Finn for short. "Name your poison, boys," he said.

"Rum and Cokes," Bobby told Finn. "Make 'em *Meyer's*. None of that rail shit."

"What did he call you?" Rudy whispered. *"The crowbar?"*

"My wife," he said. "That was her nickname for me. Finn overheard one night and has been riding me ever since. It's hard to explain. She had this old book – *The Perfumed Garden*."

"The Perfumed Garden? My ex-wife had a copy of that, too."

"You're shitting me. Really?"

"It's how we met," Rudy said. "Sort of."

"Same here!" Bobby said. "Well. Sort of."

"How weird is that?" Rudy asked.

"Weird," Bobby said.

Rudy forced himself to meet Bobby's eyes. "So… Are the two of you still together?"

"Oh, no. Didn't I tell you? I thought I told you. She died. An accident." Bobby held out one of his hands, as if checking to make sure that his fingernails had been clipped, then he reached up and scratched his head.

"Oh, Jesus, I'm sorry."

Bobby said nothing. The drinks came. Bobby took a sip, stirred it with his finger, and took another sip. "What about you, old sport?" Bobby asked, perking up. "You said *ex-*? What happened?"

"I don't know. One day we were married, and then one day we weren't. Maybe we were just too young."

"Sounds like my wife's *first* marriage."

Rudy nodded. He waited for more, but nothing more came. Bugs, searching for light, banged against the screen door. A lizard army-crawled across the bar.

"Darts?" Bobby finally asked.

Rudy'd hoped darts would set the stage for personal revelation, but this didn't happen. By his fifth rum and Coke, Rudy missed the dartboard more often than he hit it. His head started to feel puffy, as if a pound of air had been pumped into it.

Rudy picked up his sample kit and carried it to the men's room. Inside the restroom's only stall, he sat down, opened his kit, and pulled out the pilfered photo of Leila. The bathroom's bulb was dim, but after turning the photo back and forth, he finally caught a swatch of light. The longer he studied the photo, the more familiar she became. There were so many things he'd forgotten about her. Her lazy eye, for instance. *My droopy eyeball*, she called it. Or the scar on her chin, a wound from childhood. The scar was probably only a fifth of an inch long, and it was semi-hidden by a natural contour, but Rudy would touch it as gently as he would have touched a fresh wound. How could he have forgotten? There was the extraordinary thickness of her eyebrows. They were exotic, especially with that whisper of hair between them that could be seen only close-up. Rudy wiped his eyes. He was drunk – he realized that – but seeing the photo had miraculously resurrected all that he had somehow buried.

Rudy returned the photo, snapped shut his sample kit, used the urinal, washed his hands, blew his nose, blew it some more, wiped his eyes again, splashed cool water onto his face, dried off, then walked back to the bar. A shot of whiskey was waiting for him.

"You could've left that thing here," Bobby said, nodding at the sample kit. "I promise I won't rifle through it."

The bartender said, "I can't make that same promise."

Rudy stuck his finger into his shot, pulled it out, then licked his finger. "When did your wife pass on?" he asked.

"Six months ago," Bobby said. "Six months ago today, in fact."

Finn reached over the bar and squeezed Bobby's shoulder.

Bobby said, "She fell off my boat. The blades from the motor…they decapitated her. The Coast Guard recovered her body, but that's it – just her body."

Rudy wanted to ask what that meant – *just her body*. He knew what it probably meant, that they'd never recovered the head, but what were the theories about what had happened to it? Could it still be retrieved? Was anyone still looking? The more scenarios Rudy imagined, the weaker he felt at the possibilities of what might have become of it.

"What have you got in that damned thing, anyway?" the bartender asked, nodding at Rudy's sample kit.

Rudy threw back his shot. "Personal artifacts," he said.

Finn stared at Rudy. Rudy was getting the feeling that Finn didn't much care for him. Then Bobby said, "He's a rep for Artemis. You know, cleaning supplies."

"Oh," Finn said. "Isn't that a *cult* of some kind? That's what I heard, at least."

"Leila worked for them a long time ago," Bobby said. Rudy recognized in Bobby's voice the same tenor of grief that had once haunted his own voice. Everyone, *everything*, was somehow connected to Leila. All Rudy had needed – and all

Bobby needed now – was a bridge to join one subject, *any* subject, to her. "Leila," Bobby continued, "she always claimed it wasn't so much a cult as it was a pyramid scheme. We're talking fifteen, twenty years ago. I'm sure it's not like that now–" – he winked at Rudy – "– but what *she* said was that each person would rope in a certain number of people and then get a kick-back for each person roped in, and after you'd recruited so many people, you moved up this seemingly endless chain. The salesmen had to pay for their own products out of pocket, so it was a good idea to recruit as many people as possible so you could start getting some fringe benefits, like deeper discounts on the cleaning supplies. Or something like that. She didn't work for them too long, though. A year, I think."

"Was this when she was with her first husband?" Rudy asked.

"As a matter of fact, it was."

"Did he work for Artemis, too?"

"Oh yeah!" Bobby said, smiling. "According to Leila, this poor guy fell for the company hook, line, and sinker. They said jump, he jumped."

"But if you want to move up," Rudy said, "wouldn't you jump when someone said jump?"

"Absolutely," Bobby said. "Unless you're part of a pyramid scheme. Then what's the point? You end up looking like a sucker. And then your wife leaves you."

Finn said, "That's why I like my job. Someone says, 'Jump,' I say, 'Fuck you. *You* jump, shit-for-brains.'"

Bobby said, "You still keep that baseball bat back there?"

"You bet your ass," Finn said. He ran a hand over the stubble on top of his head. He smiled. In the dark recesses of his mouth were two gaps where teeth should have been. There was gold back there, too.

Bobby turned to Rudy. "Let's take a walk, buddy. I want to show you something." When Rudy reached for his sample kit, Bobby said, "You can leave that here."

"I'd feel better if I had it with me."

"Suit yourself."

The two men walked outside, then followed a stone path that curved around, and then behind, the building.

"That's my boat down there. This is where I dock it."

It was so dark out, Rudy couldn't see any of his own body parts let alone a boat. "Where?" he asked.

"Right there."

Rudy saw nothing. He followed the sound of footsteps, consciously lifting his foot high for each step so as not to tumble down the stone pathway. As soon as Rudy opened his mouth to ask how much farther it was, he ran smack into Bobby, who had stopped walking. Apparently, they'd reached the end of the dock.

"Whoa," Bobby said, turning to face Rudy. His breath was fumy from the alcohol, and a brief whiff made Rudy weak in the stomach. After Bobby composed himself, he climbed down into the boat and said, "Here, give me that damned suitcase."

Rudy surrendered the sample kit. Carefully, he made his way down into the boat. Rudy didn't know the first thing about boats. Did it have an inboard motor? Was it an inboard/outboard motor? Was the boat wooden? Aluminum? Fiberglass? At least it wasn't inflatable.

Bobby turned a key, and the engine coughed several times. Once it fired up, Bobby powered ahead, taking them quickly away from shore. A light mist touched Rudy's face. He hated to admit it, but this was nice. A boat. Maybe when he got back to D.C., he'd start pricing around. He liked this particular boat, too. It had padded seats, probably enough seating for a half-dozen people. Its headlights allowed Rudy to watch water slice and roll away beneath him – a dangerously hypnotic sight. In a matter of minutes they were far from land. Rudy, hearing something rolling around near his feet, reached down and picked up a flashlight. He turned it on, but nothing happened. After shaking it a few times, a dim spot of light appeared, surging. Bobby cut the engine, and the two men sat quietly in the listing boat, staring up at the night sky like a couple of castaways.

Bobby lit a joint. Rudy hadn't smoked since he'd been with Leila, but the familiar smell of pot instantly brought her into sharp focus. As if he'd read Rudy's mind, Bobby said, "This is the last of her stash."

"Your wife's?"

"I rolled it at the house," Bobby said, "before we left. She liked it to take the edge off. I never much cared for it."

"Me neither." Rudy, after taking a deep hit, handed it back. He held the hit for a long time, until he couldn't stand the burning in his nose and throat any longer, and then he let go.

Bobby took a hit. He said, "I was asleep when it happened."

"When what happened?"

Bobby coughed a few times, then sat with his elbows resting on his thighs, his head hung low. "The accident," he finally said.

"Was it this boat?"

"Yeah. And it happened right about here."

"*Here?*"

"More or less. We used to come out here every weekend."

Rudy and Bobby continued smoking the dope until all they were passing back and forth was an ember. "Ouch!" Rudy said and dropped it. "Well! I guess that's that." Rudy shook the flashlight, and the bulb brightened. He aimed it at the distance, illuminating only a wall of darkness. Darkness and water. He then aimed the flashlight into the water, studying the depths. The pot had unlocked a long-forgotten memory: A mythology geek he'd met a conference, a man who'd come up to him after a speech, told him that mythology was full of contradictions,

and that Artemis embodied one of them. On the one hand, she
was the protectress of dewy youth. Like a skilled huntsman,
she was careful to protect the young. On the other hand, she
wouldn't let the Greek Fleet sail to Troy until they had sacrificed a maiden to her. The mythology geek had been pleased
with himself, pleased with his knowledge. Rudy had politely
thanked him, shook his hand, and then, before the night was
through, forgotten all about him. Until now. He was about to
tell all of this to Bobby when he spotted something in the water.

"Oh my God," he said. "Look, look."

Bobby sat up. He moved to the edge of the boat and
leaned over.

"Right there," Rudy said, pointing to something that appeared to be the size and shape of a human head.

"What is it?" Bobby asked.

"I think it's her," Rudy said. "It's Leila."

"It can't be," Bobby said.

"It is." Rudy moved the flashlight until there wasn't as
much light reflecting off the water. "Look," he said. "The scar!
Just below her mouth. It's there. See it? And her eye. Look. The
lazy eye. It's her. I swear to God, it's her."

Bobby dipped his hand into the water, but the sandy
bed was too far down, way beyond his reach. He dipped his
hand in again, more desperate this time, trying to touch her.
Rudy, squinting, realized that what he was looking at wasn't
a head at all: It was only a large stone, or possibly his own
head's shadow. "I'm sorry," he said. "It's not her. I'm sorry. Jesus, what was I thinking?" Rudy leaned back. It was the pot.
He was so messed up. Why hadn't he looked a little closer
before saying anything?

Bobby removed his hand from the water. He sat down.
Rudy expected Bobby to ask how he knew about the scar, the
lazy eye, but Bobby didn't. Rudy was starting to drift in and
out of sleep. Every so often, he'd open his eyes and think, *I'm*

in a boat, I should stay awake, something terrible might happen, but then he'd slide back into the comfort of his subconscious. He was about to go completely under when he heard a voice – Bobby's: "She was going to leave me. She said I reminded her of her ex-husband."

Rudy couldn't open his eyes; the lids were too heavy. "How so?" he heard himself ask.

"Always thinking about myself," Bobby said.

"Oh."

Bobby continued talking, but Rudy couldn't hear anymore. Bobby sounded so far away. Rudy tried to picture Leila but saw only an image of himself in Chicago, snow blowing all around him. After the train had taken him to the Howard stop, Rudy stood on the platform, shivering. He turned up his collar and tucked his gloves into his shirtsleeves, but he couldn't stop shivering. He was shivering because of Leila, because he'd seen her again after so many years. He wondered what it would be like if the two of them got back together. Surely they were different people now, no longer so impetuous, and maybe it was possible to have a deeper, more mature relationship, given all that they had been through these past fifteen years. It was a silly thought, but what if? *What if?* he asked himself. *Didn't such things happen?*

Rudy had considered crossing over to the other platform and then taking the next train back to Leila's stop, but he was afraid that she, having realized her mistake, would be on her way to the Howard stop to catch up with *him*. If he moved, he might miss her. And so he waited. He let trains he needed go by. He paced the platform. He imagined her waiting for him, too. He imagined her thinking that he might be heading back to her. It was maddening, not knowing what to do. He waited almost an hour, hoping. He'd never wanted anything in his life as much as he wanted this. It was the exact same feeling he'd had when he first fell in love with her, when he was aware of every little nuance in their relationship, when he wasn't yet sure if she, too, loved him. The tightening in his chest. The shortness of breath. Rudy waited and waited, willing her to appear each time the train doors opened, but by the end of the hour, Rudy knew the truth. Leila wasn't coming. She'd had no intention of following him. Not now, not ever. And wherever it was that she was going, she was probably already there.

AT THE CHATEAU MARMONT, BUNGALOW 5

(John Belushi, 1949-1982)

Do you remember, Judy? I hitchhiked all the way from Chicago to Champaign to see you, and you drove me to Rantoul, into the country, and then you led me by the hand to a field full of acres of pot. *Acres.* I said how it was like Dorothy walking into that field of poppies, and how totally strange was that, anyway: a little girl...a field of poppies...a witch peering into a crystal ball. It's fucked-up, you had said and laughed. We stuffed eight pillowcases full because eight was all you had, and then we spent all night in your apartment, sitting on the floor and smoking from a batch you and your girlfriends had harvested the month before. "Rantoul Rag," we called it because it made us more dizzy than stoned. Remember? I must have smoked half a pillowcase worth that night trying to get a buzz on, but the buzz never came. Instead, the room circled around me, slow at first, then faster and faster. I felt sick. I felt like puking my guts out. I had to shut my eyes. What happened next is something I don't expect anyone to believe, but

I saw my future, Judy. Honest to Christ, I did. It came toward me in waves, scene after scene. A bee the size of a man. Fat samurais. A blind bluesman who may not have been blind at all. There was a castle, too, not far from an ocean, and everyone was waiting for me to come outside. Reporters, fans, even the police. How had this happened to me, the son of Albanian immigrants, a high school jock, a boy from Wheaton, Illinois? I had become someone important, someone other people actually waited to see, but what had I become? Some kind of prince? A king? I was staying inside a *castle*, Judy. I saw the future that night, and I wanted to tell you all about it, but you were lying there curled up, your head sinking deeper and deeper into one of the pot-stuffed pillows. Your eyes were closed, your mouth was open just a bit, and you were drooling. My face was only inches from your face, and I was staring intently at you. And then I got worried, Judy. I was sure you'd stopped breathing. I couldn't see your chest rising. I couldn't hear any sounds coming from your mouth. *Please, God*, I thought. *Help her hold on*. It didn't seem possible: my life without you. Was this the price I would have to pay, sacrificing you for the spoils of my future? Was this a choice I would have to make? The harder my heart beat, the faster blood coursed through me. My pulse hammered inside my ears. *Judy*, I whined. *Judy, wake up*. And you know what I did next? You really want to know? I picked up the one-hitter and lit it. I sucked in as hard as I could, and when I finally opened my mouth, the air around me filled with smoke, so much smoke that I couldn't see you or the room or even my hand that held the pipe. It was as though I existed now only inside my head, as if I were nothing more than thoughts floating through dense clouds.

The smoke is only now starting to clear, and it isn't you who's lying curled up and not breathing; it's *me*. I'm here on the castle grounds – Bungalow 5, to be precise – and there's more than just blood in my veins, it's a lethal dose of what might finally drag me kicking out of this world, away from you, and into the next. The past is like the tip of a scraped match: bright at first but already starting to die until all that's left is a sad little twist of smoke. I'm so sorry, Judy. If you were here with me, I'd tell you how sorry I really am, but no one's here. It's just me, babe, me and the sound of my own breath and my too-weak heart trying to keep the soul from shedding away. Remember that night, the two of us wading through acres of pot? Remember? A miracle, one of us had said. And then later at your apartment, when I didn't think you were breathing, after I had smoked some more dope, remember how I started crying? I was high on Rantoul Rag and crying my eyes out. I finally stumbled up and found a pocket mirror in the bathroom and held it up to your nose, and when the glass frosted over, I knew I hadn't lost you, I knew you were still with me. I rested my head next to yours on the same crisp pillow and shut my eyes, and then you draped your arm over me and pulled me toward you, as if holding on for dear life. I was a lucky man, Judy. The luckiest. Have I ever told you that?

MEN WHO LOVE WOMEN WHO LOVE MEN WHO KILL

Shortly after the switch was pulled, Thomas Roubideaux's leg started to smoke. That, at least, was what the witnesses had claimed. The electric chair hadn't been used in Nebraska in thirty-four years, so no one knew quite what to expect, but nobody expected a man's leg to start smoking.

Before Roubideaux's execution, the local news featured several segments on the chair itself: how it worked, who built it, what needed to be done to make sure that it was in working order. Channel Two even profiled the man who shined the chair's various metal attachments and mopped the floor in preparation.

That was one year ago. The next execution – the second one since the death penalty has been reinstated – is tonight, and Brandon Dawson is choosing an engagement ring for Sheila Resnick, the woman he loves.

"This is our estate jewelry," the salesman says. "All of these have had previous owners, but if you're looking for a one-of-a-kind, I'd definitely go with one of these here rather than something new. Would the bride-to-be like one of our Art Decos?" He motions to the center row of ring displays.

Brandon, however, is distracted by a display of gaudy men's rings with stones as large as jawbreakers. "Let's take a look at *that* one," he says and points to a ring that is studded with too many diamonds, the sort of ring a street-fighter calls a cutter. When the salesman hands it over, Brandon lifts it up to the light, turning it one way and then the other. The ring is unlike anything Brandon owns. "I like it," he says. "Looks like something Elvis might have worn."

The cost, according to its pricetag, is two thousand four hundred dollars, even more than he'd planned to spend on Sheila's engagement ring. When Brandon slips it on, metal snug against his flesh, he thinks again of the restraint that held Thomas Roubideaux's ankle in place, twists of smoke rising from the man's shaved calf. What he'll never forget are the witnesses, how weak and glassy-eyed they'd looked when they spoke to the press afterward.

Brandon had stood outside the penitentiary that night with Sheila Resnick, holding up a sign – AMERICANS AGAINST THE DEATH PENALTY – but he had positioned it so that his face was hidden from the TV cameras. In truth, Brandon wasn't bothered that the state was executing a man. They could hang the guy, shoot him, poison him. They could fry him or burn him at a stake. They could throw away the key, feed him or not feed him, use him as a guinea pig for science – Brandon could care less, so long as the man was never set free. They way he saw it, Thomas Roubideaux should have done his research. Some states kill you for the crimes you commit; some don't. You don't want to risk getting executed, then you should take your business to another state. In the end, Brandon couldn't muster much sympathy for someone who failed to understand the nature of cause and effect.

Brandon had leaned into Sheila and whispered, "Want some more coffee?" but before she could answer, the lights of the penitentiary dimmed and several dozen Roman Candles shot from the parking lot, arcing overhead. Shortly afterwards, Brandon learned about the smoking leg.

Now, at the jewelry store, Brandon holds his hand away from his body. He frowns and nods, squinting at the ring. He knows he shouldn't do what he's going to do, but before he changes his mind, he looks up at the salesman and says, "I'll take it."

Upon pulling into the parking lot of Superior Lobster, a seafood distributor where he is head of accounting, Brandon is nearly sideswiped by a red Chevy Nova, the same Chevy Nova that nearly sideswipes him every day. He cannot see the driver through the smoky windows, but the car has become emblematic of a certain type of asshole, and whenever Brandon happens to see a red Nova, *any* red Nova, his heart quickens and he clenches his fists.

Today, Brandon honks his horn, rolls down his window, and flips the driver the bird. When the Nova hesitates, engine revving melodramatically, Brandon regrets his spontaneous outburst. He's not prepared to fight. The only weapon he owns is pepper spray, which he has carried with him ever since getting mugged a year ago. The Nova's engine revs a few more times before the driver jerks the car into gear, leaving behind a trail of snake-like skidmarks and the stench of burnt rubber. With the threat of violence gone, Brandon takes a deep breath, holds it, counts to three, and then lets it go.

It's funny, really, how the mere sight of a particular make and model of car can actually alter the body's physiology. This had happened to him in high school, too, after his first real girlfriend dumped him. She drove an orange Volkswagen Beetle, and every time he saw one zipping by, he felt like weeping. Even now, twenty years later, the sight of one of those silly, squatty cars will cause him to spiral into melancholy, and he'll realize that his own breathing has accelerated.

Brandon doesn't want to leave Sheila's ring in the car, so he pockets the box. His own ring is blinding in the sunlight. He likes the ring, but maybe he went a little too far this time. Suddenly, he's self-conscious about wearing it. It's like coming back to work after a long vacation with a new mustache or a toupee. People get used to seeing you a certain way, and anything new ends up seeming like a costume or, worse, a disguise.

Maria Mariani, the owner's oldest daughter, greets Brandon when he steps inside the lobby of Superior Lobster. "*You* look in a good mood," she says.

"Do I?" he asks. He doesn't want to tell her about the engagement ring. For the past three years, her father, Salvatore, has tried talking Brandon into taking Maria out for a date, but Brandon feels no pulse of desire for this woman. It's a touchy issue, refusing the boss's request to date his daughter, and for this reason Brandon avoids meeting with Salvatore alone. Working for a man who insinuates mob connections and has a hair-trigger temper is hard enough; dating his daughter would only lead to disaster, the end result of which could very well be Brandon lying unconscious in a Dumpster, rotted seafood heaped atop him.

"You're late," Maria says. "I guess we'll have to dock your pay." She's joking, of course, but her jokes tend to put Brandon in his place in terms of the company hierarchy. While Maria is only a secretary, she *is* the boss's daughter and will one day run the business. In a stage whisper, she adds, "I was late, too, so I guess I can let you slide." She winks.

Brandon smiles and starts to walk away when Maria stops him. "Whoa, wait just a minute," she says. "Let me see that *ring* of yours."

"Huh? Oh, this," he says, and he holds his hand out for her. She grabs onto a few fingers and starts twisting his hand from side to side.

"Is it new?" she asks.

"Yep," he says. "I mean, it's not a *new* ring – it's used – but I just bought it."

"It's beautiful," she says. She drops his hand and looks up at him as if really seeing him, his true nature, for the first time.

"Well, thanks," he says, and if only for the moment, he feels a smidge less self-conscious.

Numbers and equations fill his days at Superior Lobster. Brandon spends most of his time hunched over his desk, either penciling in figures or punching buttons on his calculator. Part of his job is to be a watchdog, making sure that no one skims from the company. He'll occasionally hear about an employee using the company gas pump for their personal vehicle, and he'll have to let them go. The ones he really needs to watch are the guys in shipping and receiving. They're always smuggling lobsters out at night. They have somehow justified to themselves that because they spend their days dealing with the lobsters, they are entitled to take one home every now and again. They'll put lobsters into their tool boxes or inside duffel bags, or they'll tuck one inside their down-filled jackets before clocking out. Brandon knows that these men don't like him – he has more education than any of them, and he makes more money than they ever will – but being disliked doesn't particularly bother him. What bothers him is that he occasionally slips and tells them something about his own life, and this puts him in a vulnerable position. They know, for instance, that he has spent the past few years wooing a woman who is in love with a man on death row, and they know that this man, Ridgley Brown, is going to be executed tonight.

"We'll do something special to celebrate," one of them told him earlier in the week.

"Well, now," Brandon said, "an execution isn't really anything to celebrate."

"What? Are you friggin' *crazy*? Of course it is. Once they cook this guy, she's all yours, pal. Am I right? That's what you've wanted all along, ain't it?"

It *was* what he wanted, but he hated that his own employees saw his motives so clearly. And sure enough, the warehouse supervisor pokes his head into Brandon's office at noon and says, "We've got a little surprise for you, Chief."

Inside the warehouse – a room with several stainless-steel walk-in coolers, each one the size of a bank vault – the men of shipping-and-receiving huddle around a portable Coleman camping stove with a pot of boiling water on top, while Salvatore Mariani, owner of Superior Lobster, holds a thirty-pound Maine rock lobster belly-up for everyone to see. Wrapped around the lobster is a thick piece of masking tape, and written across the tape in Magic Marker is Ridgley Brown's nickname: THE HAMMER.

Salvatore says, "Any last words, Ridgley?" He shakes the lobster from side to side as if the lobster is saying *Nope, no last words*. "Well, then, it looks like it's time you paid for your crimes, son."

Just as Salvatore drops the prehistoric creature into the galvanized tub, someone nudges Brandon from behind and whispers into his ear, "Good luck tonight." Before he can turn and see who it is, everyone begins cheering and hooting.

Salvatore shakes hands all around and winks at people he can't physically reach, then says, "Now, get the hell back to work. Execution's over. The son of a bitch is dead."

The crowd breaks apart, heading for the freezers or the loading dock, but Brandon lingers a bit too long, hearing what sounds at first like a fan above his head, clicking with each rotation, but what turns out to be the lobster cooking at too low of a temperature, tapping the side of the tub with one of its claws. It's knocking lightly, like a man who's drunk and locked out of his own house but still hopeful that someone will open the door and let him inside.

Brandon turns the flame all the way up, but he can't bring himself to watch the lobster cook. He waits for the tapping to stop, turning the flame off only after the lobster has been boiled to death.

The men at shipping and receiving remind him of the men his father used to pal around with. His father drove a semi for a living, and his buddies were mostly truckers he'd gotten to know at various loading docks. When Brandon was seven, his father took him hunting with some of these men, and though Brandon didn't want to go, he wasn't in any position to argue. On their way out the door, his mother whispered into Brandon's ear, "Don't turn into them."

"Into what?" he asked.

"Men who like to kill."

Brandon owned a Daisy BB air gun, the kind that looked like a miniature rifle, and he tucked a box of BBs in his left pocket. With the weight of them against his thigh, it was impossible to forget his purpose for being there, and so for those first few hours he, too, felt like a hunter, even though all that he had ever shot were pieces of tin and tree bark, all at close range.

At lunchtime, while the men sat around unpeeling Saran-wrapped sandwiches and popping open cans of beer that had been chilling in the lake, Brandon made the mistake of asking his father where the bathroom was. Though he had whispered the question, an obvious indication that his words were meant to remain private, his father laughed and shook his head, then repeated the question for all his buddies to hear. The men roared.

"This ain't the Howard Johnson's, son," one of the men said. Brandon had liked Howard Johnson's – the orange and aqua buildings that occasionally dotted their roadtrips, the same colors as the Miami Dolphins, his father's favorite team. There was something exotic about seeing a Howard Johnson's under the gray skies of the plains, a touch of the tropics in the Midwest.

His father said, "We're standing in the world's largest bathroom, son."

Brandon looked around. He couldn't fathom what his father meant. Then his father stood, unzipped his pants, and pissed on a tree. It was the most startling thing he'd ever seen his father do. Another man said, "Mind if I join you?" and he pissed on the same tree. One by one, the men pissed for Brandon's benefit, and after they had finished, they nudged Brandon.

"Your turn," one of them said. "Go on. It's only us."

But Brandon couldn't. It wasn't so much that he didn't want to; it was a physical impossibility. The few times he had been in public restrooms when someone else walked in, Brandon felt as though a switch inside his head had been flipped, shutting off his ability to pee.

His father said, "For chrissakes, Brandon. We're not going to drive you back to town every time you need to take a leak."

Brandon shook his head. He didn't see the point of unzipping his pants and trying – not in front of his father's friends, at least. "I can't," he said.

One of the men snorted. "You got a modest one on your hands there, Charlie."

"Modest, my ass," his father said. "Sooner or later he's going to have to piss, and that'll be the end of modesty."

Three days later, Brandon was taken to the hospital for a bladder infection. His mother, furious at the men, waited in the hall. The nurse said, "This will sting a little, honey, but you'll feel better real soon." She was younger than his mother and her hair smelled like the lilac bush outside his bedroom window. She pinched the scruff of Brandon's penis, lifted it, and slowly snaked the tube up through the blazing tunnel of his urethra. Brandon tried squirming to the head of the bed, but as soon as the urine began to siphon out of him, the pain in his bladder receded, and Brandon, holding back tears, looked up into the nurse's pale-grey eyes and realized that he might be in love.

Thirty years later, Brandon awoke on a sidewalk, squinting up at the face of another nurse – Sheila Resnick. She was on her way to work at the hospital, three blocks away, when she found him on the ground, unconscious.

"What happened?" she asked. "Did you fall?"

"I got mugged," he said.

"Oh, no." Sheila crouched and looked closely into Brandon's eyes. She was close to Brandon's age, and she had a nearly imperceptible scar along her frown line. The scar disappeared each time she turned her mouth down, making Brandon want to reach up and touch it, but he restrained himself.

"He jumped out from the alley here," Brandon explained, "and then popped me on the head with a brick or something."

"Your head's bleeding," Sheila said. "And your chin needs stitches."

"My chin?"

Brandon looked down and saw that his new Polo shirt was streaked with blood. Fresh drops fell from his chin, hit the fabric, and bloomed. "Ah, shit," he said. He reached for his grocery sack, but the half-gallon of milk had exploded upon impact. The crown of his head pulsed from where he'd been clubbed.

"All he had to do was ask," Brandon said, "and I'd've given him the damn wallet." As soon as he stood, he started to sway.

"Easy, easy," Sheila said. "Here, put your arm around me."

At the hospital, Sheila led Brandon to a partitioned rectangle of space. She had him hold a dry-ice pack to his head while she scrubbed the grit out of his open chin with what felt like a Brillo pad. To divert Brandon's attention, to reel him away from the pain, Sheila began talking at length about the series of *Planet of the Apes* movies, and how for the past four nights after work she'd gone home and watched them on the "Late, Late Show" on channel 7.

"Tonight's the last one," Sheila said. "*Conquer the Planet of the Apes*. Have you seen it? No? Well, I can't seem to figure out the chronology of the whole series. The first one was pretty straightforward. Astronauts go into space, they accidentally get caught in some kind of time-warp, and then they end up years later back on Earth when apes rule the planet. But in *Escape from Planet of the Apes*, two chimps from the first movie travel back to the present, and I guess it's supposed to explain how the planet ended up with talking apes in the first place, but it doesn't make sense. You know, *logically*. It's some sort of weird logic after the fact, if you know what I mean."

Oddly enough, Brandon *did* know what she meant. An accountant's life was ruled by nothing if not logic and order. The more Sheila spoke, the less Brandon fixated on his pain. He couldn't stop watching her. Periodically, he removed the dry-ice and touched the top of his head. The lump was starting to feel like a soft belly after a large meal.

An old doctor wearing bifocals appeared through the drawn curtains, reading a chart. Without looking up, he said, "Okay, who in here wants me to sew his chin back on?" Brandon opened his mouth to answer, but Sheila placed her hand on his shoulder, gave it a squeeze, and began telling the doctor Brandon's story.

Four days later, Brandon called Sheila at work and asked her to lunch, and the day after that they were sitting together in the hospital cafeteria, garish orange trays with plates of inedible food resting between them. Sheila was in her own world, though. Her body was there, but her mind was clearly somewhere far away. Brandon saw it in her eyes, two bottomless wells. She wasn't listening to a word Brandon said.

In the lobby, just as he was getting ready to bolt from the hospital, she asked for a ride. Brandon didn't see the point of dragging on their visit, but what could he say? He shrugged. "Yeah; sure," he said. "Where to?"

"Do you know where the state penitentiary is?"

She didn't offer an explanation and he didn't ask. At the penitentiary, she opened the car door slowly and watched her own feet hit the ground, careful of her footing. Over the next few days, Brandon couldn't shake loose the image of Sheila walking to the prison gate and waiting to be let inside. He wanted to know more, so he called her at the hospital again.

"Do you want to talk?" he asked.

"Actually, I could use another ride," she said. "Would you do that for me?"

It was on that second trip when Sheila told Brandon the story of Ridgley Brown, how he had shown up at the emergency room one night ten years ago in need of twelve stitches along the brow of his right eye, and how he had told her these incredible stories about the time he had hitchhiked across the country, sleeping under overpasses and waking up shrouded in fog, or how he had caught fish in a Colorado stream using a handmade spear, or how he had filled a diary with the names of all the different kinds of birds he'd seen, or what life was like growing up in a housing project on Chicago's west side.

After the doctor had stitched his brow, Ridgley and Sheila walked to a diner for coffee, where Sheila told him about *her* life. She was twenty-three years old, and the only interesting thing that she could think to tell him was that her past two boyfriends had stalked her after she'd broken up with them, and that she was forced to get restraining orders against them. "What are the odds?" she had asked Ridgley. "Two stalkers in a row!"

Early the next morning, Ridgley Brown was arrested at the Sunshine Laundromat for rape and attempted murder. The victim, having escaped her attacker, gave a physical description that was consistent with that of a local serial rapist who killed his victims with a hammer.

"He was doing his laundry," Sheila said. "And he was with me shortly before the time that he supposedly raped this woman, and we were talking about *fishing*. We were having *coffee*. There is absolutely no way that Ridgley Brown committed these crimes. Would someone who'd brutally raped and then tried murdering a woman be doing his laundry the next morning? *Calmly* doing his laundry, I should add. I don't think so."

"Wait a sec," Brandon said. "You're not talking about the guy they call The Hammer, are you? The guy on death row? *That* Ridgley Brown?"

"I *hate* that name," Sheila said. "Don't call him that."

"But that's how he killed those women, right? He raped them and then he beat them to death with a hammer."

Sheila said, "They've got the wrong man."

"You're kidding, I hope. I mean, Christ, you're lucky to be alive. You had *coffee* with this guy?"

Sheila said, "I had coffee with *you*, too."

"Yeah, but no one calls me The Hammer."

"*His* name's not The Hammer. Do you think he gave that name to himself?" Then she told him about the poetry he had written, and how some of it had been published in a small but prestigious journal.

"He writes *poetry*?" Brandon said. "You ask me, that's reason enough alone to kill the guy!" He laughed. He was trying to lighten the mood, but Sheila was staring straight ahead now, flexing the muscles in her jaw. "Hey, look," Brandon said. "It wasn't just this one woman, the woman who got away. It was *several* women, and those women *didn't* get away. And they have DNA evidence."

"Have you ever been to a medical laboratory?" Sheila asked. "Well, I have and I can tell you that they don't know what they're doing most of the time. They're overworked and they're always mixing up samples, and the place is filthy and people are always coming and going, including janitors. Evidence gets tainted all the time."

"Oh!" Brandon said. "So what you're saying is that they mixed up Riley's blood sample with the real killer's blood sample, which just so happened to be in the lab? Is *that* what you're saying?"

"No," Sheila said. "You're not listening to me. What I'm saying is, how can you trust the *accuracy* of the results? You can't."

"Okay, okay," Brandon said. "All right. But let me ask you this. Why are you still involved with this guy? I mean, he's got lawyers. He's got a family. I'm assuming he's got other friends. What sort of a hook does he have into you?"

"Hook?" Sheila said. "I'm trying to save his life."

"Yeah, okay, I see that. But *why*?"

"Why? You want to know why? Because we're engaged to be married. *That's* why."

Brandon ran a stoplight. Fortunately, there were no other cars in sight. "Shit," he said. And then he was silent. If what she had said was meant to shut him up, it worked. He dropped her off at the penitentiary without so much as saying good-bye.

For two weeks, Brandon didn't call Sheila, but the longer he waited, the more intrigued he became. Here was a woman, after all, whose two previous boyfriends had been stalkers. Brandon believed that certain people had magnetic qualities, and that there had to be something about Sheila herself, some intrinsic quality, that attracted such men. And then there was her own devotion to this guy on death row.

Brandon didn't buy any of her theories – of *course* Ridgley Brown had killed these women – but how couldn't he help being intrigued by Sheila's unwavering commitment? Brandon wasn't able to put his finger on why exactly, but her devotion made Sheila more vulnerable, and there was something, well, attractive about vulnerability. How many people possessed the ability to overlook, against their better judgment, pure evil? And weren't vulnerability and naïveté just as worthy of being a turn-on as, say, perfume or fishnet stockings? Worthier, Brandon believed, because it wasn't something you could simply spray onto yourself or slip into. It was deeply rooted. It was who Sheila really and truly was.

At the end of those two weeks, he called her again, this time to say that he was sorry. "Do you play pool?" he asked.

"I'm not any good," Sheila said. "I'd embarrass you."

"Well, then, I'll teach you. And I want to hear more about Ridgley Brown. You brought up some good points and I was unfair. I'm sorry."

And so they fell into a routine: Brandon taught her how to play pool, and Sheila enlightened Brandon on the corruption of the prison system.

"Did you know," she said, "that if you're black, you're far more likely to get the death penalty than if you're white?"

"Really!" Brandon said.

As an accountant, Brandon was interested in statistics and the statistical methods used to reach certain conclusions. Sheila's arguments, usually delivered in the form of broad statements, were often based on an explosive combination of vague sources and raw emotion. There were times her hands actually shook when she read some of the injustices aloud. Brandon wanted to say, *Now, let's take a look at the numbers here,* or *Now, where did these figures come from?* but he knew that these sorts of statements would run counter to his ultimate goal.

Brandon showed Sheila how to do bank shots, how to slice a ball into the corner pocket, how to break without scratching. After a few beers, he showed her a few trick shots.

"Here's a little something Minnesota Fats used to do."

"Were you always good at pool?" she asked.

"I was good at math. I was good at geometry. Pool is really nothing more than Geometry plus coordination, and I've got pretty good coordination. Back when I played every day, I could almost always run the table. After the break, I'd look at the table and I could see all the shots, every last one. It was pretty amazing. I'd feel almost, I don't know, *prescient*."

"Did you play for money?"

"Money? I wouldn't even play for a beer. No matter how good you are, there's always someone better. I couldn't do it. I don't have a gambler's constitution. I'd choke." He reached up to touch her scar, but she flinched and leaned back. "How'd you get it?" he asked.

"My father," she said. "But it's a long story." Brandon expected her to tell him the story, but she didn't. She dug through her backpack instead, finding some pamphlets about executions that had gone awry. "You should read these."

"Absolutely," Brandon said.

At home, Brandon poured over the literature. There were several electrocutions that had taken more than one jolt, causing flesh to burn and sizzle, a body part to catch fire, smoke filling the room, the prisoner all the while still alive, tortured. There were prisoners who gasped far too long in gas chambers that weren't functioning properly. There were numerous lethal injections in which doctors couldn't find suitable veins and had to prod the prisoner's body for nearly an hour. Syringes full of deadly chemicals occasionally popped out of arms. There were drunk executioners. There was faulty wiring. During John Wayne Gacy's execution, the lethal chemicals unexpectedly clogged the IV tube, prompting officials to draw the curtains between Gacy and the witnesses. In such instances, prisoners would spasm and gasp for air. A few times, the prisoner, while in excruciating pain, made a second, impromptu statement to the people watching.

Brandon understood the need for a better system, but

with each report he couldn't stop thinking of the murderers' victims, and how surprise must have quickly dissolved into terror once they realized that the stranger before them was here to cause them harm. And how much did they have to endure – what sort of pain and humiliation and fear – before they were granted the peace of death, ending the torture these men had caused? Sheila was in love with a man who'd hide inside of a woman's apartment and wait for the door to unlock, the light to come on. According to the autopsies, he'd knock the woman unconscious with a hammer, rape her, and then kill her with the hammer's claw. What luxuries should we afford this man for his own death? What pain should we spare him?

Two months into the pool-playing lessons, Sheila took Brandon to his first execution. Brandon held up a sign: AMERICANS AGAINST THE DEATH PENALTY. When the prison lights dimmed and the fireworks lit up the sky, Sheila took hold of Brandon's hand and squeezed it until it actually started to hurt. If Brandon had to pinpoint the moment that he fully committed himself to the pursuit of Sheila, he'd have cited the instant that he began to feel the pressure of her grip. Thirty minutes later, witnesses filed out of the penitentiary with stories of a man whose leg smoked during the electrocution. But it was too late for Brandon to retreat. He was, against his better judgment, irretrievably in love.

That first execution was one year ago. Brandon has been by Sheila's side ever since, helping her with every petition, doing everything that he can possibly do to help spare this man's life, a man Brandon wants dead nearly as much as the victims' families want him dead. But while they want Ridgley dead for closure, Brandon wants him dead for just the opposite – a new beginning.

Tonight marks the third time that the state has attempted to execute Ridgley Brown, but this is the first time that Brandon and Sheila have made it this far, actually driving to the penitentiary mere hours before Ridgley is to be killed. The other two times ended in stays of execution several days before the scheduled date.

Sheila, slouched in the passenger seat, stares blankly as the houses along Sheridan Boulevard, the nicest houses in town, flick past. It's ten at night and the city is eerily desolate.

"I drove by the penitentiary this morning," Brandon says.

"Was anybody out there?"

Brandon shakes his head. "A few TV cameras."

"It's all so surreal," Sheila says. "Look. My hands are shaking."

Brandon reaches out and holds one. He rubs her palm with his thumb. He expects her to comment on his new ring – the Elvis ring – but she doesn't.

"Have you talked to him yet?" he asks.

"Last night. But we agreed not to speak again."

"Any news from the lawyer?"

"Nothing new," she says. "He says anything's possible, though. He said you'd be surprised what can be accomplished in the final hours."

Brandon nods; he hopes the lawyer is wrong.

At the penitentiary, they are joined by other anti-death penalty men and women. Several of the protesters are professors at the state university. Others have religious affiliations. Brandon lives in a part of the country that is overwhelmingly conservative, and the pro-death penalty advocates outnumber those who are anti-death by twenty to one. The hatred that the pro camp feels toward the anti camp is palpable, and in a city where the mayor and a number of the judges are outspoken right-wing members of the Christian Coalition, Brandon fears that if the pro camp decided to rough up the anti camp, the police would suddenly and conveniently disappear.

Tonight, one pro guy in particular is being unnecessarily aggressive. He's with a group of frat boys, and he keeps taunting the anti group through a bullhorn that's adorned on either side with the university's team mascot, Herbie Husker, an affable cartoon farm boy who wears overalls and a straw hat. "We're havin' a barbecue tonight at midnight!" the frat boy yells. "Want to join us?" Or: "We'll take our Ridgley Brown extra crispy, thank you very much." These are par-for-the-course taunts, the ones Brandon expects, but then the frat boy starts zeroing in on Sheila. "My condolences to the future widow!" he yells. "But not to worry. There are plenty of good-looking men on death row to choose from."

The others in Brandon's group remain Zen despite the taunts. They continue to huddle and peer into their candles, softly humming slave hymns. Only Brandon is glaring at their opponents, and only he is mumbling a litany of assaults he'd like to perform on the bastard with the bullhorn. The frat boy realizes this, grins, and flips Brandon off. Brandon breaks from his circle, walking in the frat boy's direction, but a cop stops him and says, "You'd do best to stay with your own folk, sir. There's no need making the night worse than it already is." The cop says nothing to the frat boy. Brandon thinks he catches the two smiling at each other, but it's too dark out to know for sure.

At Superior Lobster, men were always returning to work with black eyes or contusions from the fights they'd gotten into over the weekend. This was one of the things that scared Brandon about these men, the fact that under nearly any other condition, they wouldn't think twice before knocking Brandon to the ground and doing bodily harm to him. Brandon had an intellectual understanding of violence in that he often felt the impulse to punch someone who was out of line, but when it came to the actual punching, he suspected that he would freeze up.

In the fifth grade, Brandon had come home from school after getting beaten up by a seventh grade bully nicknamed Mongoose, who inexplicably decided one day to make Brandon the object of his aggression. During the after-school assault, Brandon had stood perfectly still, absorbing whatever punishment Mongoose doled out, hoping that his passivity would take the steam out of Mongoose's anger. He mistakenly thought that the other kids, his own classmates, would admire his unwillingness to participate in something so crude as an unprovoked fistfight. But the other kids, including his friends, yelled, "Fight back! Fight back!" and it was all Brandon could do not to break down in tears.

When his father came home from work that night, he took one look at Brandon and said, "I hope the other guy looks worse." When Brandon didn't answer, his father said, "Well?"

So Brandon told his father what had happened, how he didn't want to fight back because he didn't know why he was being attacked in the first place.

Brandon's father said, "Let me get this straight. A guy attacks you, but because you don't know *why*, you think you shouldn't fight? Is that what you're saying? Jesus Christ Almighty, Brandon, is that how you plan to go through life? Well?" When Brandon didn't answer, his father said, "C'mon. I want you to show me where this Mongoose character lives."

"No, Dad."

"I said, *c'mon*, goddamn it."

Brandon knew that his father wouldn't back down, so he gave him directions but begged him not to go there.

"You're going, too," his father said. "I want to show you something."

Brandon wished now that he had lied. He wished he had told his dad that the other guy looked worse, but it was too late. A few minutes later, they arrived at Mongoose's house. When Mongoose's father opened the door, Brandon's father ordered him to step outside and take a good look at what his son had done to Brandon.

Mongoose's father obeyed, but he looked disgusted at both Brandon and his father. "I don't have time for this shit. This is what kids do. They fight. What the hell you expect *me* to do about it?"

Brandon's father said, "Your kid's older than my kid. He's a bully. Did you raise him to pick on kids who're younger and smaller than he is?"

Brandon thought he could see Mongoose through the screen-door, crouching in the shadows of their living room, but he wasn't sure. It might have been a piece of furniture he saw. Brandon was expecting the conversation to end – his father had made his point – but then Brandon's father took hold of Mongoose's father's face, squeezed it tight, and shoved him against the doorframe. In a low voice, a voice Brandon didn't recognize, his father said, "Your son messes with my son again, I'll kill you. You hear me, you son of a bitch? I'll *kill* you." Then he let go of the man's face and led Brandon to the car, his grip too tight around the back of Brandon's neck.

On their way home, his father said, "You don't let anyone fuck with you. You hear me? Nobody."

A minute after midnight, when everyone is expecting the lights to dim, nothing happens. The warden, whom Brandon recognizes from the local news, steps outside and announces through a portable p.a. system that there has been yet another last-minute stay of execution by the governor. The warden is clearly perturbed by this news.

Sheila hugs Brandon, her tears soaking through his shirt and dampening his chest.

"Oh my God," she says. "I've got to talk to Harvey." Harvey is Harvey Zimmerman, Ridgley's attorney, a beleaguered man who has taken on Ridgley's case, *pro bono*. Brandon suspects the man is going to cash in on his experience once Ridgley is dead. Write a book. Appear on Oprah. The death penalty is always in the news, and Harvey could make a decent living doing the morning talk show circuit. Plus, there's always the human interest side of the story. Namely, Sheila's story. Brandon can already see the hook: *women who love men who kill*. It's possible that Harvey truly believes that Ridgley was given a raw deal the first time around and is representing him out of the goodness of his heart, but Brandon seriously doubts this.

Brandon and Sheila cross the highway on foot, heading for the pay-phone at Burger King. While Sheila calls Harvey, Brandon orders french fries and a milkshake. He slips into a booth and spreads the fries across the paper sack. "Shit," he says. "Shit, shit." He picks at the fries. He wags his head. He can't believe it's come to this, a third stay of execution. How many close-calls can one man get? How many loopholes are left? The lawyer is like a magician-for-hire, pulling an endless stream of kerchiefs from his sleeve – a dull and predictable trick that sooner or later must come to an end.

Sheila joins Brandon at the booth. She is full of hope. He sees it in her eyes. "The governor has agreed to look over the issue of jury tampering. He says he'll make a decision by the end of the week."

Jury tampering could lead to a dismissal of charges. This explains the hope. What Sheila isn't acknowledging is that it's an election year, and by agreeing to look over the case, the governor is giving the illusion of being fair. But he also must give the illusion of being tough on crime, which is why none of the lawyer's tricks will amount to anything. Sooner or later, Ridgley will fry in the electric chair. In the meantime, everyone will use him to advance their own agendas.

"Oh, for crissakes," Brandon says.

"What? What's wrong?"

Brandon wants to tell her to quit being so naïve. *Don't you see?* he wants to say to her, *Don't you see what's REALLY going on?* What he finally says is "It's just so, I don't know, so *frustrating.*"

Sheila says, "I know. Believe me, I know. You don't have to tell *me* about frustration."

"Excuse me," Brandon says, and he slips out of the booth and heads for the restroom.

No sooner does he lock himself inside of a stall when someone else enters the restroom, locking himself in the stall next door. It's one of those guys who likes to talk to himself in the john, as if no one else is within earshot. "C'mon, c'mon, c'mon, c'mon," he coaxes, "c'mon, oh-oh, c'mon," and then Brandon hears the muffled piss hitting the water in the toilet bowl, followed by sighing. "Oh, yeah," the voice says. "Whew, boy."

The switch inside Brandon's head – the switch that allows Brandon to pee – has been turned off, so he zips up. When he steps out of the stall, he nearly trips over a Herbie Husker bullhorn. The mere sight of it sets his heart pounding. Brandon, peering between the slats of the stall's door, sees the frat boy from the execution sitting on the toilet. He appears to be reading the graffiti and softly chuckling. When he turns and sees Brandon staring in at him, he squints and leans forward.

"Hey, what the fuck?" he says. "What in the *fuck* are you doing, man?"

The frat boy reaches for his pants and starts yanking them up, but Brandon already has his pepper spray out, aiming it between the crack. According to the package, the spray could hit a target six feet away. Brandon presses down and sprays the frat boy's face. When the boy reaches up to cover his eyes, Brandon sprays his crotch.

The kid falls to the floor, curling into a ball and screaming. Brandon pockets the spray and leaves the restroom.

Sheila says, "Did you hear that?"

Brandon squints, as if trying to hear.

"That screaming," Sheila says.

"What screaming?"

Sheila cocks her head. "Hear it?"

Brandon listens, then says, "Nope. You ready?"

They leave Burger King. He knows if he doesn't do what he had planned to do, he'll never do it, so in the parking lot, under the fluorescent lights, clouds of bugs flapping blurrily all around, Brandon pulls the ring from his pocket. He opens the box and shows it to Sheila.

"What's this?" she asks.

"I was going to wait," Brandon says, "until after, you know..." And he's about to propose when Sheila holds both hands up and starts shaking her head.

"Oh, no," she says. "I'm sorry, Brandon." She starts crying. The penitentiary glows across the street, and a floodlight makes obligatory sweeps over the yard.

Brandon shuts the ring box. "How can you love *him*?" Brandon asks. "He's using you, Sheila. Can't you see that?"

Sheila stops crying. She squints at Brandon, and at first Brandon thinks it's because of the brightness of the parking lot's lights, but then he realizes that she is looking at *his* ring. When she finally looks up, it's as if she is staring at a man she has never before seen, the same chilling clarity she must have felt looking into the faces of former lovers who, upon rejection, took to trailing her every move. Everything she's thinking is in her eyes. Her face is eerily expressionless. Her scar seems to be shimmering in the weird, unnatural light. She is about to speak but turns instead and walks away, heading for her friends across the street who are waiting to hear the news.

Brandon is driving home, but he isn't sure that he can stand being alone right now, the weight of the night bearing down on him. What has he been thinking this past year? At what point did he lose his sense of how things would pan out with Sheila? She's in love with a man on death row. How do you compete with that?

At the last second, too late to hit the blinker, Brandon veers onto Cornhusker Highway instead of driving to his subdivision. Cornhusker is the seediest part of town – trailerparks, motels with weekly rates. Brandon pulls into the gravel parking lot at Little Bo's, a townie bar, where some of guys at work hang out. On his way inside, he notices a red Chevy Nova with smoky windows, and on closer inspection he sees that it must be *the* red Chevy Nova, the one that nearly sideswipes him on a regular basis. The car is parked in such a way that it's taking up four parking spaces.

Brandon clenches his fists and walks inside. Through thick spirals of smoke, he spots Maria Mariani. She is sitting alone in a booth, a half-full pitcher of beer in front of her, along with four empty shot glasses. When she sees Brandon, she perks up and waves him over.

"Oh, Brandon," she says, standing and hugging him. "I'm so sorry," she whispers into his ear. "I saw the news." She's holding him longer than necessary, and her mouth rests against the soft spot beneath his ear. Maria is drunk, so Brandon takes her by the shoulders and gently pushes her back down into the booth. He sits across from her.

"Do you love her?" she asks.

Before Brandon can answer, a man by the pool table raises his stick aloft and yells, "Oh yeah, baby, oh yeah!" The man looks over at Maria, winks, then notices Brandon and narrows his eyes. He struts over to the booth.

"Did you win, honey?" Maria asks.

The man, still staring at Brandon, says, "You bet your sweet ass I won."

Brandon says, "I don't believe we've met. I work with Maria. I'm their accountant. Brandon," he says and holds out his hand.

The man says, "Vik," but doesn't accept Brandon's hand.

Then he heads back to the pool table.

"He's been winning all night," Maria says. "I guess I'll be marrying a regular pool shark."

"You're getting married?"

"Oh, one day, I suppose," Maria says. "Vik says as soon as he can afford it."

Brandon looks around the bar. Little Bo's is crowded, but he doesn't see anyone else he knows. He scoots out of the booth, walks over to Vik, and says, "You want to play a game?"

Vik says, "I recognize you, bub. You might not realize it, but I know who you are."

"I know who you are, too," Brandon says.

Vik says, "You want to play? Okay. 8-ball. Call your shot. No slop. Twenty bucks. Now let's see who wants to play, smart guy."

"Twenty bucks? Is that it?"

Vik looks around, laughs. "Okay. *Fifty*."

Maria has wandered over to see what's going on.

Brandon says, "That's your Nova out there, right?"

Vik huffs through his nose. "You know goddamn well it is. You flipped me off this morning, remember?"

Brandon smiles. He pulls Sheila's ring from his pocket, opens the box, and balances it on the edge of a corner pocket.

"Oh my God," Maria says. "Oh my God, would you look at that? It's gorgeous."

"You win," Brandon says, "you get the ring. I win, I get the Nova."

Maria is smiling at the ring. No doubt she's imagining what it would look like on her own finger. But then something crosses her face, the reality of what the ring means. A commitment. A lifetime with Vik. A sentence.

"Don't do it," Maria warns Vik.

Vik looks ready to back out until Maria tells him not to do it. He's left with no choice now: he *has* to do it. He surveys the bar. More people close in on the table to watch.

"Okay," he says. "Okay." He fishes his keys from his pants pocket and sets them next to Sheila's ring.

They flip for the break, and Vik wins. Vik circles the table while Brandon racks the balls. Vik checks to make sure that the rack is tight and then he breaks. The break is explosive, sending the balls ricocheting off every rail, but nothing goes in. Vik shakes his head. He can't believe that a break with so much action has resulted in nothing.

Brandon, chalking his cue, thinks of Sheila, her devotion to Ridgley Brown, faith so blind she'd step into his shoes if she could. How could you *not* love a woman like that? Tomorrow, Brandon will call her to apologize. *This isn't about me,* he'll say, *it's about you, and I'll be there for you this time, honest.* And he will. From here on out, with or without her blessing, he'll be right behind her. He'll follow this woman to the ends of the Earth, if that's what it takes. He loves her. He loves her, and soon she'll see how much.

Brandon looks down at the table now, at the configuration of solids and stripes, taking the whole of the table in, and he sees clearly his next eight shots, one right after the other.

THE SOMETHING SOMETHING

(Gene Siskel, 1946-1999)

They were the only ones in the movie theater, Gene and Roger. Gene liked it like this: sitting in a vast space but not entirely alone. He hated crowded theaters, though, and he hated when parents brought their babies to a movie. There was nothing worse than that. *Nothing.* One time, he gave the usher twenty bucks to kick a baby and its mother out. The usher, who recognized Gene, was happy to oblige. Gene could hear the mother's protests, and for a little while the baby's crying grew more intense, but once the woman and child had been taken into the lobby, Gene could relax again. He could sink back into the cocoon of sensory depravation, where the only world that mattered was the one made of light and shadow.

But there were no babies here today, thank God. He and Roger were watching a French movie. The Something Something. For the life of him, Gene couldn't remember its title. *The What What*, he wondered.

Gene sat four rows behind Roger. An hour into the movie, Gene dozed off. He had a dream that he was back in grade school and that between classes he had forgotten the combination to his locker. Did he actually have a locker in grade school? Weren't lockers more of a high school thing? He questioned this in the dream itself, but even questioning it couldn't slow his beating heart. The other students were already filing into their respective classes, while Gene continued twisting the lock's knob one way and then the other. Each time he yanked down on it, he expected it to snap open, but nothing happened. When the principal approached, smacking his palm with a thick ruler, Gene started yelling, "No! No!"

It was here that the dream world intruded upon the real world, and Gene screamed out "No!" in the theater. The sound of his own voice woke him up.

Roger turned around and gave him a look but didn't say anything.

After Gene caught his breath, he wanted to laugh but didn't. The movie they were watching – The Something Something – was awful. Gene couldn't have said what the main conflict was. Fifteen minutes in, he'd quit reading the subtitles. He wasn't sure what he was going to say about the movie when they taped their TV show. Maybe Roger would let him look at his notes, and then he could simply disagree with whatever Roger thought of it. That's what made good TV, their disagreements. That's why people tuned in. But he knew Roger wouldn't let him look at his notes. He wasn't that sort of guy. In truth, they weren't even that good of friends.

Gene slurped up the rest of his Coke. Only a few melting ice cubes remained in the cup. Even so, Gene sucked on the straw hard one final time. Roger turned around again. The light from the projector illuminated his face. He said, "If you don't like the movie, then *leave*." Gene shrugged, and Roger swiveled back around.

On screen, an unshaven man was sitting in a room and reading a newspaper while his squat, angry wife paced back and forth in her underclothes.

"Good God," Gene said.

Roger said, "Shhhhhh. Quiet."

Using his teeth, Gene started tearing apart the paper wrapper from his straw and making little spitballs from it. He inserted one into the straw, aimed it at Roger's head, and blew. The spitball shot out of the straw's barrel and landed in Roger's hair.

Roger didn't notice.

Gene loaded another spitball into the straw and fired again. This time, the spitball nicked Roger's ear. Roger reached up, touched the lobe with two stocky fingers, then put his arm down.

What could Gene do? He shot a third spitball at Roger. This one smacked his neck and stuck. Roger found the spitball, examined it, and then turned around. Gene, straw still in his mouth, grinned at him.

"Have you lost your fucking mind, Gene?" he asked. "Is that it?"

Gene laughed. The straw bobbed up and down between Gene's teeth. Roger stood up, walked to the end of the row, as far away from Gene as he could get, and, sighing heavily, sat down. Gene draped his long legs over the seat in front of him and shut his eyes until the final credits rolled.

It was snowing. In the short time that Gene and Roger had been inside, snow had piled up high. Gene loved these sorts of days – walking out of a dark movie theater and into the bright night where fresh snow reflected the moon and all the storefront's neon lights; nights where everyone seemed happy just to be outside filling their lungs with crisp, icy air.

"Look, Rog!" Gene yelled. "Snow!"

"Go to Hell," Roger said. He trudged down the snow-covered sidewalk, staring down at his feet like a man who'd stepped in something he shouldn't have. If this had been the old days, Roger would have headed over to the Old Town

Ale House and spent the night drinking with his buddies, but Roger didn't drink anymore. Gene wasn't sure what he did with his time, or who he did it with.

Gene picked up a clump of snow. It was good sticky snow, the kind of snow that was going to be around for a while. Without really thinking, he packed it into a ball and threw it at Roger. It exploded against Roger's back. Roger turned around while Gene quickly packed another ball.

"Why you son of a bitch," Roger began, and he started trudging toward Gene. Gene pegged Roger square in the face this time. Roger hesitated, blinking, but then he started walking again. Roger moved slowly and gracelessly toward Gene, like the old Frankenstein monster taking one bullet after the other. Gene, laughing, tried walking backwards but then he tripped over his own shoes and landed on his back. Snow, breaking his fall, provided a nice enough cushion.

"Don't sit on me, Roger!" Gene said, unable to stop laughing. He held up his hands. "Don't," he yelled. "You'll crush me!"

Roger fell on top of Gene, and the two men wrestled on the sidewalk. Roger picked up handfuls of snow and smashed it onto Gene's face.

"Oh, God, stop!" Gene yelled. "Please, stop!"

But Roger wouldn't stop. He scooped up more snow and slammed it onto Gene, as if trying to bury him alive. A pedestrian, stopping to watch, momentarily distracted Roger; and this was all Gene needed, a splinter in Roger's concentration, to give Gene the momentum to push Roger off him. Gene's hands were brick red from the cold. Melted snow dripped from his face.

"You thought you had me, didn't you?" Gene asked, doing to Roger what Roger had done to him, covering his partner's head with whatever snow he could reach. But Roger was stronger than Gene. It was never really any contest between them. Roger lifted Gene into the air, as if he weighed nothing, and tossed him to the side. Gene's head hit a lamppost. It even made a noise, like a gong. Everything dimmed for a moment; everything went soft and muffled. Gene lay on his back, eyes closed, silent.

"He's bleeding," someone said.

"Gene," Roger said. "Gene, are you okay?"

A minute later, Gene opened his eyes. He blinked a few times.

"Thank God you're okay," Roger said, and he fell onto his back, next to Gene.

"You hurt me," Gene said, his voice like a child's.

Roger said, "Could you imagine the scandal? Film critic kills film critic?"

"I was only playing," Gene said, "and you hurt me." He opened his mouth and let snow fall into it. By now, a crowd had gathered. Roger started to get up. Gene grabbed his sleeve and said, "Wait – watch this." He began scissoring his legs and flapping his arms.

"Oh, no," Roger said, laughing. The lenses of his eyeglasses had fogged over.

"Go on," Gene said, still flapping and scissoring. "I mean it," Gene said. "I'm not letting you leave until you do it."

Roger spread his legs and lifted his arms above his head. Then he brought his legs back together and lowered his arms. "There," he said.

"Nuh-uh," Gene said. "I mean *really* do it. Like me."

Roger sighed but did as he was told. He moved his legs apart and back together, again and again, all the while lifting his arms over his head and bringing them back to his side. When the two men finally stood up, they looked down and saw their angels flying side-by-side, one fat and one skinny, and then they took turns brushing each other off.

LOVE'S LATENT DEFECT

O nce a year, from the time I was three until I turned eleven, my father took me down to his office to show me how he spent his days. Where he worked was Quigley Realtors, the largest independent real estate company on the South Side of Chicago, and each year he'd walk me from cubicle to cubicle, introducing me to the same men and women I'd met the time before. The women, wearing matching skirts and blazers, would come over and shake my little hand and ask me questions, but the men, behind their desks with their shirtsleeves rolled up, would make some side-of-the-mouth comment to my Dad, like "He doesn't look anything like you, Frank. Why do you suppose that is?"

The last person my father always took me to see was a tall woman with long brown hair and long nails painted pan-candy red. Her name was Mrs. Van Patton, and she wore bulb-like earrings that hung from her earlobes like blown-glass Christmas ornaments.

"Oh, here he is!" she'd say, and then she'd smile, as if she'd done nothing all morning but wait for me. She came around the desk, but instead of shaking my hand, as the other women did, she'd place her palm against my cheek and then slide it around to the back of my neck. My father jangled the keys and coins in his pants pockets, something he normally did only when he was in a hurry and wanted me or my mother to *put it in gear, please,* but Mrs. Van Patton pretended not to notice.

"He's such a sweetie," she'd say. Or, in a whisper to my father, "She must be very attractive." It took a few years for me to realize that the *she* was my mother.

I never spoke. As I saw it, my job was to stand stock-still and smile. Even so, I enjoyed my visits with Mrs. Van Patton. She was pretty, her hands were soft and warm, and I liked seeing her earrings close-up when she crouched down to kiss my forehead, which she did each year and which always both surprised and pleased me. One time she whispered into my ear, "Tell your father to be nice," but later, when my father asked me what she had said, I told him that I couldn't hear her, that she was using too much breath when she talked, and that listening to her was like putting my ear up against the opening of a seashell.

My father made it a point at the end of each visit to show me his SALESMAN OF THE YEAR plaque that hung on a wall in the lobby. The year on the plaque was 1965, the same year that I was born, and he told me that whatever he did that year, whatever he touched, turned to gold.

"There wasn't a deal I couldn't close," he'd say. "There wasn't a piece of property in the whole of Chicago I couldn't move."

I knew from conversations I'd overheard that my father missed the way things used to be. "Everything changes so damned fast these days," he often said. It was 1975 now, and my father was the last in his office still wearing dark suits with slim tasteful ties and wing-tipped shoes. He genuinely cared about the job he did, and he honestly believed in such things as customer satisfaction. It wasn't about schmoozing to him. After walking a client through a house closing, he always checked back to make sure that there had been no latent defects. Telling a potential buyer, for instance, that the basement doesn't leak when you know that it does, or that there are no structural problems when you know that there are – these are serious issues. As a realtor now myself, I've seen more than one protracted legal battle over such failures to disclose. But my father went out of his way to correct whatever defect came to light. If something could be done, he took care of it without question. Often this meant doling out his own money.

"Believe you me," my father liked to say, "you *hope* money can solve the problem. Because if money can't solve it, there's a pretty good chance that *nothing* can."

And so when money couldn't solve a problem, my father handwrote apologies on company stationary. Sometimes writing a letter was all he could do, but he wouldn't be able to sleep for days afterward, pacing our house night after night, walking the halls like a man who had lost something important but could no longer remember what he was searching for.

We lived on the bottom floor of a three-story apartment complex. My father rented out the units above us. His grand plan was to save enough money so that we could eventually buy one of the brownstones in Lincoln Park. Saving alone wasn't going to do it, however.

"What I need," he said, "is for things to pick up the way they did in '65. A few years like that, and we'll be out of this damned apartment in no time."

My mother spent much of her time taking care of the household chores. Even now, thirty years later, my most vivid image is of my mother pushing her old Kirby upright vacuum around, moving her arm back and forth, a task that made her seem both determined and distracted at the same time, as if the longer she pushed, the deeper in thought she became. Some days I wondered if she was ever going to turn the vacuum off.

Since my father was often not home, busy showing houses to clients at their convenience, my mother took care of whatever maintenance problems arose in the rentals. In doing so, she became a good plumber. She also learned about electricity. I had seen her more than once holding a removed switch plate in one hand and needle nose pliers in the other, squinting into the wall's dark cave of tangled wires.

"Hand me a Phillips," she'd say. Or, "Go get me a flashlight. Make sure it works."

During that summer between fourth and fifth grade, I started biking all over the neighborhood, even beyond where my parents had designated the farthest point I could go. Evel Knievel, having recently attempted but failed to soar over the Snake River Canyon in his sky-cycle, was still teasing every kid's imagination. And so when I saw the construction site for a new complex of apartment buildings, I couldn't resist: I headed over, pushed my bike to the top of the tallest mound of dirt, got back on, and then pedaled down. The sprocket turned faster than my feet could pedal, and I had to quit moving my legs and let gravity take over.

One apartment building looked more or less completed, and one unit on the first floor was already occupied. It was eerie to see only one occupied apartment in an otherwise empty building surrounded by so many apartment skeletons, buildings whose glassless window frames revealed nothing but the occasional dangling light bulb. Each building was like an insane architect's Jack O'Lantern. I loved doing this sort of thing when I was a kid – turning something innocent into something macabre – but the way the apartment buildings' windows had been spaced, you could easily imagine eyes, nostrils, and teeth. As new features were added, I revised what I saw. Drainpipes became sideburns. The concrete steps leading to the front door were its tongue.

A father and child were the occupants of that first completed apartment building. They sometimes sat in lawn chairs on their first-floor patio and watched my stunts. The child appeared to be about three years old. I never saw the mother.

One day the father motioned me over. He had a TV tray set up outside with three ice-filled glasses and a tall sweating pitcher. A wrought-iron fence that came up to my chest surrounded their patio. The father picked up the pitcher and filled all three glasses to the rim.

"Lemonade?" he asked.

I was hot and sweating, and so, despite my parents' dire warnings never to take food or drink from strangers, I accepted the glass and chugged it down until the ice piled onto the tip of my nose, momentarily sticking there. My breath caused the ice to steam in front of my eyes.

"This is my son," the man said. "His name is Al."

I'd never met a little kid named Al. Al was the name of uncles and shopkeepers. I reached over the wrought-iron rail and shook Al's hand. "Hello, Al," I said. Al squeezed a couple of my fingers, but he wouldn't look at me. I, however, couldn't stop staring at him. His eyes were like a Siamese cat's. There was the faint trace of a smile, too, but it didn't have anything to do with what was going on around us.

I handed the glass back to the boy's father. I was about to wave goodbye when the man said, "He's special, you know. He's more special than me, and he's more special than you." He reached over and petted the boy's soft head, as if it were the head of a dog, but the boy didn't even notice.

Whenever I happened to bike past a Quigley Realtors sign and saw my father's name dangling on a shingle beneath, my heart grew fingers and tickled my lungs. It was the odd physical sensation that accompanied knowing that you were someone more than just who you were. I felt like a celebrity.

Here was my very own family name! And if I kept biking, I'd find even more signs with my name on it, all over Chicago!

My life revolved around my bike back then. It was a blue Schwinn Continental 10-speed, and though it was a little too big for me when my father first brought it home, I gradually grew into it. I was made conscious of getting taller, of my arms and legs getting longer, by how well the bike was starting to fit me. Since I spent a considerable amount of my waking hours on my bike, it stood to reason that I also spent a lot of time thinking about the bizarre nature of my body, how it was constantly stretching, my bones and neck and tongue getting ever-so-slightly longer by the second. Some days I'd sit on my bike in the sun and, with a ruler up against my forefinger, try to watch myself actually grow. I never caught myself in the act, which led me to believe that most of my growing occurred at night while I slept. One morning I woke up, and my shoes didn't fit quite right. Another morning, the sleeves of my windbreaker were too short.

I kept returning to the construction site and, in turn, to the apartment with the father and son. They didn't have any curtains, and from what I could see, there wasn't much furniture inside. The father always had a glass of lemonade waiting when I came over. I wasn't sure why, but I wanted to impress Al and his father, so I always tried to find something interesting to say.

"My grandfather has flat feet," I told them once. The next time, I said, "There's this woman who works with my Dad – Mrs. Van Patton. She likes to kiss me."

The father nodded at what I said, but I wasn't sure he was listening. Al never responded to anything I said. Usually, he just smiled while his eyes remained fixed on something up in the sky that I couldn't see.

On my fifth visit, I brought my Instamatic camera. It had a cube-shaped flashbulb, and after each picture taken, the cube rotated to the next flash. I loved looking inside the cube at the burnt bulb and, behind the bulb, at my own melted reflection. One time I got in trouble for holding the bulb up to my eye and firing off a flash. I had wanted to see what happened inside the bulb during its split-second explosion of light, but afterward I couldn't see anything out of my eye. Afraid I had blinded myself, I ran crying to my mother. My vision slowly came back, but mother took my camera away for a week.

"Look," I said to Al. "This is my camera."

Al wouldn't look. He smiled and rocked on his heels.

The father said, "Would you like me to take your picture with Al?"

"Sure!" I said. I could never talk my mother or father into taking as many pictures of me as I wanted. It had never occurred to me to let strangers take pictures of me.

The father lifted Al onto a chair so that he would be closer to my height. I climbed off my bike and over the wrought-iron fence, and I slung my arm over Al's shoulder.

"Okay," Al's father said. "Say Pocahontas."

Al said nothing, but I yelled, "Pocahontas!" By the middle of the word, I was already blinking.

I couldn't sleep that night. I lay in bed, wondering if I was growing. I'd read somewhere that giants were really just people who suffered from excessive growth hormones, and that because they couldn't stop growing, they eventually suffered all kinds of terrible illnesses. Giants often didn't live to be very old.

Lately, usually at night, I started worrying that maybe I was a giant. Maybe this growth spurt was just the beginning of a never-ending growth spurt. But how would I know unless my parents took me to a doctor for tests? It was possible, I concluded, that I was indeed a giant but wouldn't be able to confirm this fact for years.

I finally got out of bed and creaked open my door, hoping to sneak to the fridge for a glass of milk, but my father was already up, sitting at the kitchen table and writing a letter.

"A client who wouldn't take money?" I asked.

"Jesus!" he said, looking up. "Where did you come from? Why aren't you in bed?" He quickly folded the letter and rested his arm over it.

"I couldn't sleep," I said.

My father's face softened. He nodded toward the seat across from him. "I hope to God you didn't inherit my insomnia. It's a curse. It'll drive a sane man crazy."

I wanted to tell him that I thought I was a giant, but the moment didn't seem right. When he saw me looking at his letter, he folded it again and slid it into his pajama's shirt pocket. It was the first time I'd ever seen someone use any of the pockets on their pajamas.

"Let me boil you some milk," he said. "That sometimes works for me."

I hated warm milk, but I didn't tell my father that. I said, "Sure."

My father said, "But we don't want to wake your mom, you hear? She thinks I'm in bed next to her, so we need to be quiet."

"Okay," I whispered, and suddenly the night seemed like an adventure.

The next time I visited the new apartments, Al's father said, "I want to tell you why Al is special. He was sick when he was little. He was a very sick little boy, weren't you, Al?" I looked over at Al, but Al wasn't listening. He was gently prodding what looked like a mosquito bite on his arm. "He had to have surgery," the father said. "And during surgery, he died."

I must have looked frightened because the father began to nod vigorously, pleased by my reaction.

"That's right," the father said. "He died. He was pronounced dead. And just as the doctors were about to give up, he came back to life." The father leaned toward me. "He's seen things only a few people have ever seen. He's seen what comes after death. You know what that means, don't you?"

"No."

The father smiled. He said, "He's been chosen."

"For what?" I asked, but the father didn't answer. He patted his own leg, and Al walked over and sat down on it. He whispered something into Al's ear, and Al nodded. I was starting to feel queasy, but I couldn't stop staring at Al. Had he been to Heaven? Had he seen *God?* How could someone die and then come back to life? It wasn't possible.

I set down my glass of lemonade. "I need to go," I said, but the father grabbed my shirt sleeve, pinching my arm. He pulled me toward him, and I almost lost my footing.

He said, "Don't tell anyone what I've told you. You understand? This is our secret."

I nodded.

"I *mean* it," he said, and I could tell by the way he was squinting at me that he did.

I quit going to the construction site. Instead, I biked up and down streets that my parents had pre-approved for travel. My father had given me a map of the neighborhood with these pre-approved areas marked off with a felt-tip pen. These were the same maps he gave to his clients who were looking for a new home to buy.

I practiced riding my bike without using my hands. The most difficult thing about riding without hands is turning corners. You have to lean gently. You shouldn't make any drastic change to what you are doing before you start to turn. If you are pedaling, keep pedaling. If you aren't pedaling, don't start.

The first time I tried turning a corner, I leaned too hard and started pedaling faster. The front wheel pivoted entirely to the right, and I flew over the handlebars. In that airborne moment, I understood why Evel Knievel did what he did. I was flying. I wasn't afraid. A car had stopped, and the driver watched me. I smiled at him. But then I landed. And then my bike landed on top of me. A few people rushed over to see if I was okay. I wasn't okay – not for a few minutes, at least – but the time I had spent flying more than compensated for the pain. I'm fine, I told myself. I would live to tell my story.

Later that summer, my father took me to his office for my annual visit. By now I had come to look forward to seeing everyone. I knew who was who, and I knew what each person was going to say, but it was Mrs. Van Patton I really wanted to see. I had started to have small crushes on older women, including some of my mother's friends, though mostly my crushes were on women I saw in grocery stores. I would follow them from one aisle to the next, hoping they'd turn around, see me, and smile. But my crush on Mrs. Van Patton was different. I didn't want to have to follow her around to win her affection. What I wanted was for her to come to me, as she did each year. I wanted her to tell me how cute I was so that I could blush. It was funny how I used to hate hearing her talk that way to me – I never knew where to look or what to do with my hands – but at some point I had started to crave it. And so when my father took me to his office that late-summer day, I shook hands all around but barely paid attention to what anyone was saying because I was too busy imagining the various ways that Mrs. Van Patton might react upon seeing me. My heart thumped harder the closer we got to Mrs. Van Patton's office, and by the time I saw her through the plate-glass window, pouring over a stack of papers on her desk, I could barely breathe. I had paused, waiting for my father to tap on her door with a single knuckle and then walk on in, as he did each year, but he just motioned with his head for me to keep following him.

"We haven't said hello to Mrs. Van Patton," I said.

"C'mon," he said. "We're not stopping this year." He said this as if she were a monument we normally visited while on vacation but couldn't fit in this trip.

At the sound of our voices, Mrs. Van Patton looked up. I smiled. I had no doubt that she would smile back, that she would motion me inside, but I was wrong. She looked back down at her papers.

I didn't know it then, but this would be the last time that I would ever see Mrs. Van Patton. By my next visit, she would already have moved on. Two years later, my father would quit taking me to the office altogether. The annual visits would come to an end without explanation. But on that final day I gave pleading one last try.

"*Dad*," I moaned, but Dad wasn't having any of it.

"Let's go," he said. "Time is money."

The rest of that summer I spent riding my bike without using my hands. I became expert at turning corners and negotiating parked cars, but the ten-speed had skinny tires, and it didn't take much to throw the bike off its intended course. One drizzly morning, I ran over a rock. The bike's tire swung to the left, and I slammed into the car that I had been riding along beside. I landed headfirst, and though I don't remember it, I did a somersault according to one witness. I spent a few days in the hospital, under observation, to make sure that blood wasn't spreading throughout my brain. As large as my head had gotten, I wouldn't have surprised me if this were the case. I couldn't stop touching the top of my head, mostly because I could barely feel it. It was like touching a balloon that had been strapped to me. I could feel the pressure of my finger, but I couldn't feel the finger itself pressing into my head.

My mother stayed with me for the duration of visiting

hours, and it was the first time that I became aware of how little we had to say to each other, or of how little I knew about her. She spent most of those hours pacing my room.

"They should fix this drip," she said, pointing to the sink. "All it needs is a new washer. It'd probably take them two minutes."

I nodded. I hadn't even realized that the sink was dripping until she brought it up, but once she did, it was the only sound I heard.

To distract myself from the maddening plunks of water, I asked my mother if she thought I was growing too fast.

"What do you mean?"

"Do you think I'm going to be a giant?"

"Don't be silly," she said.

At night, my father popped in with my Instamatic camera.

"We need a few snapshots of your noggin, in case we sue the driver."

"It was my fault," I said. "I hit *him*."

"Nothing against the driver," Dad said. "It's an insurance issue. The driver's rarely ever one hundred percent liable, you know. The insurance companies, they'll hammer out a percentage of liability, but just in case the driver's insurance company wants to play hardball, I'll have a few photos of your head. That's how the game works, kiddo. They'll want to bluff, then we show them an ace or two."

I had no idea what he was talking about; I let him snap as many photos as he wanted. A few days later, after I'd been released, my father came home with a package from Fotomat.

"Nice," he said, flipping through them. "Your head looks *terrible*. That's exactly what we want."

"Good!" I said.

"These must be yours," he said and handed me a short stack of photos I had taken. The first was of a Dumpster. At first I couldn't remember why I had taken a photo of a Dumpster, but then I remembered the thousands of green flies that hovered above it like a toxic cloud. The problem was, I couldn't see any of them in the photo. It was just the Dumpster. There were several other photos that had the same problem. I'd snapped one of an airplane, but it was so small in the photo, it looked as though a piece of fuzz had landed on the lens. Photo after photo was a disappointment. An ant colony with several tunnels and thousands of inhabitants looked like nothing but a pile of dirt. The tips of my sneakers appeared at the bottom of that one.

The last photo was of me. It was the one Al's father had taken. Al, however, was nowhere to be seen. Al's father's forefinger covered up his son, turning him into a smudge, around which I had draped my arm. But when I looked closer, I wasn't entirely sure that it *was* a finger covering little Al. I could still see most of my arm. The shape of the smudge was the same shape as Al. Maybe Al was actually a ghost, and though I could see him in real life – I could squeeze his hand and hear him breathe – he couldn't be captured in photographs, except as a blur. Maybe Al really *had* died.

Since my bike had gotten run over by the back tire of the car that I'd slammed into, I hoofed it to the apartment complex. I hadn't realized how much better time I made by bike than by foot. I also hadn't realized how potentially dangerous the trip had been. On bike, I blew past buildings without ever noticing how shabby they were. On foot, however, I saw people looking at me out their windows as I passed. I saw kids who, bigger than me, looked like they wanted to make trouble. I walked faster. I thought of my Dad's map, and how he probably had a good reason for marking it up the way he did. He was doing me a favor, but I couldn't see that until now.

Though earth-moving equipment still surrounded the property, most of the apartment complexes looked completed. I walked over to Al's apartment, but neither he nor his father was on the patio. I climbed over the wrought-iron gate and knocked on the sliding glass door's window, but no one answered. I cupped my hands and looked inside, but I couldn't see anything in there. The apartment was empty.

A golf cart came bouncing over mounds of dirt, the same mounds I had ridden up and down on my bike, and I thought, *So it's going to be a golf course,* but the cart came zipping right up to me, stopping at the patio. A fat guy smoking a cigar said, "You're trespassing, kid. You can't be here."

"I'm looking for my friends," I said.

"What friends?"

"Al," I said. "Al and his father."

The fat guy removed the cigar, blew smoke out the side of his mouth, then jammed the cigar back inside. His lips were fat, too, and the way his mouth was turned down reminded me of a fish.

"They used to live here," I said.

"Who?"

"Al and his father."

"Where?"

"Here."

The fat guy shook his head. "No one's ever lived there," he said. "I haven't even started renting units. Maybe you're in the wrong place."

"No, it was here." I took out my photo and showed it to him. You could see some of the same earth-moving equipment in the background, as well as the wrought-iron fence of the unit next to Al's. I had thought the photo would clear up the matter, that it would prove that I was right, but it only made matters worse.

"There's no one in this photo but *you*," the man said.

"Al's right here," I said, pointing to the blur. "And his father's the one who took it."

"Listen, kid. You need to tell me who these people are. They weren't supposed to be here, understand? And I can't let squatters come and go as they please. What were their names?"

"Al," I said, and I felt like crying. "Al and his father."

"Last names, kid."

"I don't know last names."

"Where were they from?"

"I don't know."

"Do you have a phone number? Do you know where they might have gone?"

"I don't know." I was crying now. I didn't know anything.

"Okay, okay," the guy said. "But I'm keeping this photo."

"Why?" I said. "It's just me."

"That's right," he said. "And I'm showin' it to everyone who works here so that if they see you around again, they can tell me." He folded the photo once and tucked it into his shirt pocket. He blew one last stream of cigar smoke at me before driving away, bouncing over one mound of dirt after the other, eventually disappearing behind all the dust his golf cart had kicked up.

We never moved to Lincoln Park, as my father had hoped. In fact, we stayed on the bottom floor of our apartment until I was thirteen, the year my father's health took a turn for the worse. Only then did we relocate but not to the nice part of Chicago. Instead, the three of us moved to Victory, a small town in Southern Illinois, where my father could afford to quit working.

It was here in Victory that my father lived out his remaining days – fishing along the banks of the Mississippi, strolling the town square, paying visits to the proprietors of each business. Whenever there was an open house, he made it a point to stop by and look around, sometimes offering advice. And every Sunday he put on his bifocals and carefully read over the real estate advertisements in the *St. Louis Dispatch*.

My father developed glaucoma the year before he died, so I would take him by the arm and walk with him, helping him search the streets for Realtor's signs, and though he could still see, I would describe each house to him. Nice fretwork on this one. Flaking paint on that one. Rotted shingles. A cornucopia of leaves blooming from a downspout.

He lived the last three years of his life in Victory. He never admitted it, but I suspect he spent a good part of those days thinking about that one magical year, 1965. *What was it about that year?* he must have wondered. *What did I have that year that I didn't have all those others?*

I kept hoping one day he would tell me what had happened to Mrs. Van Patton, but he never mentioned her name again, and I feared asking him. I imagined Mrs. Van Patton showing up at his funeral, standing in the distance and dressed in mourning, but on that gray March day it was just me, my mother, and a priest we didn't know beside the grave as the coffin was lowered into a plot my father had bought only a month earlier. He'd purchased it from a widow who, planning a cross-country move, was determined to put her old life behind her. While my father sat across from the widow at her kitchen table and counted out crisp ten-dollar bills, I typed up a receipt on an ancient cast-iron typewriter she kept in her sewing room, using a sheet of purple carbon paper from a dusty box to make a copy. When I returned to the kitchen, I could tell my father was pleased by the deal he had struck. I saw it in the way he twisted around in the thin-legged chair and said, "Ah ha! Here he comes!" as if I were someone more than just his son. My father, squinting, signed both copies of the receipt, the widow signed both copies, and I signed them as witness.

My father said, "Here, let me give you my card, in case you need to reach me," but he must have realized as soon as he said this that he didn't have cards anymore. He shrugged and put his wallet away, and then they shook hands, my father and the widow, and wished each other luck.

SAMSONITE

(Richard Joseph Daley, 1902-1976)

On Michigan Avenue, outside the Conrad Hilton Hotel, policemen wearing short-sleeved sky-blue shirts and sky-blue helmets backed protestors up against the large plate-glass window of the Haymarket Restaurant. After the window broke and some of the protestors tumbled inside, several officers climbed through the jagged frame and chased them through the restaurant and into the hotel lobby.

This was August, 1968. Chuck Kipper, checking out of his room at the Conrad Hilton, pulled a handkerchief from his back pocket and blew into it as one of the shaggy-haired protestors ran past him. The man, who wasn't wearing a shirt, was followed closely behind by a police officer wielding a Billy club.

Forty-five years old and unemployed, Chuck had traveled to Chicago on his own dime to interview for a job that had seemed so promising over the phone. If all had gone well, he would have been a copywriter for the Leo Burnett Agency. Leo Burnett himself was the genius behind the Jolly Green Giant, the Marlboro Man, and the Pillsbury Doughboy. It didn't get any bigger than this!

The interview, however, *didn't* go well. It quickly devolved into four bored men looking over his mock-ups. No one smiled or offered encouragement. Chuck couldn't help,

even as the men were wrapping up their talk with him, silently calculating how much the trip had cost: the airfare, the new
suit, the hotel. He spent the afternoon after the interview staring vacantly at green sea turtles and moon jellies at the Shedd
Aquarium – the only refuge he could find from the city's noise,
the only place to calm his nerves. He couldn't summon the
energy to call his wife, Mary, and when, later that evening, she
called his hotel room, he didn't pick up.

Chuck had met Mary Holtz at the Currency Exchange in
Wichita, where she worked behind bullet-proof glass. It had
been a slow day, affording her the opportunity to chat with
customers through the slatted speaker-hole that separated her
from them. She was lonely, she told Chuck later. She felt like
a woman in prison, waiting for visitors to come in and talk
to her. When her supervisor returned from lunch, the door's
buzzer announcing his arrival, Mary placed a folded sheet of
paper into the stainless-steel trough for Chuck to take with
him. On it was her phone number. Just when he'd begun to
accept his fate as a man who, with his collection of matchbook
covers and mason jars full of buffalo nickels, would spend the
rest of his years alone, love came slamming into his life.

Leaving his luggage behind, Chuck walked away from
the Conrad Hilton's front desk, following the noise coming
from outside – the sirens, the screaming. The luggage had
been a wedding present from Mary's parents, and this was the
first time he used them. "Oh, look," Mary had said the next
morning when she opened the big box. "They're Samsonite!"
On this trip, whenever he caught sight of the pair of avocado-
green suitcases, he heard his wife's voice, and he remembered
thinking how strange it was that the luggage had excited her
so much.

They're Samsonite! Chuck thought ruefully now, opening
the hotel door and stepping out onto the sidewalk of Michigan
Avenue. Several young men across the street waved Viet Cong
flags. A man half Chuck's age sat astride a statue in the park

and flashed the peace sign. On the sidewalk in front of the hotel, a group of protestors yelled profanities while a row of humorless Chicago policemen advanced toward them.

Chuck stood between the two opposing groups. He took a deep breath, ready to ask someone what the problem was when he felt a sneeze about to overcome him. He bent forward, squinting and reaching for his handkerchief, and in the split-second that the sneeze seized him, the police charged the protesters. They tackled some while hitting others with their clubs. *Get back inside the hotel*, Chuck thought, but he had no sooner finished thinking this when a club came down hard on the back of his head. It caught him by surprise, a blow from behind, and as his knees gave out and he started to go down, he shut his eyes and saw a little boy riding an antique bicycle with a huge front tire down a quiet street lined with bungalows – and then Chuck's world crumpled to black.

Little Richie Daley rode the high wheel bicycle all over Bridgeport, but mostly he stayed on South Lowe, where he was born, or on Thirty-sixth Street. The bicycle belonged to his friend, Colin McVickers, who had taken a trip to Memphis with his parents. Colin had asked Richie to take care of the bicycle, and Richie, who was seven and didn't own a bicycle of any kind, agreed. The bicycle, according to Colin, was over thirty years old and had belonged to his father when he had been their age.

The summer of 1909 had come and gone, and Colin still hadn't returned from Memphis with his family. *What had happened to them?* Richie wondered. *Would they ever come back to Bridgeport?*

The bicycle's pedals were connected to the center of the tire's spokes, but the tire itself was so large, Richie's feet almost didn't reach the pedals. After his father explained to him that a bigger tire meant he could cover more ground per rotation than someone riding a bicycle with a smaller tire, Richie fantasized about a bicycle with a front tire so large he would need a ladder to climb up onto the seat. A single rotation, and he might end up in Indiana!

"Be careful you don't take a header," his father warned each time Richie took the bike out. Because Richie sat so high off the ground, it would be easy to fall off if he hit a rock or if a squirrel ran in front of him, and more likely than not, because of the way the bike was made, Richie would end up breaking the fall with his head. *That*, his father explained, was a header.

One afternoon, while Richie rode the bicycle down Thirty-sixth, going two blocks further than he normally went, three boys stepped down from a front stoop and forced him to a stop. He knew them by reputation: Theo Crawley, Nathaniel Borst, and Quintin Brooks. They were Protestants, and more than one of Richie's classmates had had run-ins with them.

With Nathaniel and Quintin stationed at the rear wheel, Theo stood in front and held the bike steady. "Get down," he said. "This is ours now."

Richie's upper lip began to quiver. He couldn't get down because the bicycle wasn't his to hand over. A duty had been entrusted him, and he would honor that duty.

Quintin said, "I don't think he heard you."

Nathaniel, who was the fattest of the three by at least fifty pounds, laughed. "Oh, he heard him. Look at 'im. He's gonna wet himself."

"Down!" Theo ordered. "Now!"

Richie tried pedaling, hoping to break free, but when two sets of arms grabbed him from behind and lifted him into the air, the bicycle collapsed beneath him. Nathaniel and Quentin held onto Richie, allowing Theo to run off with the bicycle. Then Nathaniel and Quintin let go of Richie, walking slowly away but still facing him, shaking their heads. The look they gave him said, *Don't even THINK of trying anything... or you'll be sorry!*

Richie ran home and told his father, explaining in great detail everything that had happened, even providing the culprits' names. Throughout Richie's short-of-breath recitation, his father's face didn't change expression.

When Richie finished, his father said, "You'll have to come to your own solution." Richie knew what this meant: their conversation was over. There was no debating in the Daley household, no second chances to make one's point. If his father told him that it was up to him, then it was up to him.

That night, Richie kneeled beside his bed and prayed for the return of his bike. He stood and looked out the window, but the bike wasn't there. God was telling him the same thing his father had told him, that he, Richie, would have to come to a solution on his own.

Richie lit a candle. On top of his bed, he pieced together an imaginary city, the same city he worked on every night, a city where streets had hills (ripples in the blanket) and where a snow-capped mountain (his pillow) sat majestically at the edge. He pulled out from under his bed a box of wooden blocks, and he lined them up like houses – one over here, one over there. He put one of the blocks on top of the mountain because this was where the Daleys would one day live. Richie knew this city well because he'd been thinking about it for the past three years. He knew which imaginary adults lived in which imaginary house, he knew what each person did for a living, and he knew how many kids each family had. The people who lived in his imaginary city were all Catholic, and most of them were Irish. But tonight, as he lowered the last block into place, he set it down beside another block, the way the houses in his real neighborhood sat, side by side and with just enough room to stretch your arms out without touching either house, but not much more. Then Richie removed the pillow – there were no snow-capped mountains in Bridgeport – and he straightened out the bed sheet since there were no hilly roads, either. Carefully, using everything he could find in his room (pencils, an eraser, matches), he meticulously recreated, house by house, South Lowe Street, after which he worked on Thirty-sixth Street, all the way from where he lived to where the three boys had sat on the stoop. His heart actually seemed to grow at the realization of all he knew about where he lived – his neighbors, their houses, their pets' names, the types of hats they wore, the firmness of their handshakes.

As his plan grew in scope, Richie's heart pounded faster. On a sheet of paper, he made a list of every boy he knew, and then he tried remembering the names of adults who'd suffered some indignity at the hands of these hooligans. It was possible that they would want to help him, too. There was Mr. Conklin who ran the corner grocery store, always a soft target for thieves. And there was Mr. McCaskill who owned the funeral home and whose front window had been busted out no fewer than three times. But when Richie tried to think of the name of the man who worked in the feed store, the only name that came to mind was Samsonite. It was an odd name, one Richie wasn't sure he'd ever heard before, but he liked how it sounded. "Samsonite," he said, trying it out. The word rang in his ears, as if someone from the future were whispering it to him. *Samsonite*, he thought and added the name to the list, though he was certain he'd just made it up.

With his plan of action firmly in place, Richie could go to bed now. Tomorrow, he would go door to door, gathering all of his friends and compatriots, dozens of them, and together they would walk down Thirty-sixth street and show the little thugs who was boss. He folded the list and tucked it into an empty shoe; then, before blowing out the candle, he lifted all four corners of his blanket and, in one fell swoop, destroyed the city he had so lovingly created.

PLANETARY DANGER

When the bartender flipped the switch for the neon sign, green light rolled like smoke through the looping glass tube, and Tommy was reminded again of the poison that had streamed through his veins the night his wife served him orange juice spiked with radiator fluid. Once he had realized that something had gone awry inside his body (his breath labored, his concentration splintering), and after she had told him what she had done, smiling the whole while, Tommy became frighteningly conscious of his own blood – namely, how fast it could absorb and transport, and how impossible it seemed to stop what was now set in motion. In the ambulance, on his way to the hospital, he lay on the gurney and imagined the ghoulish network of veins inside him, thousands of miles' worth, tangled and criss-crossed, an interstate system designed by a madman.

That was over three years ago – he and his wife were now divorced – and yet Tommy still didn't feel quite himself. Whenever anyone asked him how he was doing, he told them that he felt *off*. There was no other way to put it: he just felt *off*.

It was almost eight p.m., and Tommy was The Alibi's only customer tonight. He was finishing his third pitcher – or, by his best calculations, his eighteenth beer. The Alibi, sand-

wiched between Brenneman's Auto Parts and All-Pets Grooming, was a storefront bar in the otherwise nearly-vacant town
square of Belvedere, Illinois. Mounted and hanging around
the bar's main room were a dozen heads of large animals, each
head wearing its own hat: a deer in a Santa cap, a moose in a
derby. It was the sort of detail that Tommy found more unset-
tling as the night wore on.

Since neither he nor the bartender had said much of
anything, Tommy hitched his thumb in the direction of the
business next door and said, "All-Pets Grooming. Do they really mean that? *All* pets? You know what I'm going to do? I'm
going to bring a friggin' crocodile over there and tell them I'd
like it groomed. What do you think they'll do?"

The bartender fixed herself a Bailey's and coffee, her
fourth since Tommy'd arrived. She squinted at him and said,
"Probably take it out back, hose it down, then charge you thirty
bucks."

"Uh huh. Well, thirty bucks isn't bad for a hosed-down
crocodile." He pushed a ten dollar bill toward her, her cue to
refill his pitcher.

"You know what?" she said. "You're hardcore. I'll give
you that much."

"I'll take that as a compliment," Tommy said. "Thank
you."

What the bartender had meant was that no one else was
crazy enough to head for the bars in these conditions. A blizzard, pushing across Iowa, would start pounding southern Illinois any minute now, and if the satellite map on the news
could be trusted, the worst of that blizzard would approach
The Alibi as a snake would a rodent, capturing it quickly, then
swallowing it whole.

Tommy took a credit card out of his pocket, walked over
to the large plate-glass window, and began shaving away frost,
enough for a porthole's view of the street.

"So tell me," the bartender said a bit later. "What do people call you?"

"Depends on who you talk to," Tommy said. "My mother and my ex-wife, for instance. They call me different things." Though he thought about her all the time – every day, several times an hour – Tommy regretted bringing up his ex-wife in conversation. Talking about her to strangers was like getting sucked into a black hole: once he started heading in that direction, he might not ever return. He did, however, have enough sense not to tell the bartender that, even as they stood there, his ex-wife was across the street and drinking at the only other bar in town, a stand-alone building in an empty field. In fact, he could see her right now through the freshly shaven porthole.

The bartender said, "Okay. Let's start with your mother."

"Tommy," Tommy said, settling back onto his stool.

"Nice to meet you, Tommy. *My* mother calls me Lauralynn." They shook hands.

Tommy pointed at the books leaning against her cash register. "What are those?"

One by one, she picked them up and read the titles: "*Guinness Book of World Records, 1978 edition. The Mystery of the Loch Ness Monster. The Great Houdini.*"

"Jesus," Tommy said. "Does the owner order his books from Scholastics or *what*?" He was trying to be funny, but Lauralynn wasn't laughing. It was possible, he supposed, that the books were hers. "Okay, okay," Tommy said. "Give me the *Guinness Book*."

She pulled up a stool to watch him read.

Tommy peeled open the fat book. "Moustache at least 102 inches long," he read. "Look at that!" He showed her the picture.

"Don't show me the one with the fingernails," she said.

"What page?" Tommy asked.

"I don't know," she said. "There's an index. Look up *longest fingernails*."

Tommy peeked up at her, then continued flipping through the book until he found the photo. "Holy Toledo," Tommy said.

"Let's see," she said.

"You just told me you didn't want to see it."

"I know what I said," she said, "but let me see it, anyway." Tommy showed her. She groaned and turned away. "The way they *curl*," she said.

"Hey, listen to this," Tommy said. "He gave each one a name."

"Of course he did," she said.

"How do you think he, you know, takes a whiz?" Tommy asked.

Lauralynn said, "How do you think he unzips his pants *to* whiz?"

"Get this. World's longest moustache and world's longest fingernails – they're both from India. India! Do you think they know each other?"

Lauralynn stopped blowing into her drink. "That should go without saying," she said.

"Longest hiccoughing," Tommy said. "Charles Osborne from Iowa. His first wife left him and he was unable to keep in his false teeth."

"Want to know what you do with a guy like that?" Lauralynn asked.

"What's that?"

"Stuff him into a burlap sack and dump him in the river. *Adios, amigos!*"

Tommy nodded. "Or poison him," he suggested. He glanced out the porthole. The window across the street had frosted over, but he could still make out his ex-wife's ghostly silhouette. Six months after they'd married, she had secretly decided to quit taking her anti-psychotic medication. Part of the problem, however, was that she had never told Tommy that she was on anti-psychotics, making her accusations impossible to interpret. One week, Tommy was supposedly sleeping with other women; the next, he was conspiring to kill her; within a month, he and a man from a local television commercial had begun plotting acts of terrorism together, and the man's monologue in the commercial was a code that only Tommy understood.

At first, Tommy thought that she was joking, that all of this was coming from some dark side that she hadn't previously revealed. He kept hoping to pick up on its nuances and be able to play along, but when this didn't happen he began ignoring what she said, assuming that she was venting in metaphors, a phase that would surely end soon. Eventually, though, he feared that she had gone crazy. Since he'd never been around a crazy person before, he didn't know what to do, so in the end he did nothing. How, after all, did you tell a crazy person that she was crazy?

A sharp wind slammed into The Alibi, and the large plate-glass windows, encased in ice, sounded as though they were about to shatter. "Shit," Lauralynn said. They watched the shivering windows, waiting for whatever would happen next, but when nothing happened, Tommy returned to the book.

"Here's one," Tommy said. "Most tattoos. Some guy named Sailor Joe had 4,831 tattoos."

Lauralynn said, "4,831. And I thought *three* tattoos were decadent."

Tommy looked up at her and smiled. He liked this woman. She was leaning closer to him, eyelids droopier by the hour. "4,829 more tattoos and *you* –" Tommy poked her gently with his forefinger "–you can beat that worthless sack of crap, Sailor Joe."

Lauralynn gave him a free pitcher, courtesy of her tip jar. She fixed herself another Bailey's and coffee. "Tell me something about your ex," she said. "If you could pick only one thing to tell me about her, what would it be?"

Tommy said, "She has incredibly thick hair."

"That's it? Thick hair? Of all the things about her, that's the one thing you'd pick?"

"No; listen," Tommy said. "One night we were both drinking pretty heavily. We came home and she passed out. I couldn't find any floss, so I plucked one of her hairs and used it."

Lauralynn said nothing. She stirred her coffee. Apparently, this wasn't the sort of thing she was looking for.

"I was drunk," Tommy said for clarification. "And I have a bridge here that I have to floss under every night. The dentist calls it a food trap. That strand of hair? Worked like a charm. And no one was the wiser in the morning."

"Hm."

Tommy decided to start chugging his beer, but as he leaned his head back to finish the last of what was in his glass, he met the eyes of an elk. Atop its head was a red-felt Shriner's fez. The odd thing was, the elk looked positively overjoyed to be there.

Tommy shut his eyes, finished his beer. Pouring himself another, he asked Lauralynn if she anticipated any more customers.

"The only people we're likely to see tonight," she said, "are Eskimos, the Abominable Freaking Snowman, and a couple of escaped convicts."

"My kind of people," Tommy said. "So tell me about those tattoos of yours."

"I've got a tiny cat on my ankle," she said. "It looks like a shadow. And I've got a bleeding heart on my arm here." She sipped her coffee, then dabbed the corners of her mouth with the bar towel.

"What about the third one?"

"The third one? You really want to know?"

"Absolutely."

"The grim reaper," she said.

"No joke? The grim reaper?"

"It's on my right shoulder blade, only it's not done yet."

"Run out of money?"

"Not money," she said. "*Luck*. The guy who was doing it, he doesn't live here anymore."

"Why don't you get somebody else to finish it up?"

Lauralynn smiled. *You don't get it,* the smile said. It was the exact same smile his wife had given him when he asked her why she had poisoned him.

"My friend," Lauralynn began, "the guy who started it, he's the only one who can get it right. He's not just a tattoo artist. He's an *artist* artist. Once you've seen his grim reapers, all the others look like cartoons. His reapers look, I don't know, *real* somehow. Alive. But he's in jail now. They haven't sentenced him yet, so I don't know when he'll be out again."

Jail. Tommy didn't ask. His ex-wife was lucky that *she* wasn't in jail. The ambulance took Tommy to St. Luke's that night, where they ran a series of tests to check the level of toxicity. *Ethylene Glycol*, the doctor had told him. That was the poison. It was used in radiator fluid to increase the boiling point and to decrease the freezing point. The doctor said, *You can imagine what it does to a person's body*. They stuck an IV into his arm, hooked him up to an ECG to watch for arrythmias, poked his finger for blood at regular intervals. Tommy hoped that he was wrong, but he thought that everyone around him looked a little nervous – the doctors, the nurses, the interns. They all looked like they knew something that Tommy didn't.

Is it that bad? Tommy asked, but the doctor told him to relax, that getting excited would only complicate matters.

Tommy didn't tell the doctors that it was his own wife who'd poisoned him. From St. Luke's, between tests, he called her parents, who drove in from St. Louis and checked their daughter into St. Luke's later that same night for psychiatric evaluation. To Tommy's surprise, they knew well of her affliction. Later, Tommy would learn that all of her old friends knew, too. Her high school teachers knew. So did her aunts and uncles, her therapist in college, her old roommate, her first fiancé. Everyone, except for Tommy, knew.

In a few days, when his health permitted, he wandered the hospital in a robe until he found the psych ward. *Honey*, his wife said when she first saw him. *Are you all right?* She asked this as if she hadn't been the one who'd poisoned him. *Well, no, not really*, he said. *I feel kind of off.* She wrapped her arms around him, pressed her cheek against his chest, and said, *My poor Sweetie. My poor, poor Sweetie.*

Who could have imagined that, among the disinfected halls of St. Luke's, only a short time after one had tried to kill the other, they would enter their second honeymoon stage? While his wife shimmered through her days in a medicated haze, Tommy bought her bouquets from the gift shop, he smuggled his leftover desserts from his wing of the hospital to hers, and once they even feverishly made out in her room, ghosts of their teen aged selves, until a tired older nurse, waiting to take her temperature, knocked on the door and loudly cleared her throat. But then, during the final two weeks of her stay, before he could bring himself to ask her any of the questions that had begun to plague him, an odd thing happened. She didn't want to be touched anymore. She even flinched when he reached for her. Only later, after she was released from the hospital, did word, floating down the hospital corridors like a strain of bacteria, reach Tommy, word that she had begun spending time with an intern who worked the graveyard shift, the man who literally tucked her into bed each night.

Tommy said, "The grim reaper, huh?" He smiled now at Lauralynn. "I'd like to see that one." It wouldn't have surprised him if she took off her blouse right there to show him. He was having better luck with women these days, but it was for the most unlikely of reasons: he just didn't give a shit anymore. Back in the days when he *did* give a shit, women wouldn't have much to do with him; now that he didn't, they actually sought him out. Lauralynn wasn't having any of it, though.

"You'd like that, wouldn't you?" she said.

"Hey, I'm no different than the next man. I enjoy a good-looking grim reaper every now and again."

"What about your ex?"

"She won't mind."

"I mean, does she have any *tattoos*?"

"Oh. *Tattoos*. No. No tattoos."

Tommy could tell that his answer pleased her. Nearly all the women he knew were like that. They thrived on competition with women they'd never met.

Tommy walked to the window again and scraped away fresh frost. His ex-wife appeared to be dancing. He couldn't actually *see* her dancing, but her silhouette was gliding one way and then the other, and he could tell that her arms were over her head. He imagined that she was trapped inside of a frozen lake, the plate-glass window across the street now a lid of ice keeping her from getting out. Instead of dancing, she was swimming. Instead of having fun, she was panicking, running out of time.

He returned to his seat and said, "Have you ever been so glad to get rid of someone who was ruining your life, so unbelievably fucking glad that you couldn't stop *thinking* about them, you couldn't stop *fixating* about them, even though you were glad?"

"Absolutely," Lauralynn said. "My creditors. I paid them off, but I still want to kill them. Some mornings I wake up and the first thing I think is what I'd like to do to them if I had the chance. The problem is, I don't know who the hell they are exactly. They're like that movie *The Blob*. I mean, it's coming after you, but *what* is it and *where* do you start attacking?"

"*The Blob*," Tommy said. "Guess what they call *The Blob* in France."

Lauralynn shrugged. "I don't know. *Le Blob*?"

"Nope. Good guess, though – *Le Blob*. Actually, it's *Dan-*

ger Planétaire."

She stopped pouring herself another drink. "What the hell's that mean?"

"Planetary Danger."

"Oh." She resumed pouring.

Tommy said, "I saw it in a revival theater in Paris about ten years ago."

"You?" Lauralynn said. "In France? You're lying."

"Lying? Why would I lie?"

"You've never been to France," she said.

"I haven't?" he said, as if the possibility existed that she was right. He could see her point: it was preposterous that anyone who'd ever spent time in Paris would now be spending time in Belvedere, Illinois.

"Watch yourself, bub," she said. "I can smell a rat a mile away." She smiled, shook her head, and said, *"The Blob* in France. Nice try."

By the end of the night, Tommy had consumed nearly thirty beers, plus three shots of rail whiskey. His peeing-to-beer ratio eventually reached two-to-one. At the urinal, he thought of the man with the world's longest fingernails. And then he thought of poor Charles Osborne hiccoughing while his wife packed her suitcases in another room.

At two in the morning, Lauralynn and Tommy said their good-byes.

"How do you feel?" Lauralynn asked.

"Off," Tommy said.

"Off? What does that mean?"

Tommy shrugged. "I don't know. It means *off*. You know. *Off."*

When Lauralynn flipped the switch for the neon sign, the smoky-green evaporated, leaving the tube as gray and empty as a vein drained of life. Tommy dragged a bar stool across the room, climbed up onto it, and removed a hunter's cap from the head of a buffalo.

"I'll bring it back," he told Lauralynn, pulling the cap onto his own head and unsnapping the flaps so that they covered his ears.

"Sure you will."

"I will. Promise. Scout's honor." He raised his hand and gave her the scout symbol.

Two feet of snow had fallen since he'd arrived, requiring Tommy to lean all of his weight into the front door to push it open. He struggled the few steps it took for him to reach his pick-up. He decided against brushing away the snow or scraping the ice that covered the windows, deciding in favor of sitting in the truck's cab with the heater blasting and the rear defroster on, hoping everything would melt without him having to lift a finger. Fiddling with the heater's controls, he realized that what he'd given Lauralynn wasn't the gesture boy scouts gave for honor; it was the Vulcan greeting from *Star Trek*. He knew, even as he stood in front of her with his hand raised, that it felt wrong, but he didn't know why. "Ah, Christ," he said and looked over to see if his ex-wife was still across the street, but the bar appeared to be closed.

Why had she decided to self-medicate? What had made her decide that she *didn't* need the medicine anymore? Why had she never told him about the medicine in the first place? It was during dialysis, trapped in that wretched chair for five or six hours at a stretch, connected to a machine that was draining his bank account faster than it purified his blood, that Tommy started fixating. The more he clenched his fists, the faster the blood pumped out of him, and the faster the blood pumped out of him, the more he wanted answers.

Shortly after their divorce, Tommy was fired from his academic advising job. A sorority girl – a Chi Omega – had smelled vodka on his breath and reported him to the dean. Unable to afford anywhere else to live, Tommy cashed in his retirement benefits, quit going to the dialysis center, and bought himself a camping trailer that was small enough that he could tow with his pick-up. Without dialysis, he would die sooner than later, but without a job, without a place to live, he didn't really have a choice.

Tommy wasn't asleep long when he heard someone knocking at the window. *The police*, he thought, but when he opened the door, he saw Lauralynn shrouded by the exhaust that was shooting from his truck. She was hopping from one foot to the other and patting her arms to keep warm.

"My battery's dead," she said. "Kaput!"

"Hop in!" Tommy said, cheered to learn that the night wasn't over.

All Tommy needed in order to drive was to be able to see the road ahead of him, so he flicked on the wipers and knocked two half-moons of snow from the front windshield. While Lauralynn buckled her safety belt, Tommy put one foot on the gas pedal and the other foot on the brake, alternating between the two, trying to get enough traction to set the truck in motion. Once they started moving, Lauralynn said, "Lucky for me you were still here."

"Lucky for both of us," Tommy said.

"How so?" she asked, but since Tommy couldn't remember what he'd just said, he didn't know what she meant.

"What?" he asked.

"How's it lucky for you?"

"I don't know. Did I say that? I don't think I said that. You still thirsty?"

"I could use another drink," she said. "But we can't go to my place. I live at my mother's. It's just a temporary thing, but I don't want to wake her up."

"My place it is!" When the windshield started icing over again, Tommy squirted it a few times with wiper fluid, but that only made things worse. According to the radio, which was on low, the wind-chill was eighty-below-zero – a record.

"Christ Almighty," Tommy yelled. "Eighty-below! You know," he said, "the thought of going to hell doesn't bother me. I don't mind heat. But cold. *Jesus.*"

"I can't see through the windshield," Lauralynn said. "Can *you* see?"

"Like a bat," Tommy said.

He turned into an entrance for a forest preserve, plowing through fresh snow, not slowing down for fear of getting stuck. A few seconds later, he fishtailed into his parking space and skidded toward his trailer. The truck stopped just shy of smashing into two propane tanks, which would have blown the two of them up.

"Whoa, baby," he said.

"Where are we?" Lauralynn asked.

"Campground," Tommy said. "The place is small, but the price is right. And like you said, it's temporary."

But as soon as he said that, it became obvious that neither of their situations were all that temporary. Tommy believed that if he could figure out why all of this had happened to him, then he could move on with his life, start rebuilding what was left of it. There were times he wanted to stop his ex on the street and yell, "*Why? Why?*" over and over. He imagined a crowd gathering, waiting to hear her answer. But the truth was that he would *never* ask her directly because he wouldn't have believed what she told him, so he followed her instead, keeping to the shadows, hoping that an answer would reveal itself in time, but so far he had learned nothing. By all accounts, his ex-wife's new life with the hospital intern was a happy one, and yet they had moved five times in three years. Five times in three years! How happy could they be? When they moved the fifth time, they did so at night when Tommy wasn't watching, but he found them. They were here. In Belvedere.

So maybe that's why he and Lauralynn ended up so easily in bed together – the frightening prospect that their situations were actually permanent. For Tommy, the only variable in his life these days was where he parked his trailer; everything else was a constant. Whatever the reasons, it didn't take long before they were crushed up against each other on one of the camping trailer's narrow beds, kissing and fumbling in the pitch-black. Tommy unbuttoned Lauralynn's blouse. Then he slipped his forefingers into the elastic waistband of her pants and panties. She arched her hips to help him out, and Tommy rolled them down her legs.

"You never told me what it was your ex-wife called you," Lauralynn said, jerking on his belt until it unhooked.

Tommy was about to tell her what his wife used to call him – *Sweetie* – but the light of those first few years always got snuffed out by the night she poisoned him. "Shhhhhh," he said.

The trailer was poorly insulated, and the walls were blocks of ice. The bed itself was so small, Tommy had to stand up to take off his clothes. When he slipped back into bed, naked and freezing, he started rubbing his palms up along Lauralynn's body. One side was smooth, but the side of her body against the wall was covered with goosepimples. It was like being with two different women at once. Two different bodies. One soft; one not so soft. She turned over, onto her belly, then positioned herself for him – right foot planted on the floor, left knee on the bed.

Tommy was going through the motions, but he was drunk and tired and starting to drift off. At some point he started to dream that he was with his ex-wife, only she wasn't his ex anymore, she was still his *wife*, and they were back together, having survived what seemed like the worst nightmare imaginable. Miraculously, here they were, on vacation – camping! – and they were drunk, *very* drunk, and having sex, the best sex they'd had in a long, long time. Tommy reached up and grabbed a fistful of hair the way she liked, and he tugged on it with just enough force so that it stung but didn't actually hurt, that precarious middle-ground she always expected him to find. He was doing all the things she liked, finding that gray area that gave her the most pleasure, and he was about to whisper her name when the high-beams of a passing car swirled by, illuminating the two of them, and what Tommy saw wasn't his wife, it was the grim reaper. Although there were no eyes, only empty sockets, the reaper appeared to be staring up at Tommy, staring and smiling, all teeth and bone. The scythe was raised, and in the split-second play of light, the blade seemed to move ever so slightly toward him.

Death had been his constant companion ever since the night the EMTs arrived at his house. They had worked on him in his living room, then placed him onto a gurney. While they quickly packed their gear, Tommy's wife leaned down and kissed him full on the lips. He expected her to whisper *Sweetie* into his ear, but what she said was *Dead man*, so soft that only Tommy could hear, and then she waved good-bye.

"Are you okay?" It was Lauralynn. She had turned over, onto her back, to see what was wrong. The car was gone, leaving them in the dark again, and now that he was no longer inside her, Tommy started to shiver.

"Oh, baby," Lauralynn said, rubbing him with her palms to warm him up. "You're freezing."

"I'm all right," he said, his first lie of the night, and as he lay beside Lauralynn, cradled in her arms, he thought of that summer in Paris and how, spending his days and nights going to movies, it didn't matter that he couldn't understand the language. When people kissed, they were in love. When they screamed, they were frightened. But Tommy had no sooner stepped out of the theater, into the night's swampy heat, and he was back in a world he knew all too well, a place where prisoners of war spent years chained to walls, and where a man could be tortured every day, month after month, and still never reveal the truth in his heart.

SWEETNESS
AND
THE FRIDGE

(Walter Payton, 1954-1999)

Here's a story I never told.

It happened a few months after the Super Bowl, after the champagne, after the championship rings, after it had all died down and what we were left with was a buzzing in our ears, what I realize now is the post-rush zing of adrenaline still flowing through our veins, the kind of buzz that comes with fame and power and everyone wanting to lift you into the air and carry you across town, except that the people are gone now and all that's left is this low-level drone. It's like a ringing in your ears after a concert when you're back home, all by yourself. So me and Walter, we decided to drive down south together. A roadtrip to get away from it all. Walter had gone to Jackson State, after all, and I'd gone to Clemson. It was like a homecoming, only we hadn't told anyone. I did all the driving. I didn't mind. I did the speed limit the whole way, too. We'd just driven through Memphis and crossed over into Mississippi when Walter turned down the radio and shifted in the passenger seat.

"Hey, Fridge," he said. "Why'd you do it?"

"Do what?"

"Why'd you try carrying me into the end zone?"

"Shit, man," I said. "You don't know?"

We both laughed. He was talking about our game against the Cowboys. Week eleven of the season. I was riding high. Everyone knew me by then; everyone knew the Fridge. And Coach, well, he wanted this one *bad*, and boy did we give it to him. Forty-four to nothing. Worst loss the Cowboys ever saw. We rubbed their faces in it.

"No, really," Walter said. "What *possessed* you?"

I looked over at him, but his face was back-lit. The sun, starting to sink into the river, was huge – dull and bright at once. I'm not even sure I can explain it. I could see the outline of Walter, but I couldn't *see him* see him. It was like he was resting his head back into this big, orange cushion that glowed. I loved that guy. We all did.

"You were so close," I said.

"First and goal," he said.

I said, "You looked so small. It looked so easy. Just pick him up, I told myself. Just pick him up and carry him over, and that's six more points for the team."

"It cost us ten yards," he said and laughed.

"We did okay," I said.

I looked over at him again, but I still couldn't see his face. Not seeing him – not knowing what he was thinking – made me nervous. I wanted to tell him the truth, but I wasn't sure where to begin. What really happened was this: I had looked down at Walter that day, and it was like that story of the footprints in the sand, two pairs side-by-side, and how suddenly there's only one pair of footprints. God says, *That is when I picked you up and carried you.* And that's how it is, isn't it? God lifts you up and carries you when your burdens are too much. And here's where it gets difficult, because I don't want people thinking that I thought I was God out there on the field that day, but if you've never been out there on the field on a day when you're destroying the other team – and not just *any* team...we're talking the *Cowboys* here – and if you've never known what it's like for everyone in the country to know your name or recognize you at a glance or want to touch you and squeeze you when they see you, if you've never known that kind of collective love, the love of millions all at one, or what it feels like to do no wrong, the way I felt in the fall of 1985, if you've never had so many eyes on you at once, so many people *thinking* about you, so many people chanting your name... well, then, I'm not sure I can make you feel with words alone what I felt that day when I looked down and saw my friend on the ground clutching the ball. He was this close to the end zone. *This close.* And so I picked him up and carried him over the line, and it was like lifting nothing, like reaching down and cupping air, and I wanted him to know that I would have done anything for him, that *that's* how much love and respect I had for that man. *I'm bringing you home,* I had thought. *I'm bringing you home where you belong.*

"Hey, Walter," I said now, hoping to tell him a sliver of what was on my mind, but he didn't answer. I glanced over at him again, and this time the sun had dropped enough that I could finally see his face. He was sound asleep and looking like I'd never seen him before – every muscle relaxed, a whisper of air whistling from his lips. Like a child he looked. Like sweetness personified.

I turned on the headlights and let the man be.

REMAINS OF THE NIGHT

I'm his butler. You know him, of course: the Silverfish.

A *Sun-Times* columnist calls him the *creepy* superhero. He's not the first insect superhero, that's for sure, so why *creepy*? Is it the antennas? Is it the fact that he crawls instead of walks? Hard to say, but I'd wager it's the whole package – the way he looks, the way he moves. Women in peril are hesitant to accept his help. Men committing crimes have been said to soil their pants at the sight of a six-foot fish-like insect slithering down the street after them. He doesn't photograph well, either. No smile. No hands in the traditional sense. A little too blob-like. A little too bottle-shaped. "He looks more like the villain than the good guy," a famous talk show host has noted, and it's true, if only because his suit is too life-like. I tried telling him this once, suggesting that maybe a skin-tight body suit with the *image* of a silverfish embroidered on it might be the way to go, but he wouldn't have any of it.

"I'm not a poseur," he replied. "When I'm the Silverfish, that's what I am."

I tried explaining to him that *real* silverfish, the small ones, are known to cause psychological distress to people, so just imagine what people think when they see a 250-pound one barreling toward them!

"Is that my problem?" he asked. "And what do you mean by *real*?" He wagged his head and glided out of the room.

I have seen The Silverfish out of costume only a handful of times. He's a normal-looking fellow, unassuming, even slight of build, but make no mistake, he's still the Silverfish. In costume or out, he eats glue, paper, sugar, hair, dandruff, and dirt – anything with starch in it, anything with polysaccharides. I'd walk into his library and see him with a book cracked open, licking the adhesive holding the pages together.

"Oh...uh...*sorry*," he'd say, caught, embarrassed.

Unlike most butlers, who keep their houses impeccably clean, my job is to maintain a certain level of untidiness. Furthermore, the house is to remain humid year-round – ninety, ninety-five degrees most days. These are non-negotiable duties. It's not easy to live here. I'm always short of breath and kicking shit out of the way, but the pay and benefits are good, and although he can't offer a 401(k), he's set up a modest trust-fund for me that activates at retirement age, so long as I remain with him until then. And for the past twenty years I've imagined myself staying until the bitter end, but lately I'm not so sure. On nights when the Silverfish is out doing what he does, I sometimes sneak away and meet up with other butlers and maids, usually at El Mar Bowl, where we can get ourselves a lane and enjoy a few pitchers of cheap beer for those few pilfered hours we have together.

And so here I am tonight at El Mar with Tommy and Oula. They both work for the enemy, but that's what most people don't get: just because you work for an asshole doesn't mean that you yourself are one. Take Tommy. He's Spiderhole Man's butler. Spiderhole Man is a notorious terrorist who lives in hand-dug holes in the ground, and it's Tommy's job to keep each place in order and stocked with necessities. But who in their right mind, other than someone in desperate need of employment, would spend his life living in one dirt hole after the other, keeping it stocked with fresh ice for refrigeration and diet cream soda (Spiderhole Man's favorite)?

And then there's Oula: she's maid to The Silverfish's

arch-enemy, Earwig Man. Earwigs are predators to silverfish. In a perfect world, I should pledge my undying loyalty to my boss and keep my distance from Oula, but once you put aside the superheroes and the villains, you realize that the rest of the world exists in shades of gray, and that every day we must trudge through the murk that is our hearts and desires. The truth is that I'm in love with Oula and have been for years, though I have never told her. For all she knows, we are good friends, nothing more.

"Oula," I say, "your turn," and point to the bank of bowling balls.

She's distracted tonight, and I want to reach out and squeeze her arm, but I don't. I offer her my small smile of encouragement, my bowler's curt nod as she walks up onto the lane.

"Concentrate," I tell her as she blows her hands dry.

Oula has been with Earwig Man as long as I've been with The Silverfish: twenty years. Neither The Silverfish nor Earwig Man knows that we know each other, let alone go bowling together. I know things about Earwig Man that only Oula knows. For instance, how most of his underwear is over ten years old, and that he recycles. He's not all bad, she assures me, and I believe her. I told her The Silverfish once ate his own molted exoskeleton. "But isn't it just a costume?" she asked, and I had to tell her that I could say no more, that I wished I could, but that I'd said enough already. I couldn't tell her about the enormous silverfish farm in our basement, hundreds of thousands of the little buggers wiggling around down there, or about how Mary the seamstress miraculously patches up our hero's silvery blue costume using the real silverfishes' recently shed body scales. Mary's not as fast as she used to be, and The Silverfish and I both fear what will happen when arthritis finally gets the better of her. This is all the more reason for me not to bank on that trust fund. Mary is the key, really, to The Silverfish's success. No Mary; no Silverfish.

Oula throws the first ball, too straight down the middle, and though there is power in her throw, she is left with a seven-ten split.

"Ouch!" I say, and Oula shakes her head, already defeated. She waits glumly for the ball to pop out of the mechanical chute. She picks it up and, without taking the necessary time to consider strategy, runs gracelessly to the line and releases. The ball rockets into the gutter.

"Wow," I say. "The power!"

She walks past me and plops down in the hard plastic row of chairs, slumping down.

"What's Earwig doing tonight?" I ask.

"Oh, you know, being a pain in somebody's balls. What about The Silverfish?"

I shrug. "Same 'ol same 'ol," I say.

Tommy, standing to retrieve his ball, says, "Goody two-shoes shit."

"That's it in a nutshell," I say.

"He ever get laid?" Tommy asks, then looks over at Oula and says, "Pardon my French. Just wondering if there are ever going to be any little Silverfish running around."

"It's not that easy," I say. "He leaves these – how shall I put this? – gossamer-covered sperm capsules around for a female to fertilize, but it's not like there are any female silverfish hanging around. It's pretty disgusting, actually."

Oula sits up in her seat, suddenly interested. "So he really *is* a silverfish?" she asks.

"Kind of," I say. I shrug. "Sort of." I realize I've said too much already. "It's complicated." I stand with the empty pitcher, ready to change the subject. "Is Bud Light okay?"

Later, after we stumble across the parking lot and say our goodbyes, I get into my car – a fifteen year old Toyota Corolla stick-shift. The car has over two hundred thousand miles on it, coughs thick blue-gray exhaust into the eyes of the drivers behind me, and shimmies when it goes over twenty-five, but I can't bring myself to ask for a company car. For all the press he gets, The Silverfish hasn't figured out yet how to cash in on his fame. He had a manager for a while, but the only endorsement offers that came in were from exterminators.

"Fuck that shit," The Silverfish said. "What do I look like – some kind of punch-line?"

He was dressed as The Silverfish when he asked me, and his antennas were nervously tapping the ground.

"No," I said. "Of course not."

On my way home from the bowling alley, I'm followed by a cop for a good two miles before we go our separate ways. The last thing I need is to get pulled over for a DUI while The Silverfish is out making the world a better place to live. For all he knows, I'm home baking cookies for him or boiling rice. Sugars and starches: that's what keeps my boy sharp, that's what keeps him on edge.

I park on the street in the same spot where I was parked when he left home earlier tonight. At the front door, I ease my key inside the lock so as not to wake Mary, hoping to sneak in unnoticed, but when I open the door, I see that The Silverfish is waiting for me. He's sitting in the living room, the way my old man used to wait up for me in high school, ready to ground me for staying out after curfew.

"Where were *you*?" The Silverfish asks. He's holding the Mega Glue Stick in his hand, as though it's a bar of chocolate-dipped ice cream. Mary and I use the Mega Glue Stick to make congratulatory posters for the Silverfish, posters that say things like, "Another Evil-Doer Down. Yay!" or, for his birthday, "300 Million Years Young!" The Mega Glue Stick is in the same receptacle as a stick of deodorant. The Silverfish, keeping his eyes on me, twists the dial until a good inch of glue appears, and then he raises it to his mouth and takes a bite. "What if the house caught fire?" he asks. "What if someone called?"

"We have voice-mail," I say.

He says, "I wasn't out *playing* tonight, you know. I diverted a nuclear missile. I sidetracked a civil war. I removed a cat from a tree."

I know that only the last thing he says is true, so I ask, "What kind of cat?"

The Silverfish stops chewing his glue and stares at me. Then he resumes chewing.

"I'm not a prisoner here," I say. "I should be able to take a night off every now and then, and go bowling with my friends."

"Bowling!" he says and snorts. "You went *bowling?* With *who?*"

I leave the room. I head downstairs. Mary is still awake, darning the exoskeleton. I can hear the low-grade hiss from the thousands of real silverfish squirming over one another, searching for a morsel of sugar or a strand of hair to nibble on. I have all the respect in the world for Mary, but I sure as hell wouldn't want to be her. She has no goals of her own; she expresses no desires. To her, The Silverfish is our new messiah. She sees none of his faults. She questions nothing he does. Like that time a photograph of The Silverfish appeared on the front page of the *Trib*. He was in a seedy-ass motel in Cicero with a crack pipe stuck jauntily into his bug mouth. Behind him, slumped on the bed, sat a hooker wearing a faded denim mini-skirt and a tube-top. This was his Marion Barry moment, and it almost caused our little empire to come tumbling down, but when I tried commiserating with Mary about it, all she said was, "He has his reasons." Mary sees The Silverfish only in light of the bigger picture – the greater good he accomplishes – while the rest of us, well, we are all just little people. Our job is to serve.

I'll admit that whenever I think of Mary's blind faith, I end up feeling pretty damned petty for thinking ill of him. Every man has his demons, right? So what if a six-foot insect smokes the devil's dandruff with a skanky crack whore in a twenty-five dollar cat-piss-smelling motel room? Given all the good he's done, was that really so bad? Who among us, at one time or another, hasn't stooped so low? But my guilt lasts for only a flash, a blip, and then the dark truth slow-burns inside me: the longer I'm with The Silverfish, the more I hate the bastard.

I wake up the next morning, the cobwebs of a hangover filling my mouth and throat. The extent of my pain is such that my head feels as though it's giving birth to another head. I can hear the tap-tap-tap of The Silverfish's old manual typewriter. He is upstairs working on his damned manifesto. If there's one thing I've learned over the years about manifestos, it's that things never end well for the person writing one. Until now, I had considered it his hobby, something he liked to chip away at in his spare time, but lately he's been spending every waking minute in his room, hammering out page after page with no apparent end in sight.

I make the mistake of saying something to Mary about it while I pour my coffee, but she just stares worshipfully up toward the ceiling and says, "I'm sure it will be his masterpiece!"

"Yeah-yeah," I say, yawning. I shift my weight from one leg to the other, stifling the pending explosion of gas from last night's microwaved burrito. I pour my coffee into a Styrofoam cup to go.

"I see you're hung over," Mary says, staring at me now. "Again." She turns away from me and says, "You're acting more and more like a homeless person."

I shrug, and a peep of gas leaks out. Since it sounds like the creaky hinge on a door, I turn and pretend to see who's coming. I don't tell her about the time The Silverfish drank an entire bottle of Mad Dog and then slithered across the Eisenhower Expressway underneath a speeding semi, nearly getting squashed and causing a pile-up. Or the night, after polishing off a bottle of peach schnapps, he drunk-dialed his arch-enemy the Earwig to see if he wanted to go clubbing. Despite his reputation for unusually cruel methods of torture, The Earwig is notorious for his sobriety and politely declined.

I go upstairs. The curtains are pulled shut. They are *always* pulled shut. I open them just enough to look out with one eye. There's an exterminator's truck parked in our neighbor's driveway, and the man from Orkin is carrying inside two jugs of boric acid. "Oh no," I say. Some of our silverfish from downstairs must have gotten out and made their way to the Johnson place. It's hard to catch and kill the little bastards, but boric acid and sugar will do the trick: sugar lures them; acid kills them. I shut the curtain.

As I walk past The Silverfish's room, the typing stops. "And where are *you* going?" The Silverfish asks from behind a closed door.

"Out," I say.

"Could you pick up a few more of those Mega Glue Sticks?" he asks. When I don't say anything, he adds, "Pretty please?"

"If the Dollar Store has any more," I say. "It's not high-quality glue, you know. I can get Elmer's when I do my next Target run."

"No, no," he says. "Mega Glue Stick, please."

I wait a second, thinking he wants to say something else, but then the typing resumes, and I leave the house. The house is just a 1950s ranch, a little bigger than most because of an addition built on in the seventies, but we're not talking a castle here by any means. It's no fortress. It's no stronghold. We have neighbors; we have a lawn that can be mowed with a push mower; we have a short driveway with a two-car garage. No one, in fact, knows who really lives here. They think it's just me and Mary.

Like I've said, The Silverfish isn't rich. He's not one of

these trust-fund superheroes. His parents worked at the old 3M factory on Harlem Avenue. A psychologist would have a field-day with that detail: parents who worked at a place that made adhesives, a child that grows up craving the very thing his parents once made... But it's all too convenient, this explanation. If you ask me, that's Monday-morning-quarterbacking The Silverfish's life. He eats glue because silverfish eat glue. Sometimes things are simply as they seem.

Outside, Mr. Johnson calls to me from his lawn as the exterminator backs out of his drive.

"Do you have a silverfish problem?" he asks.

Do I, I'm tempted to say but shake my head instead. "Nope. I don't think so."

"Keep your eye out," he says. "I woke up this morning and found *thousands* of them in my basement."

"Will do," I say and then give him a tiny salute.

From a payphone, I call Oula to see how she's feeling.

"I can't talk now," she says. "The Earwig might be listening." Then, in a near-whisper: "Meet me at Duke's at noon."

Duke's is a local Italian beef sandwich shop, an unlikely haunt for Earwig Man or The Silverfish to appear. I tell her that I'll see her at noon, and then I give Tommy a jingle, but reception isn't good. He's down in a hole somewhere in Oak Park, waiting for Spiderhole Man to return from a car bombing.

"Can you hear me now?" he asks.

"Yeah-yeah. Can you hear *me*?" I ask.

"What? Say that again."

"I'll call you later," I say.

"You're breaking up," Tommy says, and I return the receiver to its cradle. There's no sense prolonging the misery of a bad connection.

At noon, I meet Oula at Duke's. I can tell she's been crying, but I wait until we order our beef sandwiches before I ask her what's wrong.

"I can't take it anymore," she says.

"What?" I ask.

"I love him so much, it's killing me."

"Who? *Earwig?*"

"No," she says. "The Silverfish."

"The Silverfish?" I say. "Really?" My breathing grows shallow. I pull out my inhaler, put it to my mouth, and knock back a blast of albuterol sulfate.

"I know, I know," she says. "It's not even realistic, is it?"

I shrug. "Anything's possible," I offer, though I'm not sure I really believe this.

Oula grabs hold of my arm and presses her face against it. She's weeping uncontrollably now, and everyone who's in line to order their food has turned to stare at us. I feel, for the first time since I was a teenager, empty, and I can't help shivering like the lovelorn fool that I am. *What now?* I wonder. *What now?*

I drive to Oak Park and find Tommy's hole in the ground. The hole's cover is a Styrofoam cooler lid with fake plastic flowers poking up out of it. There's no room on the lid to knock, so I just push on it until it falls into the hole.

"What the fuck?" I hear, and then, "Oh, hey, it's you."

"Want to get a drink?" I ask.

"Sure, sure," Tommy says, "just give me a hand out of here. Spiderhole Man took the ladder so I couldn't get out. I know he's a terrorist and all, but sometimes he's just a regular run-of-the-mill asshole to boot."

I offer Tommy my hand and hoist him out of the hole, and then we drive to Bar Louie. In a few short hours, we are annihilated.

"And another thing," I yell. "The Silverfish isn't that bright. No, really. I was reading his manifesto, and he doesn't know the difference between *its* possessive and *it's* as a contraction. Fucking *its* and *it's*. It's not that hard, my friend. It's not rocket science, that's for damned sure!"

Tommy slams the counter with his palm and says, "Where's his goddamned grammar handbook?"

"No shit," I say, and then I motion to the bartender for another round.

"Listen," Tommy says, his voice low. "You know all these stories about Spiderhole Man's car bombs? Well, I'm starting to think they're not all true." And then Tommy tells me how Spiderhole Man went off his meds while in the Iraq War, and how it was shortly after he was dishonorably discharged for shooting bottle rockets out his ass and accidentally burning down a few tents in his unit's bivouac that Spiderhole Man emerged in the States. "The timing," Tommy says, "is suspect, to say the least. I mean, yeah, sure, he blows shit up every now and then, but you want to know what I think? I think he isn't so much a terrorist as he is a compulsive liar with a trust fund."

"Get the fuck out of here," I say. "Get. The. Fuck. Out. Of. Here."

"No, really," he says. "Just a rich bastard who needs some Prozac. That's all."

I wag my head, but the motion of my swaying head messes with my equilibrium, and I almost fall off my barstool. "Whoa!" I say, grabbing onto Tommy, who, in turn, almost falls off *his* barstool.

"Time to go, li'l fella," he says.

We stumble back to my car, and after I drop him off at his hole, I drive home. I have to keep one eye closed most of the way so as not to see two sets of Harlem Avenues. I pull into the driveway, a bit too fast, and almost hit the garage, but I manage to stop with just enough room to slide a sheet of paper between bumper and garage door.

Inside, as I stumble past The Silverfish's room, the typewriter pauses, as if taking a breath from talking. "Did you get those Mega Glue Sticks I asked for?" he says.

"Shit," I say under my breath. Then, "I'm sorry, but they were out."

"Out?" he asks. "Are you sure?"

"I couldn't find them," I say.

"Did you look in school supplies?"

"Of course," I say.

"How about home repair?"

"I looked everywhere," I say. "I *scoured* the whole damned place, okay?"

"Don't get touchy," The Silverfish says. When I look down and see one of his antennas slipping under the door and starting to feel around for me, I back up. "Where are you?" he asks.

"Listen," I say. "I'm tired. I need a nap before my shift starts." As I walk away, the antenna retracts back under the door and into its room.

That night, I toss and turn, unable to fall into any kind of deep or meaningful sleep. I wake up at three in the morning. The Silverfish is already out for the night, saving the world and what-not. I'm supposed to have been awake, keeping an eye on things, but my afternoon bout of drinking had gotten the better of me – that, and a dark depression over Oula's revelation. *Jesus*, I think.

I get out of bed. I put my flask of whiskey in my back pocket. I pick up my cell phone and walk upstairs, my feet pushing all the licked envelopes out of the way. The Silverfish, before going out, needs his fix. He's done this before. I've seen him do it, too – lifting the flap with arms that narrow like miniature pool cues, then swiping his mouth across the adhesive. Whenever he sees me paying the bills, he insists on licking the envelopes. We'll sit side-by-side – me writing checks, the Silverfish waiting impatiently.

"Can you go any faster?" he'll ask.

"Don't rush me," I'll say. "You'll make me put a check in

the wrong damned envelope."

After each lick, the Silverfish lets out a barely-audible orgasmic moan. His antennas vibrate for a moment, and then he sighs. One time I left the room to find some stamps, and when I came back, he was eating an envelope. Real silverfish don't have well-built mouth parts for chewing. What they do is sit on top of paper and gradually grind down the surface. If you pick up a book and find words missing from its pages, you know a silverfish has been there already, snacking. But the big guy, he uses some combination of his own human mouth with the silverfish's, giving him a variety of ways to ingest his daily nutrients.

I go into The Silverfish's office. His manifesto sits on the desk, a pile of drivel. My cell phone vibrates. It's Tommy.

"Dude," I say. "I'm so hungover."

There's silence. Then, "Spiderhole Man hasn't come home. I've got a bad feeling."

"Where are you?"

"I'm standing outside the hole," he says. "I couldn't breathe anymore."

"Any idea where he was going?"

Tommy says, "He said something about blowing up a CVS, but I just figured he was getting his Viagra refilled."

"Spiderhole Man uses Viagra?" I ask. This is news to me.

"You don't think this is serious, do you?" he says. "I don't know why I thought you would. I mean, you work for *him*."

"Yeah; well," I say, and I'm about to unload a few of my own problems, but Tommy hangs up.

I sit down at The Silverfish's desk and flip through the manifesto while Mary snores loudly in the room below. His new working title is *Everything I Learned I Learned in the Paleozoic Era: Notes from a Much-Maligned Insect.* I flip through chapters on subjects as diverse as the failures of the American penal system and the three years The Silverfish spent in college downstate shrooming his ass off. Near the bottom of the pile, in chapters he must have typed these past few days, I find a chapter titled "The Butler Did It." My hands shake as I remove this section from the rest of the manuscript.

In "The Butler Did It," I am described as one of his many charity cases, a man who, without the assistance of The Silverfish, would probably still be living in his parents' basement. I'm a sad-sack, according to the text. But worse: I may not be stable anymore. Lately, he's been suspecting that I'm suffering from some kind of mental deterioration with possible psychotic episodes. "I would dismiss him," he writes, "but twenty years is a long time to be with someone without feeling some moral sense of obligation toward them. Even so," he continues, "he's under the delusion that I've set up a trust fund for him, and that, upon retirement age, he'll start collecting monthly checks. These delusions worry me, of course, but worse are those times, like right now, when I know he's standing outside my door listening in on me. What's he up to? What's he planning to do?"

I return the chapter to its proper place in the manifesto. My cell phone is blinking. It's The Silverfish.

"Hello?" I say. I take the flask from my back pocket, uncap it, and take a swig.

"Guess where I went tonight," he says.

"How should I know?"

The Silverfish says, "I went to the Dollar Store. They were closing, but a cleaning crew let me in."

"Of course they did," I say.

"And you know what I found in the aisle with all the school supplies?"

I say nothing. I know where this is going.

"No guesses?" he says. "Okay, I'll tell you. I found Mega Glue Stick. A whole wall of them on hooks. Probably two hundred of them."

"Your point?" I ask. I take another swig from my flask,

then cap it.

"No point," he says.

"Where are you now?"

"I'm waiting for someone," he says. True to his nature, when The Silverfish waits for an enemy, he stands in the bathtub or sits in a sink. Imagine, if you will, opening a door, turning on the light, and, bam, there he is: The Silverfish in your tub!

I shut my phone. A few seconds later, he calls again. The phone blinks for a good thirty seconds before stopping. He hates when I hang up on him. *Hates* it. I go outside and light a cigarette. I've been trying to quit, but I still carry a pack around with me in my shirt pocket – Marlboros – and tonight I need one. My hands are shaking.

"Jesus," I say, and I no sooner finish hissing the Lord's name in vain when I see them, a caravan of tiny silverfish making their way from my house to Mr. Johnson's. The moon is bright enough and my eyes have adjusted sufficiently for me to see that they're heading toward a metal cookie sheet near the Johnsons' downspout – but then I also see, just around the bend, the two jugs of boric acid and, on top of their picnic table, a pound of sugar. I snuff out my cigarette and tiptoe over to the Johnsons' yard. I tuck the sugar under my armpit and lift the two jugs of boric acid. Then I tiptoe away.

I make the short trek to Stevenson Park over on Eighty-fifth and State Road. I squeeze myself inside the jungle gym and, walking in ever-widening circles, sprinkle all the sugar onto the ground. Following the same swirling motion, I empty only one jug of the white powder boric acid onto the sugar granules. Then I make the call.

"Yo," The Silverfish says. "Whazzup?"

I take a deep breath. I say, "I heard on the police scanner that there's a hostage situation at Stevenson Park."

"What time is it?" he asks.

"Four-twenty," I say.

"A.M. or P.M.?" he asks.

"A.M.!" I say. "Four-twenty in the *A.M.*"

"Okay, okay," he says. "I've been sitting in a dark room all night. And I forgot to bring my watch." This is no surprise: The Silverfish's short-term memory is no better than his namesake's. On more than one occasion, after I have berated him for leaving his keys at home or forgetting to take along an umbrella on a cloudy day, he had replied, "I live in the moment!" – as if this were a strength and not a weakness.

"So?" I say. "Are you coming?"

"I guess," The Silverfish says. "Do you think I should?"

"It's a *hostage* situation," I say. "What do *you* think?"

"Hostages." He sighes. "All right then. I'll be right over."

I camp out on the park's outskirts – one jug still full of boric acid, one empty. So this is what it's come down to: I'm going to kill him. Tonight. The Silverfish will die. When he comes to the park and realizes that there is no hostage situation, he'll get a whiff of all that sugar, and then how can he resist? He'll glide between the jungle gym's bars, and while the lethal white powder starts tugging him through that murky space between life and death, I'll emerge with the full jug of acid and finish him off. After he's dead, I'll remove his suit and put it on for myself, and then I'll slither over to Oula's and whisk her off her feet. I'll wrap my antennas tightly around her and shimmy away with her. She'll get her wish; I'll get mine. And then, in a few days, when it becomes clear that The Silverfish's longtime butler has disappeared for good, I'll hire Tommy. It's a perfect plan, and I'm so happy with how the pieces are falling into place, I remove the flask from my back pocket and take a celebratory nip. I don't want to pound it, that's for sure, but the longer it takes for The Silverfish to arrive, the deeper my swigs become. I open my phone and call The Silverfish. No answer.

"Shit," I say. "Where the hell are you?"

"I'm right here," he says, and when I look up, there he is,

wrapped around a thick tree branch and peering down at me.
I drop the cell phone and knock over my flask.

"Oh no," I say, but it is too late: The Silverfish falls from
the tree and lands on top of me, his squishy legs holding me
in a grip from which I cannot break. "Ease up," I yell, "you
got me," but he squeezes harder. With my face pressed flush
against his flaking underside, I can barely breathe. I fear he's
going to snap my spine and paralyze me. As the world begins to pulsate and blur in front of me, I realize that I have no
choice: I take a bite of his scaly flesh, and because I have nowhere to spit, I chew it quickly and swallow. Still, he doesn't
loosen his grip. I take another bite, confirming my suspicions
that The Silverfish, like every other insect on this planet, feels
no pain whatsoever – nothing at all. With all the air squeezed
out of me, I start blacking out. I honestly never thought it
would come to this, a man being smashed by an insect, and
yet here we are – my fate in The Silverfish's hands. "You win,"
I say before finally slipping under.

It's not bad here, I guess. I room with a guy who scratched
his arms until they bled and then tried to hang himself with
the cord to a heating pad, so now they belt him in each night
for his own safety, not to mention for the safety of others. Since
I don't sleep well, I tell him stories about The Silverfish to lull
him to sleep. I tell him the big stories, the ones about daring
rescues he made or disasters he averted, not any of the small
stuff, like how his favorite TV show is *Dog the Bounty Hunter*
or how he likes to sing show tunes when he thinks no one's
listening.

When Tommy finally comes to visit, we have to stay inside. I haven't yet earned outdoor privileges.

"Whatever happened to Spiderhole Man?" I ask him.
"Did he ever come back?"

"What?" Tommy asks. Then, "Oh-oh, yeah. *That*. Turns out I was just overreacting. He went to a movie. Some Iranian film playing at The Music Box."

"And Oula? Do you still see her?"

Tommy averts his eyes. He squints over my shoulder, as if reading a posted sign. "No, no," he says, but I can tell he's lying. I get the feeling she and The Silverfish have finally hooked up, a thought that makes my knees turn to jelly and my heart kick into overdrive, but I don't push him.

"You want to play chess?" I ask.

"I...," he pauses, thinking. "I better get back. Spiderhole Man has a little, you know, *project* to take care of today."

"Oh; okay," I say. "Sure. No problem. Will you come again?"

"You betcha," he says, standing. He pats my shoulder, but when I stand and move in to hug him, he takes a step back. "It's great to see you," he says. "You're looking good."

I want to ask him why he's treating me like the crazy one when it's him that lives in a hole. But I don't go there. "Good to see you, too," I say.

I sit alone at a table in the recreation room. This place is clean. And it has air-conditioning. No more sweltering heat. But lately I've started to miss the mess, and my body craves both heat and humidity.

"It's so *cold* in here," I complain, and an intern says, "It's seventy-five. It's the perfect temperature."

I shiver all day, and when I get into bed, I ask for more blankets. I feel changes taking place inside me, and my skin has become dry and brittle. I know what's happening to me. Even so, I don't tell anyone that I ate the flesh of the Silverfish. It's nobody's business, really.

Every morning at eight, after breakfast, I sit in a semi-circle in Conference Room B with six of my fellow floor-mates, and we share stories about what was going on in our lives in the days just before we were forced to come here. Bill set his house on fire one afternoon for no reason he can remember other than that he was watching a TV show in which a house was on fire. Larry swallowed everything in his medicine cabinet, beginning with all the prescription drugs but working his way to the tropical-flavored Tums and giant bottle of expired Gingko Biloba tablets. Jimmy shot a flare gun through his neighbor's window and then watched the whole family come running outside, screaming. Jimmy still chuckles when he tells that part of his story, a pretty good sign that he's not ready to leave the facility any time soon.

When it's my turn, I tell them simply that I was butler to The Silverfish and that we'd had a falling out.

"No big whoop," I say.

The therapist stares at me, but she doesn't press. She thinks I'll eventually come around and tell the whole story.

Every morning at eleven we work on our arts and crafts. Some days, we nail together prefab birdhouses. Other days, we paint coffee mugs and then send them off to get glazed. Today, we're making posters for patients in the oncology wing of the hospital. I have scissors, construction paper, and glitter to choose from. I have Sharpies, Crayolas, and little jars of tempera paint. But I don't have what I want, what I *need*.

I stand up and walk over to Tiffany, who is working on her own poster. Last month, from what I've been told, Tiffany got into her car and ran over every mailbox on her street, and then she drove as fast as she could into a power line tower, knocking it down and causing an entire city to lose its electricity for the day. Two boys playing basketball almost fried to death when the whipping live wires brushed against them.

Tiffany stares up at me now, her cold eyes speckled black and white in their centers, like a guppy's tail. "What," she says flatly.

"Mega Glue Stick, please," I say and point.

She gives me the once-over, her eyes taking in the whole of me, moving from head to toe and then back to head, like a scanner. She's cute, I think. Her hair, thick and brown, looks edible. When she begrudgingly leans over for the glue, I lick my forefinger and gently touch a piece of dandruff stuck to the back of her blouse. The sight of it clinging to my finger causes my eyes to water; it makes saliva pool up inside my mouth. I wipe the white flake onto my pant-leg and take the glue from her.

"Thank you," I say and walk back to my project.

I uncap the glue stick, spin the dial to adjust the size, and start smearing it all over the poster board. When no one is looking, I raise the Mega Glue Stick up to my mouth and take a bite. I start to take another bite when I notice Tiffany watching me from her end of the table. As though it were a phantom limb, I feel the antenna I don't yet have reach over and pat her on the head, letting her know that everything is all right, that with every passing day I'm feeling a little stronger, and that any day now I'll be slithering out of here under my own steam, disappearing into the dark and clammy night.

ASCENSION

(George Pullman, 1831-1897)

This was before men transported George Pullman to Graceland Cemetery, his already-decomposing corpse safe and secure in a coffin lined with lead and reinforced with steel-and-concrete; before cement was poured into his grave, so fearful was his family that his employees would find where he was buried, dig him up, and desecrate his body, dragging it ceremoniously through the town of Pullman where Pullman himself had turned from friend to foe, cutting his workers' wages by one-fourth while refusing to lower rent in the houses he owned or decrease the cost of utilities, which he controlled. This was before all of that...but not by much.

Here is the story of when an ambitious man's heart quit beating, finally giving out, the way Pullman's own sleeping car, carrying the body of Abraham Lincoln, stopped at long last in Springfield after a seemingly never-ending journey across the country: one final sigh, like a man's breath, pouring from the train's nose. You might think a person might reflect upon his family, his spouse or his children, when the cloak starts to drape before his eyes, but what George Pullman thought about was a hotel called Tremont House.

They said it couldn't be done, the raising of Tremont. Chicago had been built on a swamp, the worst possible land on which to build a city; and each time it rained, men and their horses, or women out shopping for scarves or hats, would get sucked into the unholy brew of mud and shit, unable to move, requiring assistance from strangers standing on more solid ground to uncork them. And so the city needed to be raised six to eight feet, and George Pullman was hired to do it.

With jack-screws lining its base, each man responsible for quarter-turning four of the screws at the sound of Pullman's whistle, a building would be raised, inch by inch. As the months went by, and then the years, more buildings were raised, until most of Chicago had been lifted up out of the bog, but no one thought Tremont House could be budged; no one thought it possible. It was the largest structure in the city: five-and-half stories tall, brick, and taking up over an acre of land. To compound matters, the hotel's owner – a man named John Drake – didn't want to interrupt business. The guests, among them a U.S. Senator, were not to know what was happening. *Could this be done?* John Drake asked. The year was 1861, and George Mortimer Pullman was thirty years old: Anything was possible.

Thirty-six years later, his heart stops, the last breath is taken, but he doesn't think about his wife, Harriet, or his beloved daughter Florence, for whom he named a hotel in the now-despised town of Pullman, or the daughter named after his wife, or either of his twin sons, George Jr. or Walter. What he thinks of is Tremont House, as if this distant part of his life were only a moment ago. He is a young man again, still ankle-deep in the muck, watching the hotel from across the street and wondering what the guests must be feeling, guests who are unaware that the building itself is rising from the ground, four, five, six feet – probably unaware that anything at all is amiss save for inexplicable, periodic dips in their stomachs, a collective exhalation from being ever-so-gently lifted, the way a child feels when a parent comes up from behind and hoists him up without warning. The tea in their cups barely ripples and the large chandeliers sway imperceptibly, and then – *ah!*

– they feel that dip in their lower bellies. The guests are light-headed today; they're giddy – or so Pullman imagines as he peers at the hotel rising higher and higher, standing like a pharaoh who, having loaded his crypt full of gold and alabaster and jewels, watches helplessly as it ascends to the afterlife without him.

THE
MEMOIRIST

If you could step inside my brain this very second, you may wonder why I'm so interested in a splinter of wood, or the rusty nail-head, or the length of time before a flake of snow turns to water after it falls. Where is he, you may ask yourself, and what is he doing?

Earlier today, after the TV show that I was a guest on finished taping, I removed the remote mike and set it on the chair. I walked past the host, who wouldn't look at me, past the producer, who was trying to get my attention, and past my publisher, who appeared on the precipice of tears but hadn't yet allowed herself to give in. I grabbed my coat from the green room, then found a side door that opened onto the staff parking lot. "Jesus Christ!" I said and took a deep breath. I held it and began to count.

As a child, whenever I had gotten caught doing something I shouldn't have been doing, I would hide inside the closet, or wiggle snake-like under my bed, or climb inside the empty steamer trunk in the basement and shut the lid, and then I would hold my breath until dots started pulsating before my eyes and the world faded mercifully to black. What I was doing was trying to disappear inside myself. For a brief moment today – a flash, really – I had feared the studio audience was going to storm the stage. Something in the air shifted, a nearly palpable mutation of molecules, and I thought, *I'm a dead man.* But the rules of civilized behavior remained intact, and by the time I had walked outside, I was all alone – alone and safe. I let go of my breath.

A man wearing an old snorkel parka and holding a stack of paper cut to look like money came up, peeled off one of the fake bills, and handed it to me.

"Free drink," he said.

"Where?" I asked.

He pointed. "Two blocks thataway."

Drinking: It had been a while. But I needed it today. Oh God did I need it. I took the coupon. I started walking away when I noticed that several men were standing around the building, all holding stacks of coupons. They must have been waiting for the audience to emerge, I thought, but after walking a block, I turned back to look and the men were gone.

I don't know Chicago at all, so I can't even say now where the bar was, but it had a porthole window on either side of the entrance. I stepped inside, into a large, cold room with walls draped in dusty red velvet. The bartender squinted at me. With his drooping mustache and shiny dome of a head, he looked like a circus strongman who'd gone soft in the belly. I handed over the coupon, and the bartender nodded. I ordered a beer and a shot, quickly downed them both, and then ordered another round. I had forgotten how much I enjoyed whiskey in winter. I had forgotten how much I enjoyed whiskey, period. And bars. I love bars and hated when I had to give them up. Especially bars like this one, old and poorly-heated caverns where no one knows you, and where the smell of a spent match can make you both melancholy and wistful at once.

During my first five rounds of drinks, the bartender dialed his cell phone and left whispered messages. Every so often, he would look over at me. There was only one other customer in the joint, but I was a stranger among them and, as such, the one they needed to keep an eye on. I didn't take offense. The bartender could probably have cupped my entire face in his palm and squeezed it to pulp, if he wanted. He wore a Chicago Bears Super Bowl Champions sweatshirt – twenty years old, I calculated – and each time he rinsed off glasses, he pushed up one of the frail sleeves and then drove his arm into the sudsy water. On his forearm was a tattoo of a stick man.

I was hoping that the whiskey would calm my nerves, but it didn't. It was as though I had been an insect this morning pinned to a board and dissected for the entire class to see. I'm not saying that what I did was right, but did anyone die reading my book? Did otherwise well-fed children go hungry? Did the world stop spinning? Besides, as I had tried to explain when confronted, there are various approaches to the memoir, and mine is an *interpretation of memory* as opposed to a *literal transcription*. (A stretch, I realize, but I was forced to come up with something off the top of my head. No one had warned me that my former friend – I use the word loosely – might turn foe on me.)

After my sixth whiskey, I pointed to the bartender's tattoo and asked, "What does it mean?"

"What does anything mean?" he said. "What does it mean that you have a beard? What does it mean that you came into *this* bar instead of the one across the street?"

"Are you angry with me?" I asked.

"Why would I be angry with you? Is there a reason I should be angry with you?"

"I don't know," I said. "You *seem* angry at me. Have I done something to offend you?"

He shook his big bald head, *no*. He made a few more phone calls, then came over and said, "Listen. Sorry about before. I'm a little stressed out."

"You and me both," I said.

"Name's Terry," he said.

I told him mine.

"Friends?" he asked. He reached across the bar, and I shook his hand. I was right: He could have killed me with his grip alone. "Listen. I need some help moving a pool table," he said. "I won't kid you. It's the heaviest goddamn thing you'll ever move."

"Sure; okay."

Terry stared at me a good long while before saying, "You'll have to take a ride with me, though. Do you think you can do that?"

I nodded. "Not a problem," I said. It was like the old days all over again, where every offer from a stranger was an adventure, the writer inside me always willing to go, more than eager, in fact, to follow the syntax of the night to its final and decisive period or exclamation point, common sense be damned.

I stood. Terry slapped the bar to summon the attention of his only other customer, a man who'd been drinking steadily since I arrived but was now falling asleep. "You know how to mix drinks, Bob?" he asked.

Bob looked up from his own mixed drink and smiled. "If I don't, then I'm one sorry son of a bitch."

"Good," Terry said. "Call my cell if you run into any trouble."

Bob eased himself gently off his stool, as if he had been sitting all day on a box of explosives, and limped around to the other side of the bar.

"Okay, then, let's hit it," Terry said to me.

We exited through the stock room, and Terry pointed to a Lexus parked next to a Dumpster. I'm not sure why I was surprised to see a Lexus, but I was. I was expecting an old hatchback, I supposed, a rusted-out junker rife with litter. Instead, a small plastic bag for garbage slumped peacefully between us, like a calm house pet.

"Don't smoke in here," Terry said.

"Where're we going?" I asked.

"A little ways out," he said. "You'll see."

We turned onto a street that quickly morphed into an expressway.

"Which way are we headed?" I asked.

"West," he said. "Why?"

"Just a little turned around."

"If we were driving east, we'd be at the bottom of Lake Michigan right now." He cut his eyes toward me. "Drowning," he added.

"I'm not from around here," I said.

Terry nodded. "No shit." Before I could respond, he pushed in a CD. It was a Books-on-CD of a novel I didn't recognize. Whatever it was, the actor read it in a theatrically ominous voice. I pivoted to get a better look at Terry. Who the fuck was this guy, I wondered, and what the hell was his problem?

"Something wrong?" Terry asked.

"No," I said. "Not at all."

"Do you like to read?" he asked.

"Now *that's* a funny question," I said.

"Why's that?"

"Well, actually, I'm a writer."

"Oh, really? A writer!" Terry glanced in the rearview mirror, as if checking to see if we were being followed. I turned around but didn't see anything. "Aren't we all, though?" he asked.

"What?"

"Writers."

No, I thought. *We are not.* But I'd had my fill of arguing for the day, maybe even for a lifetime. The issue that had really burrowed under the host's skin was the portrayal of my girlfriend's death. In my book, I claimed that she had died one way when in fact she had died another. Since the girlfriend was indeed dead, I failed to see the host's point. The girlfriend had taken her own life; the method of suicide was of no consequence. While the host belabored her point, I started to think about my first royalty check, which I had not yet received but soon would, and how I could buy a small island and disappear altogether. The amount of money the book had earned was beyond any figure I could ever have imagined, but since I hadn't yet received the first check, it all remained nebulous. I was a blind man being told an operation would give him sight.

"I'm a writer, too," Terry added.

He didn't elaborate, and I didn't push it. Time and again, stacks of poorly proofread pages have been foisted upon me. It's happened in airports, barber shops, taxi cabs, funeral homes, and elevators, all from would-be writers who otherwise earned their keep as doormen, sushi chefs, CEOs, Elvis impersonators, and locksmiths. What you learned was that everyone had a story to tell. Most, however, were not worth reading.

Chicago's skyline receded behind us. Soon, we were zipping past corporate suburbia. As a child, I had envied those men and women who worked all day in glass and mirrored buildings, as if they were somehow already living in the future and knew things I might never know. But even these buildings grew sparser, and before long we were the only car on the road. The sun had all but disappeared in front of us. Snow-covered fields lined either side of the highway. My buzz had mutated into a muffled, growing throb inside my frontal lobe. I saw cows and thought, *When is this going to end?*

"I didn't realize we'd be going this far," I said.

"Why not?"

I shook my head; I wasn't going to answer. The actor narrating the novel continued his dramatic interpretation, as though reading a ghost story to children, though the best I could tell the plot involved a husband and wife on the brink of divorce. If Terry had been a different man, a man not prone to rhetorical questions asked in a hostile tone, I might have brought up the issue of *listening* to a book as opposed to *read-*

ing one. Is listening really comparable? Reading a book, you get to experience the tangles of clauses, the face-to-face encounter with the unfamiliar word, the text as a microcosmic world populated by idiosyncratic punctuation, paragraphs of varying (and sometimes startling) lengths, even distinct typography to provide, like wind or sun, the mood. Listening to a book, on the other hand, you get the story but not much else; all the nuances simply wash over you. It's the difference between walking through a jungle and watching one on TV. Give me a pith helmet any day of the week, I say. Give me the rifle, give me the net. Some may call me elitist, but if being elitist means absorbing art more fully, more *sensually*, well, then, so be it. I'm an elitist.

Terry sniffed the air then made a face. He narrowed his eyes at me and powered down his window. "Was that *you*?" he asked.

"Possibly," I said.

"Good God. I'd hate to see what your diet looks like."

"It's bottled-up stress," I said.

"Bully for you, but uncork it somewhere else, pal – not in my Lexus. I need to drive home still."

I waited for him to correct himself – to say that *we* needed to drive home still – but either he didn't realize his mistake or there was something he wasn't telling me. Just as I was about to ask him to pull over and let me out, Terry took an exit ramp without braking. It was one of those long-dead interstate exchanges: the skeleton of a gas station next to a hamburger shack with no remaining windows. An old Stuckey's had been transformed into a 24-hour Triple-X Adult Bookstore, but even this had been boarded up, its parking lot unplowed. Someone had spray-painted "Jesus Saves" across the entire front of the building.

"It's sad," I said, "to see that happen to a Stuckey's. I miss the pecan rolls."

Terry grunted; I wasn't sure he'd even heard me. A few

miles later, Terry said, "We're here," and he pulled behind an abandoned barn. A dozen cars and motorcycles were parked scattershot around it. Terry turned off the Lexus, and the actor's voice stopped mid-sentence. A part of me wanted to know what was going to happen to the married couple. Would they get back together? Would they go their own ways? The actor had sucked me in against my will, after all.

"Who *are* all these people?" I asked.

"It's just a club I belong to," he said.

"What kind of club?"

"A book club of sorts. I wanted you to meet them."

"So you know who I am?" I asked.

Instead of answering, Terry honked three times then stepped out of his car. When I got out, he pushed the button on his key chain and locked the doors. "Meth labs all around here. Cars are always getting stolen. Fucking meth," he said. "It's destroying this place."

I nodded. My buzz was completely gone now, replaced by whiskey's dark and unforgiving shroud. "I need to pee." I said it like a little boy asking for permission; I hated myself for it, too.

"Hurry it up then," Terry said, and he motioned toward a stand of trees.

As I stood some ways away, trying but failing to pee, I heard what sounded like a swarm of bees, an arrhythmic drone nearby. I knew it wasn't bees. In the heart of winter, the only surviving insects would have been those tunneled into the earth, trying to hold out until thaw. Unable to produce even a drop of urine, I zipped up and walked back to Terry, shivering the entire way. The closer to the barn we got, the louder the drone.

"Jesus. How many people are in there?" I asked.

I took a deep breath. Make the best of it, I told myself. Terry pushed open the barn door, revealing several dozen men and women. Except for a circle of chairs, flickering kerosene lanterns, and piles of hay, the barn was pretty much barren. Shadows climbed the walls, bending up onto the ceiling and rafters, looking like vapors.

"Hello!" I said, far more enthusiastically than I would have greeted an auditorium of adoring fans. "Welcome, readers!" I continued. "It's good to be here!"

The men and women continued pulling up chairs and settling down. Only a few looked over at me. They were, by any objective account, a motley crew. More men than not sported long, straggly beards. Women wore black leather vests. And then I noticed on one young woman's arm a stick man tattoo. It's a gang, I thought. But *what* gang? Hell's Angels? Or maybe a splinter group of the Angels, a snobby offshoot that enjoyed the occasional good book and espresso.

"We are survivors," a man wearing a leather Greek fisherman's cap said. I saw the stick man's blue-inked feet dangling from his frayed, pushed-up sleeve.

"Oh!" I said. "Veterans?" I asked.

"You could say that," Terry said.

I nodded. I didn't prod. I had learned in rehab that your own tragic story was always more interesting than someone else's, and that, more often than not, you ended up feeling embarrassed for the person who unloaded all of their sorrow at once. The most difficult part was accepting that you were probably just as much of an embarrassment the moment you opened *your* mouth. Once I realized this, I had started to embellish. If it's a story that they wanted, then I would give them a doozy of one! Embellishing, I learned, made me feel less foolish. In fact, embellishing put me back where I wanted to be – *in control of the moment*. I became the puppet master, as it were. I could tweak a mere word or two and then watch my fellow addicts cry.

"You see," Terry said, "everyone here has lost someone close to him."

"I'm so sorry," I said, and I tried looking genuinely sympathetic, meeting their eyes while gently nodding.

"They all died the same way, too," added Terry.

"Which was?" I asked.

"By hanging themselves." He pushed up the sleeve of his sweatshirt that revealed the stick man. Then he pushed up his other sleeve. On it was a tattoo of gallows.

Oh God, I thought. It had been a day of accumulating miscalculations – one poor judgment after another: agreeing to do the TV show, accepting the free drink coupon, going to the bar, taking the ride with Terry. His tattoo, I realized now, wasn't just a stick man. It was a man about to be hanged. I had been privy to only a shard of the story. The writer in me berated himself for not being open to the possibility of a more complex narrative.

"Your girlfriend," a bone-thin woman said, pushing up her other sleeve and revealing the tattooed gallows. "She didn't hang herself, as you said in your book."

"She didn't die by hanging," a man with muttonchops said.

"No," I said. "But she did *die*. She did *kill herself*."

"But not by *hanging*," the woman emphasized.

"No," I said.

"Not as you said in your book," the man said, pulling his chair closer to me.

"Well; no," I said. "But I don't think the *specifics* are important. I was trying to capture something *larger* in my book. Something, I don't know, closer to the truth than the truth itself."

"Bullshit," Terry said.

"I beg to differ," I said, but I had barely completed the last word when someone sneaked up behind me and slid a noose over my head. I started to defend myself, but the noose tightened. Another man restrained my arms, twisting them behind my back, while the bony woman quickly bound my wrists together.

Terry lifted a ladder that had been lying on the floor, half-covered with hay. It was wooden and A-framed. A second ladder went up beside it, a stainless-steel one this time, also A-framed but much taller than the one I was on. A man wearing a cowboy hat flung the long end of the rope that was attached to my neck up and over the rafters, and then three men started pulling. I had no choice but to climb the wooden ladder.

The first rung nearly broke under my weight. The ladder was probably as old as the barn. The wood had started to rot. It wobbled with each rung I climbed. The cowboy climbed the newer, sturdier stainless-steel ladder beside me.

"Keep going," Terry ordered, and the men pulled the rope harder. Up I went. I realized for the first time how precariously the head was connected to the neck and shoulders: a few bones, some muscle, veins. Mine felt as though it was about to come detached. "Higher," Terry yelled, and the men pulled again. I choked out a cough. When the ladder began to sway, the cowboy snickered. His breath warmed my face.

Only after I had reached the very top of the ladder, the peak of the A, did the men stop pulling. The cowboy, who stood as high as the rafter, looked it all over, then yelled down, "Give him another little yank," and they did. I was on my toes now, trying to maintain my balance. The cowboy yelled back, "Perfect," then took what was left of the rope, the part the men had been pulling, and began swinging it around the rafter, over and over, until there was barely enough to tie a knot. Then he climbed down and moved his ladder to another part of the barn.

I could breathe more or less okay so long as I remained on the tips of my toes, but anything less than the tips and I began to choke and cough. Also, the ladder required me to stay perfectly still in order to remain alive. I started to speak, but the mere vibrations that my voice produced caused the ladder to shake, so I shut my mouth and concentrated on breathing through my nose.

The thin woman said, "This is for your girlfriend."

Muttonchops added, "And for all of our dead."

"We want you to think about what you've done," Terry said. "See how it feels. We'll be back tomorrow at ten. If you're still among us, we'll let you down and set you free."

One by one, they filed out of the barn. They left behind only one kerosene lantern. At first, I couldn't see much at all. I was being forced to stare up into the darkest recesses of the barn, but eventually my eyes adjusted.

I can't say for sure how long everyone has been gone, but I would venture to guess it's been only a few hours. The slightest move and I will surely die up here. But if I don't die, I have vowed to write about this night. So that's what I'm concentrating on – every splinter of wood, every nail-head, every shivering web – a million seemingly unimportant details, each one now as vibrant as my own small life. I want to get it right this time, too.

Which way does the snow drift when it seeps through a crack in the roof?

How do my toes, already quivering, feel after two hours?

What, my love, does the truth sound like when you're the only one listening?

THE END IS NOTHING, THE ROAD IS ALL

(Nelson Algren, 1909–1981)

Jimmy Delaney saw kids every day, but there was something about this particular one that bugged the hell out of him. The kid looked short for his age, fragile, and you could see his pink skull through his greasy yellow hair. It was a delicate skull, flimsy, the kind of skull that might crack in half if you stared at it too hard. His nose was always running, his dull eyes rheumy and wanting.

Why did he bug Jimmy? Maybe it was the way the kid would peek over at him, give him that pathetic hangdog look and then turn away. It was a look that said, *I see you when the others don't and I feel sorry for you but I'll never be you.*

The little shit, Jimmy thought. The little turd. Every day, except for weekends and holidays, the kid shuffled down Wabansia Avenue with his other snot-nosed friends, and every day Jimmy wanted to reach out from his place under the shrubs, collar the little sissy, and ask him why the hell he thought *he* was so special. The kid couldn't have been more than eight or nine. Ten, tops. He didn't have the right to give Jimmy a look, *any* look, sorry or otherwise, and that's what got under his skin. The kid should have just ignored him, like all the others.

Jimmy knew it was the junk talking to him, it was the

needle in his arm, the swirl of blood, it was the hunger and hal-
lucinations. Lately, he saw animals in the shrubs, lemurs and
boa constrictors staring back at him. This was Chicago's West
Side, and Jimmy knew that these animals probably weren't
there, but still they came to him as he lay on the freezing cold
dirt. He had no choice but to sweat the evil bastards out.

"Hey. You holding?"

Jimmy looked up. It was Raoul. Unlike most people,
who weren't even aware that a man was living between two
shrubs, Raoul knew exactly where to find him.

"No," Jimmy said. "Nope."

"You loaded?"

Jimmy smiled. He shook his head. *Nope.* He was lying,
of course. He was feeling the first bang right now; he was getting a kick. Raoul was a junkie, too, but he was a low-life, a
moocher, too lazy or stupid to panhandle. He was a stool pigeon and a fag. The fag part didn't bother Jimmy – a person
did what they needed to do – but being a stool pigeon was
another story. Stool pigeons ended up gut-stabbed. Jimmy'd
seen it before – blood pouring from a wound, trailing down
the curb and into the street's drain.

"Well," Raoul said. "You look like shit. You look like shit
on a grill." He smiled. "You look like shit on a *stick* on a grill."

"How about if I kill you?"

"Try."

Jimmy should have. He'd fought in the Battle of Normandy. A bullet was still lodged in his shoulder. He used to
tell girls that if they thumped the scar tissue hard enough, if
they flicked it with their finger, they'd feel the bullet. If they
put their ear close enough, they might even hear it, too. Kill
Raoul? What the fuck did he care? He'd killed a German in the
war. He would kill Raoul, too, and not think twice.

But that was that. Raoul was gone. How long had he
been gone? An hour? A week? Jimmy wasn't sure. He knew it
was a weekday because kids had walked to school that morn-

ing. The rheumy-eyed kid had looked at him, as he always did. He carried a lunch box in one hand, a book bag in the other. He had offered a fleeting, tight-lipped smile and then turned away.

A man with his sleeves rolled up crouched in front of Jimmy, gave him a dollar bill and a cigarette, and introduced himself as Algren. He wore glasses and had a receding hairline, but the hair he did still have was thick. He appeared to have no upper lip, just a fat bottom one. He lit Jimmy's cigarette for him then lit one for himself.

"So tell me, friend, what's your story? What're you doin' out here? You live in those goddamned bushes or what?" Algren took a long drag from his cigarette and said, "Wanna cup of coffee? You take it black?"

"Sugar," Jimmy said. "No cream."

And so the routine began: Algren brought coffee, Jimmy listened to what Algren had to say. Jimmy always waited until Algren was gone before reaching into his paper sack and pulling out a Syrette filled with morphine. The Syrette looked like a small toothpaste tube except that it had a needle where the cap would have gone: puncture the seal with a small needle, pinch your skin, insert hypo at an angle, and squeeze the tube. This was the same shit medics used on Jimmy when the Germans shot him on D-Day. Now they sold it on the streets of Chicago – one buck each if the supply was good, two bucks if the city was dry.

The next time Algren showed up, he was in a good mood. Jimmy had heard leaves rustling before he saw Algren's shoe parting the shrubs that hid him.

"Hey there, buddy. Brought you a cup of Joe. Lotta sugar, the way you like it." He reached into his pocket and pulled out a dollar bill. "Go on," he said. "Take it." And then Algren told Jimmy about how during the Depression he'd hitchhiked around the country and ended up in New Orleans, how in the French Market men who made soup would decapitate turtles right there in front of you, how the whores were so desperate you could sleep with them for a pork sandwich, how he'd gone broke as a door-to-door salesman and ended up in Texas, how there was a time in his life that all he lived on were bananas because bananas were all he could get his hands on, how Chicago was his home and would always be his home, how he wrote books that nobody read but what the fuck were you going to do about it, how he couldn't help believing that it was better to write something worthwhile than write the sort of crap that so many other fakers and sell-outs wrote. Algren shook his head. "It's been a long road, pal. You could say I've been to Hell and back," he said, "and let me tell you, it ain't pretty."

"What's not?"

"Hell."

Before Jimmy could tell him about his own life, Algren was gone. One of these days Jimmy would have to tell him about his years before the war when he worked on a Mississippi tugboat that pulled a barge. It was a small operation, usually just Jimmy and Red. The barge was full of trash. It was nearly impossible to have a good opinion about people after spending the day among their stinking, rotting refuse. People were disgusting – and wasteful. Red skippered the tugboat when he wasn't blind drunk, and he told Jimmy, in detail that left nothing to the imagination, about all the women he'd ever laid. He was eighty-three years old, and the litany of women who'd had the pleasure of Red's services went all the way back to 1875, starting with this squirt of an Irish gal named Ruth. "Good Lord," Red had said. "We were together for only one night. Hard to believe. One night! She was only two years older than me, but she taught me damned near everything I know today, son. That's a fact." He then proceeded to describe all that they had done, every nuance of the night, up to and including the moment Ruth gathered her shabby clothes and left his cold, bare room. Listening to Red was like sitting at the feet of Scheherazade: 1001 one-night stands, one story after the other discarded, disappearing into the tugboat's frothy wake.

When Red died, he was cremated in St. Louis. Jimmy watched from the tugboat as Red's boss, Mr. Gardetta, dumped the ashes from a box no bigger than a milk jug. When Mr. Gardetta finished, he tossed the box onto the barge's steaming heap of trash, clapped ashes from his hands, and said, "That's that, I guess."

In February, it was colder than shit. As soon as his piss hit the ground, it turned to crystal. *Not right,* Jimmy thought. He discovered a city library, one of the smaller branches that people sometimes forgot about. Junkies spent days like these searching for warmth, a soft glow somewhere, a swatch of heat. They sought out foyers, city buses, the subway platforms downtown. In the library restroom, Jimmy doused his face with warm water and wiped himself off with stiff paper towels. The library could support one bum, two at most, but only as long as he kept quiet and, at the very least, pretended to read. It was a public building, after all. They couldn't very well deny someone, even a bum, the right to read, could they? And so Jimmy would get himself the newspaper or a book plucked at random, and he would stare at the words until all the letters turned to fuzz and then blotched together. On days when he fell asleep, a security guard would nudge him awake with a nightstick and then prod him outside, back into the cold and the dusk's blue light. It wouldn't have been so cold if not for the wind off the lake. The lake made the city arctic, almost uninhabitable. *The fucking water,* Jimmy thought. *Always the fucking water.*

Algren came to Jimmy almost daily now. "I was born in Michigan," he said one day, "but Chicago's my home. Chi-

cago's full of real people, like *you*. You were in the war, right?
And now look at you. I'm sure you weren't born with a silver spoon in your mouth like some of these assholes I meet,
were you? Of course not. Here," Algren said and handed over
a dollar bill. It was true what Algren said. Jimmy's mother
stayed at home, raising Jimmy and his seven brothers and
sisters. Jimmy's father was a high school teacher. He taught
Greek and Roman mythology to elementary students. As a
child, Jimmy was often lulled to sleep by tales of Pandora, At-
las, or Hercules. Jimmy's favorite story, however, was that of
Charon, who silently ferried the dead past Cerebus and into
the River Styx. "Corpses would be buried with a coin under
their tongue to pay Charon," his father told him. "So don't go
putting any money in your mouth until you know it's your
time." One morning, Jimmy's father woke up thinking he was
Tiresias, the blind soothsayer of many legends. "I just saw
Athena bathing!" he exclaimed to all eight children, and when
Jimmy's mother walked into the room, his father tried gouging
out his own eyes. According to a doctor, his father had managed only to scratch his corneas with his fingernails. After four
hospital orderlies fastened him to a bed with leather restraints
and administered a tranquilizer, the doctor sealed up his eyes.
"The eye heals fast," the doctor explained, "but every time you
blink, you wipe away the progress." Jimmy's father remained
at the Catholic hospital for another a week before being trans-
ferred to the state psychiatric hospital, from which he never
emerged. Two years later, he died.

    "You and me," Algren said, walking backwards. "We're
probably a lot alike." He winked at Jimmy, then turned to face
the direction he was headed, whistling as he left.

    In the library, Jimmy thought he could smell the trash
from the barge, that rotting meat-and-fruit stink that wouldn't

leave your nose for days, but the barge had been years ago, before the war. Strolling the aisles, Jimmy saw two books on the
shelf with the name Algren on their spines. He brought them
to his table. *Too eagerly?* he wondered. The guard, seemingly
unable to stop smoothing down his shirt sleeves, kept a close
eye on him. Jimmy could see the question in the guard's eyes:
Why two books? Taking two books was a deviation for Jimmy.
When the guard wasn't looking, Jimmy carried them into the
restroom and tucked them under his shirt. He'd heard of junkies who stole used books at one store and then took them to
another, selling them for enough cash to score some weed or
Benzedrine or yellow jackets, but you couldn't sell a library
book with its "PROPERTY OF" stamp and tidy pocket glued
inside. Library books were good only for reading.

Back under the shrubs, Jimmy thumbed through one of
Algren's books but couldn't concentrate. His arms itched. He
clawed and clawed them. Lemurs and boa constrictors stared
at him. The world was rotting – a spinning ball of putrid decay.
Then Algren showed up with a woman – solid, matronly, older
– maybe even older than Algren. She was the sort of woman
people called handsome.

"Simone," he said, "I want you to meet my friend..." He
stared hard at Jimmy, as if a name might materialize.

"Jimmy," Jimmy finally said.

Algren nodded, then completed the introduction. "Jimmy? Simone."

Algren, Jimmy noticed, was paying closer attention to
Simone than to him. He watched everything she did, the way
she brushed hair from her eyes, the way she squinted one
of her eyes when she said to Jimmy in a thick French accent,
"Please to meet you." She leaned forward and shook Jimmy's
hand.

"Her English," Algren said, laughing. "It needs a little
work, don't you think? I hung up on her three times when she
first called me. Wasn't sure what the hell she was jabbering

about. Thought it was a wrong number, for chrissake."

Algren gave Jimmy a five dollar bill and a fresh pack of cigarettes before heading down the street, leading Simone with his palm flush against her spine. It was starting to snow. Jimmy opened his mouth and let it fall onto his tongue. The French woman's perfume helped mask the unrelenting stink of the barge. When a group of boys walked past the shrubs, Jimmy reached out for the pink-skulled boy's ankle but wasn't fast enough. The boy saw what Jimmy was trying to do and almost fell down trying to get away. Jimmy laughed. "Sissy!" he called out.

"Who're you calling a sissy?" It was Raoul, coming from the other direction. "So what if I am!" he said. He sashayed his hips and puckered his lips, lips Jimmy wanted to smash. "Still mad?" Raoul asked. "Still mad at the sissy? Well, you won't be when you see what I've got for you." He tossed Jimmy a bag. Inside were Syrettes, except these weren't Army-issue; they looked homemade. "Don't look at me like that, Jimmy. It's new stuff. *Better* stuff."

"What do you want me to do for it?" Jimmy asked.

"Nothing, honey."

"When'd you get so generous?"

"Questions, questions." Raoul tisk-tisked. "If you don't want it..."

Jimmy, clutching the bag, leaned back deeper into the shrubs. "I didn't say that," he whispered.

It was D-Day again, and Jimmy was a paratrooper getting ready for battle, one of the 150,000 men sent to drive the Germans out of France. General Eisenhower even came down in person to speak to the 101st Airborne. Jimmy was close enough to smell his breath, too, but for all of his swagger and finger-pointing, there was still fear in the man's eyes. The weather wasn't good that day, for starters. Too much rain. Too much wind. Eisenhower knew; the paratroopers knew. But maybe what Jimmy saw was merely a reflection of his own fears; maybe you always saw in your leaders' eyes your own doubts, your own second-guesses.

Hours later, when Jimmy jumped from his plane, he was so far off his mark he had no idea where he was going to land. Half his gear had come off midair. Some of the men were shot on their way down: fresh corpses still subjected to gravity even as their souls rose. Below Jimmy was what looked like a dead man floating belly-down, his chute open like an absurdly large umbrella, but when Jimmy landed in the water next to him, he saw that it was actually one of the rubber dummies from Operation Titanic that had been dropped earlier that morning to divert the Germans. But why had he, Jimmy, been dropped near a dummy paratrooper? And why was he landing in water? He remembered Eisenhower's eyes: the General must have known he was looking at dead men.

Spring in Chicago: snow, hard-packed and filthy, still clung to the sidewalk. On a day when it looked as though it might start snowing again, Algren returned. He arrived with an extra cup of coffee and a pack of smokes. "Here ya go," he said.

"Where've you been?" Jimmy asked. He didn't mean for his question to sound so desperate, but the sight of Algren made him realize how much he'd missed him.

"Back from New York," Algren said. He shook his head. "Women. Jesus Christ. They'll pull your heart out with their bare hands and then eat it right there in front of you." He lit two cigarettes, then handed one to Jimmy. "Remember Simone? Just spent sixteen days with her. Happiest sixteen days of my miserable life. But she's killing me, Jimmy, I swear to Christ. I love that woman. I love that woman so much I feel it in my blood. Ever feel that way? The cabbie thought I was her husband, so that's what she calls me now. Her husband. But she won't leave this guy she's with in France. Maybe you've heard of him. Sartre? Maybe not. Why would you? An existentialist, whatever the holy hell that is. I bet you could teach that bug-eyed motherfucker a thing or two about existentialism. You and me both." Algren squinted toward a part of the ground Jimmy had hollowed out; this was where he stowed Algren's books. "Hey, hey," Algren said. "Where'd you get those?"

"Library."

"Sonovabitch," he said and laughed. He crouched and said, "Listen. That kid. You know the one."

Jimmy nodded. He knew. The little snot-nosed bastard.

"Just keep your eye on him," Algren said.

"Okay. I'll watch him."

"Watch *who*?" It was Raoul. "Talking to yourself again?"

"I'm talking to my friend," Jimmy said. He motioned toward Algren, but Algren wasn't there.

"I'm surprised you're still alive," Raoul said. He tossed Jimmy another bag of the new shit. "For the war hero."

"How do you know what I did in the war?"

"You traded me your Purple Heart for a pack of smack. Remember? Last year?" When Jimmy didn't say anything, Raoul shook his head. "Poor Jimmy. *Brain like a sieve.*"

Brain like a sieve. Fucking Raoul. Raoul was a mosquito, blood-fat but thin-skinned. An irritant. Slap him and he'd explode. One day Jimmy would reach out while Raoul was talking, sink his fingers into Raoul's eyes, and try digging into the man's brain. What did Raoul know about the infinite ways there were to die? In the English Channel, off the coast of Normandy, floating next to a paradummy, Jimmy was certain he was going to die but wasn't sure how. He might drown, or he might get shot. Later, his buddy Melson told him about what had happened on Omaha Beach, how they unloaded from the landing craft too soon and men started drowning, and how the soldiers who didn't drown were sitting ducks for the Germans up on the mountain. While Melson struggled to make it to shore, he saw Rickie Lipton's head explode: "One minute Rickie was looking at me, this look like, *Oh shit this isn't how it's supposed to happen,* and then, I don't know, a second or two later, some Kraut blew his head off." Omaha Beach was bad news, but the paratroopers didn't have it much easier. The ones who weren't shot while still in the air were surrounded by Germans the second their feet touched ground, and the ones who weren't surrounded landed so far off their destination that their mission became a moot point.

Later that day – or maybe later that week – Algren showed Jimmy a letter. "Look at this," he said. "She writes, 'My Beloved Husband.' What did I tell you? She's *killing* me, buddy. She's *killing* me. I won't see her again until September. I'm a weak man, Jimmy." He wagged his head.

Jimmy knew what Algren was going through. He knew a thing or two about love. Before getting shot, before killing the German, before D-Day, there had been Martha. They'd had a son together. Everyone thought the boy looked like her: same eyes, same hair, same teeth. Later, Jimmy learned that Martha had already begun seeing her future husband, that she was probably with him on D-Day, that he may even have been in bed with her, raking his nails down her back the way she liked while Jimmy floated in the ice-cold Channel, a God-forsaken wind blowing him further from a shore he needed to reach but didn't want to step foot on for fear of getting shot. Everyone had told Jimmy not to think about it, and for a long time he didn't, but lately he couldn't help it. It wasn't Martha he thought about or, for that matter, the bastard she was with, her new husband – the banker. It was his own boy – Mark Delaney. *Markie*, she and Jimmy had called him. Yeah, Jimmy could tell Algren a thing or two about getting your heart ripped out.

Jimmy finally read a chapter from one of Algren's books. It was okay, nothing great. It was no Aeschylus. It was no Aristophanes. The books were getting mildewed and starting to reek. Jimmy's attention span was short. Sometimes all he could read was a sentence or two before he wanted to claw off his own skin and then crawl howling down Wabansia Avenue. The junk running through his veins didn't feel right; he wasn't even sure it *was* junk. But he wanted more of it.

"You want more of it?" Raoul asked.

"Are you reading my mind?"

Raoul smiled. "You're talking out loud, friend. I've been here for an hour, listening to you." He pretended to look somber, but Jimmy knew it was an act. Raoul said, "I'm sorry about your boy. Markie. Tough break."

"Quiet," Jimmy said. "I mean it."

"If he looks anything like you, I bet he's a real cutie."

"Keep talking and I'll kill you."

"Kill *me*?" Raoul laughed. "I'm the one who's doing the killing around here." He tossed Jimmy another bag. "You must have the heart of a thousand men, Jimmy. I'll give you that much."

After Raoul left, Jimmy pierced the Syrette, pinched out some of the junk, and sniffed it. What the hell *was* it? And where was Raoul getting it? Jimmy quickly squeezed the rest of it into his mouth, afraid some of it might drip on the ground. Wasteful, Jimmy thought. And there was no need for that.

D-Day: The man sitting next to Jimmy on the Troop Carrier C-47 leaned forward and vomited all over Jimmy's boots. "Nice," Jimmy said. Jimmy looked away and took a deep breath. He was hyper-conscious that the things he thought about during this flight over the Channel could very well be his final thoughts; it was entirely possible that by day's end he would be dead. He had always imagined that a person would naturally start thinking about God and the afterlife in such moments, but Jimmy couldn't concentrate on a single idea. He thought about the time Red, using a bamboo pole, fished a used condom from the mound of trash on the barge and said, "Oh, the tales this little fella could tell!" and then flung the wilted rubber into the Mississippi. He thought about the time Dr. Dettlofson swabbed Jimmy's arm with alcohol and then inserted the needle. Jimmy didn't flinch or cry. He was four years old and couldn't take his eyes off the needle in his arm, at the blood swirling into the syringe. He wondered if Hitler's mother would have suffocated her own child if she knew what horrors lay ahead. *Could* she have? He wondered how many babies lying in their cribs this very second should probably be sacrificed for the good of mankind. He wondered why the guy next to him had to vomit on *his* boots and not the boots of the guy on his other side.

Lately, Jimmy'd become aware that there were points in a person's life that caused everything after it to shift. Sometimes the shift created a positive ripple, but most of the time it was negative. What, he wondered, was the first major dividing point of his life? Was it the day he took the half-dead mouse out of its trap, carried it into the back yard, and choked it with a pair of pliers? Was it the day his sister, Lenora, and her friend, Betty, called him into the bathroom and made him take off all of his clothes so that they could look him over? Lenora had said to Betty, "See? I told you," and then the two girls silently left the room. Maybe it was the night a group of grammar school boys performed short scenes from classic Greek drama. For his contribution, Jimmy had played Oedipus. He was ten years old and understood only a fraction of what he was saying, but he was good at memorizing lines. His parents had sat in the front row, and each time Jimmy looked down at them, he saw his father tapping a tooth with one of his fingernails. He'd never seen his father do that before and didn't know what it meant.

Jimmy performed the scene in which Oedipus learns from the Herdsman that he had been adopted. In this truncated version of the play, Jimmy ended his scene by pretending to gouge out his eyes. For days afterward, Jimmy's father wouldn't look at his son, but he kept repeating the Herdsman's answer to Oedipus' question about what it was he did. "The best part of my life I tended sheep," his father would say at unexpected moments, as if Oedipus himself had just whispered into his ear. Jimmy never responded, but each time his father spoke the line from the play, Jimmy silently asked the follow-up: *What were the pastures thou didst most frequent?*

What fucking pastures indeed, Jimmy thought now, vomit on his boots. Jimmy's father, after losing everything in the Depression, tried holding on as best he could, which turned out not to be very well at all. He had lost his inheritance, of course, but he had also lost Jimmy's mother's inheritance. Six months after the night his father had sat in the audience tapping his tooth with his fingernail, he announced to his children that he had just seen Athena bathing, and when his mother walked into the room, he tried gouging out his own eyes. Two years later, he was dead.

The best part of my life I tended sheep, Jimmy thought. And then he jumped from the carrier.

Time: What does it mean to a junkie?

There were days when time seemed not to move at all, when watching someone walk down a street took what felt like the better part of an afternoon, and then there were times when a month would slip past, or an entire season, without Jimmy barely noticing.

Jimmy knew who Sartre was. He knew a little something about Existentialism, too. He wasn't an idiot. But he didn't believe for a second that the woman Algren was seeing was also seeing Sartre. Surely Algren didn't believe this malarkey. But maybe it was Algren who was messing with *him*. Maybe it was some sort of sinister game: fuck with the junkie.

Jimmy wasn't even sure what season it was when Algren and Simone showed up one morning, hand in hand. No coffee, no dollar bill – just the two of them, as if their love alone was enough to sustain Jimmy and keep his heart beating through the long days ahead.

"You remember Simone, dontcha?" Algren tipped his head toward her and grinned. He seemed almost shy around her.

"Tell him our plans," Simone said.

"Our plans? What plans?" He squinted into the air between himself and Jimmy. "Oh-oh, *those* plans. Well, Simone here, she's coming back next year for a longer visit, and so we're going to take her on a trip down the Mississippi, just like Huck Finn, only not on a goddamned raft. She's used to cocktail parties and socialites and all those places that wouldn't even let you and me into, Jimmy." He rolled his eyes for Jimmy's benefit. "Well, I'm going to show her the *real* America. She hasn't been to Mississippi. She hasn't seen New Orleans."

"And then," Simone said, "we go to Mexico!"

"That's right," Algren said with less enthusiasm. "Mexico."

"My father," Jimmy said, "thought he was Tiresias."

Algren cut his eyes toward Simone, then back to Jimmy. "Tiresias, huh?" Simone tugged Algren's arm and Algren added, "Well...we'd better go, pal. Time is at a premium when Simone's in town."

"*Au revoir*," Simone said. She kissed two fingers and then waved at him. She made a point of looking into Jimmy's eyes before turning away.

Why did Jimmy feel compelled to tell them about his father? The words just popped out of his mouth before he could stop himself. It wasn't any big deal, he supposed, but it had left them with the wrong impression. And he felt like a fool. *Stupid*, he thought. *How unbelievably stupid!*

Jimmy pulled himself out from under the shrubs. Days

like these, he felt as though he'd never walked before, each
step uneasy, his balance questionable. He weaved down Wabansia, stumbling like a rabid animal. He walked this way for
two miles, until he reached the brownstone. He climbed the
steps and knocked. When no one answered, he knocked harder. When the door opened at last, a boy stood looking out at
him.

"Markie?" Jimmy asked.

The boy nodded.

Jimmy cleared his throat. "Do you know who I am?"

Before the boy could answer, a man appeared behind
Mark. He had a thick mustache and wore a tie. His eyebrows
looked like living organisms. It was the banker. He pulled
Markie behind him, pushing him deeper into the house. "Stay
back," he told the boy. To Jimmy, he said, "Get away unless
you want me to call the police."

"I killed a German," Jimmy said, "with my bare hands. I
choked the son of a bitch to death."

"Okay, now," the banker said. He tried shutting the door,
but Jimmy wedged his foot inside, then shouldered the door
open.

Martha stood by the staircase, clutching the boy to her.
"Oh my God," she said. "Jimmy?"

"I just want to know," Jimmy said. "What were you doing on June the sixth, 1944?"

"June *what*? What are you talking about?"

"D-Day," Jimmy said. "Fucking *D-Day*. Where were you?
What were you doing?"

Martha took a deep breath. Her hand lay draped over
the boy's head, like a spidery flesh-colored hat. "Just leave,
Jimmy. Go before it's too late."

"Too late? And what the hell's *that* supposed to mean...
too late?"

◎

What Jimmy found out later: the banker had come up from behind and struck him while he was talking to Martha. A cop explained that the weapon had been a coal shovel from their fireplace. "The next time," he added, "you might not get so lucky." They kept Jimmy in jail only until they saw that he was starting to convulse from withdrawals, and then they let him go, fearing they'd have to clean up a mess if they didn't.

Lucky, Jimmy thought. He kept an eye out for Raoul on his way back to the neighborhood. A stool-pigeon-junkie-fag like Raoul might be anywhere, but he wasn't anywhere Jimmy was looking. Passing the Y, he heard someone calling his name. It was Algren with Simone. Algren's hair was wet and slicked back, and he was carrying a paper sack.

"You holding?" Jimmy asked, walking closer.

"Holding?" Algren asked. "Holding *what*?" He put two cigarettes in his mouth, lit them both, then handed one to Jimmy. When Jimmy stepped forward, Simone gasped.

"Your face," she said. "It's bleeding."

"Christ," Algren said. "You get rolled?" He handed the bag to Simone. "Wait here."

With Algren inside the Y, Jimmy stared at the crumpled sack. He couldn't bring himself to look up at Simone, who was a liar. If she wasn't a liar – if she really *was* seeing Sartre – then she was both a liar *and* a cheater.

"What's in the bag?" he finally asked.

"Oh, Nelson doesn't have a shower in his little apartment. He comes here." She sighed. "So silly." She reached up to touch Jimmy's hair, but Jimmy flinched and the hand retreated. "You were in the war, no?"

"Yes," Jimmy said.

"Normandy?" she asked. "Were you there?"

"101st Airborne," Jimmy said. "Paratrooper."

"You have been shot?"

Jimmy nodded.

When Simone reached up again, Jimmy willed himself

to remain still. She rested her palm on his cheek. "Thank you," she said.

Algren burst through the Y's door. "Try finding a clean goddamn towel in there...I swear. Here," he said, giving the towel to Jimmy. "This'll take care of the blood."

"I'll do it," Simone said. She crumpled the towel and began scrubbing. The fabric felt like sandpaper against his face, but Jimmy didn't move. His mother cleaned his face the same way when he was child. *There could be only one puddle outside,* she would say, *and you'd find it, wouldn't you, Jimmy?*

On their way back to Wabansia, Algren told a story about a whore in New Orleans who didn't have any arms. "You'd think she'd have charged half price," he said, "but she actually got twice the going rate. You ask me, that's New Orleans in a stinking nutshell, my friends."

Jimmy, arms itching, stopped walking. "I need to find someone," he said.

"Oh; okay," Algren said.

"We will see you tomorrow?" Simone asked.

"Take care of yourself, now," Algren said.

Jimmy nodded, then bowed goodbye before stepping into a blind alley.

The moon woke him. He was back home now, between the shrubs. He hadn't found Raoul but he'd found Emmett, who could spare four Syrettes – enough, normally, to get him through the next few days. But Emmett's shit was weak. Whatever it was that Raoul had been giving him had raised his tolerance to new heights. Jimmy might as well have been shooting water into his veins.

"Raoul!" Jimmy yelled. "Raoul! Where the fuck are you?"

"I'm here!" Raoul yelled in return.

"Where?"

"Here!" There was laughter, Raoul's and another man's. "I see *you*, Jimmy. Do you see *me*?"

"Where are you?" Jimmy was on the brink of crying; he could hear it in his voice, that splintering of timbre.

"I'm *here*, Jimmy. I'm *here*." More laughter.

And then the street got quiet. Jimmy waited for more of Raoul's taunts, but none came. "Raoul?" Jimmy called out. "Raoul?"

Nothing.

The next morning, the ghost-touch of Simone's hand still on his cheek, Jimmy woke up determined to give up the junk. Maybe Algren could spare some clean clothes; maybe he could help Jimmy get into the Y for a hot shower. Jimmy would have to scrub a long time to get some of the grime off. He remembered how, when he came home after helping old man Tomlinson paint his fence, his mother soaked a rag with kerosene and told him to shut his eyes while she wiped him clean. Jimmy, no more than ten at the time, would take slow but deep breaths, compulsively sucking in the kerosene's fumes, until the inside of his head seemed to expand ever so slightly. He loved standing with his father at the gas pumps, too, sniffing while his father filled his car. Jimmy always had a headache afterward, but it was the *moment* that he cared about, the *now*.

Across the street, Jimmy spied Raoul. His first impulse was to yell out to him, to ask him to come over so that he could score a little something to get him through the day, but he willed himself not to speak. *No*, he told himself. *Don't*. But then he noticed that there was a boy on the other side of Raoul, and that Raoul was holding the boy's hand. Was it his son? Did Raoul have a past as Jimmy had a past – hidden, all-but-intangible? Jimmy crawled out from under the shrubs and padded across the street for a better look. It must have been a weekend the street was so quiet – that, or the end of the world. It was

possible. Jimmy had seen photos of Hiroshima's aftermath...
the leafless trees and gray skies, radioactive black rain, skin
burning as far away as two miles from the blast. The end of the
world was the new reality.

When Raoul crouched to the boy's height and took the
boy's face with both hands, whispering and motioning with his
head toward the abandoned building beside them, Jimmy saw
that it was the pink-skulled boy with the greasy yellow hair.
Eyes still rheumy. Nose running. Algren's words came back to
him: *Just keep your eye on him.* Until this morning, Jimmy had
thought Algren feared the boy might do him harm, but it was
clear now that Algren feared something might happen to the
boy. And Algren knew that Jimmy was in the best position to
survey the situation, to assess and then, if necessary, to act.

"Raoul!" Jimmy called out.

Raoul swung around. He looked down at the boy, "Remember what I told you, okay?" And then he said to Jimmy,
"The early bird, eh? Would you like a worm this morning? Is
that it?"

Jimmy's first punch connected with Raoul's throat, causing him to drop to his knees. It was the same punch he'd
thrown at the German after he'd finally washed ashore, after
he'd made his way to what he thought might be a safe haven.
There were no safe havens, he soon realized. The German had
been waiting for him, hiding. Jimmy had sensed movement,
spun around, and punched him in the throat. The German had
tried reaching for his weapon. Jimmy, whose own weapons
had been swallowed by the Channel, did the only thing he
felt could stop the man: he grabbed hold of the German's face
and sunk his fingers into the man's eyes. Putting out a man's
eyes was harder than he thought – up to a certain point. After
that point, the fingers slid all the way in with ease, as deep as
brain, and then it was only a matter of how much damage you
wanted to do. Jimmy didn't want to risk it. He pushed in until his fingers disappeared. That's when another German shot

him, leaving him for dead.

Raoul was quiet now. Jimmy's hands – his arms, even – were covered in blood. The boy had run away. Jimmy thought of Oedipus: *No more shall you behold the evils I have suffered and done. Be dark from now on, since you saw before, what you should not, and knew not what you should!* Jimmy removed his fingers and looked up. Algren and Simone were peering out their window, down at Jimmy. He wasn't sure how much they had seen. He hoped they had seen it all. To see only part of what had happened would have been worse than not seeing any of it.

Jimmy patted down Raoul and found the bag of Syrettes inside his coat. After crumpling the bag and shoving it into his own sagging pocket, he looked up at Algren and Simone again and shook his head, as if to say, *It wasn't about the bag,* but Simone was crying while Algren, angry or disappointed, jerked the curtains shut.

Jimmy walked due west until, a short while later, he reached the Chicago River. At the river's edge, Jimmy leaned forward and washed away the blood. He splashed water on his face. He opened the bag of Syrettes, took one out, punctured the end of the hypo, pinched his skin, and stuck himself. He squeezed the Syrette and felt himself loosen. It was as though the river he was staring at had possessed his own body, swift rapids running through his veins. In the Army, one Syrette was all that an injured or dying man needed. One Syrette, and he'd wake up later in a hospital, already tended to...or he wouldn't wake up at all. Jimmy took out a second Syrette, punctured the open end, and shot it. He took out a third and shot it, too. He would have done a fourth, but the bag slipped from his fingers and into the river. He, too, was starting to slip, unable to hold on. He slid into the river.

Unlike that day in the Channel, when blood and water churned together and men kept dropping from the sky, Jimmy refused to fight. He had no objective today, no goal. The water, clean and cold, felt good on his skin. The current was especially strong. The more Jimmy relaxed, the faster the current carried him. Before slipping under for the final time, he heard Algren ask Simone, "Where do you think we're going?" but Jimmy refused to answer. He would just keep rowing. *Let them wonder*, Jimmy thought. *Let them mull it over.* There was no more need for talk, anyway. Soon, they would be where they needed to be. And then, after they crossed over...then what?

He would kiss his friends' foreheads.

Gently shut their eyes.

Remove the hidden coin from under each tongue.

CONTRIBUTOR'S NOTES

John McNally was born in 1965. After attending a famous writers' workshop in the Midwest, he worked as a short-order cook, bouncer, grave digger, lumberjack, carnival barker, florist, disc jockey, and busboy. Most recently, he was employed as a groundskeeper. He has no permanent place of residence. He owns a 1976 Ford LTD, inside of which he could, if necessary, store all his worldly possessions. This is his first published story.

I'm more than happy to write a word or two about my story. Given the pantheon of great writers before me who have added their own contributors' notes, I have to admit that I feel out of my league. I'm a newcomer, a nobody, and whatever I have to say about the origin of my story will pale when placed alongside another writer's comments. That said, I will do my best.

What I *don't* want to do is pull a Rick Bass. Don't get me wrong. I love the guy's work—he's one of my all-time favorite writers—but do we really need to be taken from the precise second the germ of a story pops into a guy's head all the way up to the day he rides his horse to the First Bank of Montana to cash his *Paris Review* check? No. I think not.

There's really not a hell of a lot to say about my own story except that one day the idea came to me, and the next day I wrote it. I could talk about how it was a gift, how I was merely the conduit through which the story moved, or I could go on about how many tens of thousands of drafts I put it through, how I wrote this story with my own blood, but I honestly don't remember working all that hard on it. In fact, I barely remember writing it all.

Maybe what I should do is simply say a few words about the story's dedication and leave it at that. I'm sure there's more than one reader out there who'll want to know why my story is dedicated to Frank Mason. Believe it or not, Frank is an old buddy of mine. I knew Frank way before that prodigious month when the planets aligned for him and three of his short stories appeared, one after the other, in *Zoetrope*, *McSweeney's*, and *GQ*, turning him overnight into that dreaded cliché, "A writer to watch!" I knew Frank when he was a writer *nobody* watched. We were roommates our first year together in that famous and mythical Writers' Workshop, the one surrounded by cornfields and farm houses and long, flat stretches of sun-blistered interstate.

It was almost dusk the day I pulled into town and located the Victorian on Brown Street. After getting out of my car and touching my toes a few times, I took the front-porch steps two at a time. I ran my finger across the names on the mailboxes, searching for Frank's apartment number, then stepped into the foyer and started pounding on the door. *Frank*, I thought. *Frank friggin' Mason.* Since all of the arrangements for us to live together had been made long-distance over the phone, we hadn't yet met, and so I wasn't sure what to expect.

Frank opened the door wide, cocktail in hand, as if I were the first guest at the party. "Hello, hello," he said.

I know it's hard to believe, but Frank used to be a thin bastard. You could see even then that he had the potential to balloon up, but when I met him he was thin and clean-cut. He always wore white T-shirts underneath his pinstriped oxfords, and he always wore penny loafers the proper way—that is, with a penny inserted into each one.

"You must be John," he said, shaking my hand and grinning. "Damned glad to meet you. *Damned* glad." Still holding my hand, he leaned in close and said, "This is probably a historic moment. One day biographers will write about the moment John McNally and Frank Mason first met. And here it is!" When he let go of my hand, he clapped my back and laughed.

I nodded. I wasn't sure what to say.

Frank said, "Think about it, *amigo*. Think of all the other writers who've come through this city. And here we are, me and you, a part of that history!"

"You know what?" I said. "I really need to take a leak."

"Oh. Sure. Down that hall, last door on the right."

I sat in the bathroom, and with the frosted window cracked a good inch, I smoked a cigarette. Biographers? Jesus. Who did this guy think he was? After my smoke, Frank helped me unload my car. I had only a few small boxes and a modest selection of clothes—not even enough belongings to break a sweat.

"Holy shit," I said once we were done and I began to walk around the apartment. "Look at all these goddamn *books*." I nodded toward his bookcase.

"Yeah; well," he said. "Occupational hazard, right?"

I pulled a few out, pushed them back in. It took me a while to realize what was so curious about the way he'd arranged them, but when I stepped back and looked at his collection as a whole, I saw what he'd done. He'd put them in alphabetical order by publisher. Atlantic Monthly Press, Black Sparrow Press, Capra Press, Ecco, New Directions, North Point, Norton, Penguin, Soho, Sun and Moon, Vintage Contemporaries. I found Raymond Carver in four different sections, including the bleak section consisting of one lonely McGraw-Hill book, an early Carver paperback with one of the ugliest covers I'd ever seen.

I thumped a few spines and said, "So tell me. Who're your favorite writers?"

"Contemporary?" he asked.

I shrugged. "Whatever."

"Hm." He scrunched up his face, as if he'd tasted something he expected to be sweet but was sour instead. It's a look, I've come to learn, that the privileged make when they're weighing a question of intellectual import. When he was ready to answer, he cleared his throat, took a deep breath, and said, "I really like what Rick Moody's doing. He's our generation's Nabokov. A great stylist. Amazing. And David Foster Wallace. He makes John Barth look like a little boy playing with Tonka trucks. Wallace is a genius. Hands down. I think William T. Vollman's work is staggering—mercilessly dark, intense—and, uh . . ." He paused. "Why are you making faces?"

"What?"

"Each time I say an author's name, you make a face."

"No, I don't."

"Yes, you do. If you don't like them, just say so."

"No, no, they're fine."

Frank squinted at me; he wasn't buying any of it.

"Really," I said. "You like those guys? Cool. It's you're opinion, bud. What's it to me? Why should I care?" I laughed. "I mean, *really*."

"All right," he said. "Okay. So tell me. Who do *you* like?"

"No one you'd care for."

"Try me. Who?"

"Nah." I shook my head and smiled. "Tell you what. Forget I asked, okay? I never saw someone get so up in arms over such a simple question." Frank was about to say something else, but I held up my palm. "Shhhh. Listen. Where's the phonebook? I could use a pizza. How about you? Are you hungry? I'm so hungry, I could eat a goddamn *horse*. I'm not kidding. A horse! Hooves and all. My treat."

Everyone always asks me if the Workshop is really as competitive and mean-spirited as it's rumored to be, and I honestly have to say that I don't remember much about the Workshop. Oh, I remember a few classes. I remember the director holding up one of the stories, as if it were a soiled undergarment, and asking if anyone else in the room smelled what he smelled. I remember a woman breaking down in tears and bolting from a classroom, never to be seen or heard from again. I remember a famous visiting editor telling a student that his novel didn't hold his interest beyond the first word, that no one would ever publish it, and that in the entire three hundred and sixty pages he saw only one vaguely interesting sentence. I remember how the people who won the top fellowships all hung out together while the ones who didn't get funding weren't invited to anything unless it was open to the public. But other than those few episodes, I really can't recall much and so couldn't say one way or the other if its reputation is earned.

What I *do* remember is the way sunlight would stream in through the bay window of our high-ceilinged Victorian apartment, and how some days a single beam of light illuminated my desk, as if God himself had singled me out to say, "YOU! YOU'RE THE ONE WHO'S GOING TO MAKE IT! THAT'S RIGHT—YOU!" I only noticed this beam of light because I wasn't actually sitting inside it. I was usually across the room, eating a bowl of Frankenberry or Count Chocula. Still, I liked how that beam hit my desk and made all the papers on it look as though they had caught fire, a sight that was either celestial or apocalyptic, I couldn't decide which.

One day, while I was admiring the beam of sunlight and imagining all the things that God might have been saying to me, Frank walked over to my desk and started reading a manuscript I had left next to my computer. He casually read the first page, but then something caught his eye on the second page, and he picked up the entire manuscript and started flipping through it. It was the manuscript I had submitted as part of my application to gain admittance into the Workshop.

Frank turned to me and said, "My *teacher* wrote this."

"Really? He was your *teacher?*"

I couldn't remember the author's name. I'd found the story in a book that had been out of print for twenty years. I had scanned it and fixed the typos, and then I'd sent it off to the Workshop with the rest of the junk they had asked for. I had *wanted* to send one of my own stories, but none of them seemed, well, ready. Fortunately, I had left my name off the copy of the manuscript that Frank was holding.

"That's funny," I said. "You know that John Gardner exercise? The one in *Art of Fiction*? You know the one—find a writer you admire and type up the entire story so that you get inside the *mind* of that writer? Do you know what I'm talking about? Yes? No? Anyway, that's what I did. What you're holding is my all-time favorite story from my all-time favorite book. That book changed my life. I'm not kidding. I found a copy in a used bookstore in Poughkeepsie. I was visiting my cousin at Vassar, and I popped into the store and there it was, that book, on the dollar rack. I'd never even *heard* of this guy before. And so I took the book back to my cousin's, read it in one sitting, and wham, it just blew me away. I mean, it's because of him, because of his book, that I decided to become a writer. It's because of him that I'm here. And you *know* him? Huh!"

"That's so *weird*," Frank said.

"It's not *that* weird," I said.

"No, I mean, what are the odds? His book's been out of print *forever*."

"Well, like I said, I found it in a used bookstore, and it's my favorite book, so it's not so weird when you look at it like that."

But Frank wouldn't drop it. Over the next few weeks he

kept bringing it up. "I can't get it out of my head."

"What?"

"That story you typed up."

"What story?"

"My professor's."

"What the fuck? Are you obsessing over this or *what?*"

"I have to be honest. Don't take this the wrong way, okay? When we first met, I didn't like you. But when I saw that story and you told me how much that book meant to you, I started thinking that we were destined to be roommates."

"Hm." I lit a cigarette. I nodded. "Well then it's fate, I guess," I said, and Frank, squinting from the smoke I blew at him, smiled.

I started dating a poet. Carrie Wilcox. I liked dating poets. They were always so screwed up emotionally but wild in bed. It seemed to me that you couldn't have the wild part without the screwed-up part, though it was certainly possible, even likely, to have the screwed-up part and not the wild part. Anyway, this poet was both screwed up *and* wild, and when we hit the sack, she liked to talk dirty, which was fine by me, but after the third time I was convinced that she was talking dirty to me in iambic pentameter. I don't think she *realized* what she was doing, but on around our fifth time together I reached off to the side and, with my fist, pounded the stressed words against the nightstand, and sure enough, it was iambic pentameter.

One night, after sex, she asked, "Why are you always pounding the table?"

"Huh? Oh, well, I'm trying to get into a rhythm."

"You need to pound the table to do that?"

"Sometimes," I said.

Another night, the two of us naked, each smoking a post-coital cigarette, Carrie asked, "Who are your favorite poets?"

I blew three smoke rings, then watched them bend and melt. "I don't read poetry," I said.

She didn't say anything for a while. I could hear her sucking on her own cigarette and then exhaling. Finally, she said, "*I'm* a poet, or did you forget that?"

"*You* know what I mean," I said.

"Oh. So you only read poetry if you're banging the poet? Is that it?"

I was momentarily paralyzed by the truth, but I knew Carrie didn't want me to tell her that she had figured it out.

"Oh, for Christ's sake," I said, sitting up and trying to act indignant. "All right. Who's your favorite nineteenth-century novelist?"

"Dickens," she said.

"Okay. *Twentieth*-century."

"Edith Wharton."

"No, no. *Living* twentieth-century novelist."

"Joyce Carol Oates."

"Shit!" I said, foiled at every turn. I tried thinking of a poet whose work I had read and remembered, any poet, any poet at all, but I couldn't think of a single name. It was as if that part of my brain had been surgically removed. "Ah, to hell with this," I said. "It's bullshit. That's what it is. Bull . . . *shit*." I rolled out of bed and started pacing the apartment. "Quizzing *me*," I said. "The nerve!"

Frank was over at his girlfriend's house—she was a poet, too—and so I walked over to Frank's desk and started reading a story that he was working on. It seemed only fair, since he'd violated my workspace. I knew that Frank didn't like for anyone to read his stories in-progress, but what the hell, it was only a story.

And so I picked up his latest opus, a novella, and flipped through it. There was a footnote after the first word in the story, but the footnote itself went on for the next twenty-two pages. Then came the second word and another twenty-two-page footnote. Then, well, you get the idea. It was revolting.

"Are you coming back to bed?" Carrie called out from the bedroom.

"In a sec," I said, but I never made it back to bed that night. I stayed up reading Frank's awful story, until my brained burned from reading so many single-spaced pages, my eyes bubbling inside my skull from his criminally small font. By the time I finished reading I knew that my life would forever be inextricably tied to Frank's, but not because we were friends. Oh, no. We *weren't* friends, we would *never* be friends, and I saw that now with perfect clarity.

The next night it was me and Frank and Carrie and Frank's girlfriend, Phebe, all of us out drinking at the Boar's Head. I liked Phebe. She was named after the shepherdess in *As You Like It*, as she was prone to add after being introduced, thereby defusing any questions. She was pale and had long, straight hair and big eyes, and whenever she spoke, you had to lean in close to hear what she was saying. The four of us were having a good time shooting pool, feeding the jukebox, and sharing drinking stories. I was having the best night I'd had since coming to town until Frank began to talk about writing.

"Let's go around," Frank said, "and tell each other about the worst thing we've ever written." He grinned slyly, his beady eyes darting from me to Phebe, from Phebe to Carrie, and then back to me.

"Oh, Frank," Carrie said. "What torture!"

Phebe said something, and when I said, "Huh? Didn't catch that," she leaned across the table and whispered into my ear, "*I like torture.*"

Frank chuckled. He twined his fingers together, like a schoolboy. He was wearing a Rolex, and every time he set his hands down, the watch's band clunked against the table. After the sixth time, I wanted to rip the goddamn thing off his arm and flush it down a toilet.

Carrie sighed and said, "Okay, I'll go first," and she told us about a poem she'd written when she was in high school, a love poem about a worm cut in half that, after regenerating, falls in love with its other half, as if the two parts had never been one.

"Oh my God!" Frank said. "That's *awful*. I love it!"

Phebe, offering mock sympathy, took hold of Carrie's hand and patted it.

I sipped my beer, lit another cigarette. My head was starting to throb.

Phebe went next. In a voice so soft you were forced to read her lips, she told us how she had always admired Sylvia Plath, and so she'd decided to tackle her own version of "Daddy," except that her version was titled "Uncle," and it was about her own abusive uncle, a Vietnam vet, whom she compared not to a Nazi, as Plath had done, but to the Khmer Rouge. Phebe took a drag off her cigarette. "Uncle," Phebe whispered. Cascades of smoke flowed from her mouth, her nose. "I was seventeen," she said. "I read it at an open mic, and everyone thought it was a parody and started to laugh. I was mortified. But who could blame them?"

"Uncle *Pol Pot!*" Frank bellowed. "*Priceless!* Absolutely *priceless!*"

Carrie leaned into me and said, "No more bare foot, Uncle!"

I nodded. I didn't know what the hell she was talking about.

Frank said, "Okay, my turn. I wrote this story back when I thought Hemingway and Fitzgerald were gods." He rolled his eyes, then wagged his head. "Anyway, I wrote this story about a boy named Ernie who goes fishing and meets a young lad named Francis, and they have this conversation about fish, but what they're really talking about are their own aesthetics. I wrote the passages from Ernie's point-of-view in the stripped-down, deadpan Hemingway style, and Francis's in this lush, rolling prose. Oh, and there was this not-so-subtle homoerotic subtext running through their conversation. I was playing with some things Hemingway had written about Fitzgerald in *A Moveable Feast*." His watch band clunked against the table, and he let out a long sigh. "What in the world was I thinking?" He laughed nervously.

No one said anything for a moment, and I was thinking it was because we were all embarrassed for the poor schlub, but then Carrie, pausing after each word, said, "That. Is. *Brilliant*."

Phebe kissed Frank's cheek. "My genius," she said.

Carrie turned to me. "*You're* a fiction writer. Isn't that a brilliant story idea?"

Frank held up his palm. "Stop it! Please! Stop! It's *awful*." He looked at me with fake desperation in his eyes. "Save me, John! Tell us your story. Hurry."

"I don't have one," I said.

"No fair," Carrie said.

"What I mean," I said, "is that they're all pretty bad. It would be hard to choose." I smashed my cigarette into the ashtray, twisting it back and forth.

"Be that way," Phebe whispered. She stuck her tongue out at me.

After last call, long after Phebe and Carrie had helped each other home, Frank and I burst out of the Boar's Head front door and stumbled down the stairs. I turned to Frank and said, "Rick Moody is a *terrible* writer," and I punched him as hard as I could in the mouth, dropping him to the ground. I had no idea what had come over me, and I immediately regretted punching him. "I'm sorry, I'm sorry," I said.

"Jesus *Christ*," Frank said. Blood trickled out the corner of his mouth.

"Oh, shit," I said. "Give me your hand."

"Get away from me," he said. "What the hell's your problem?"

"I don't know," I said.

"Jesus Christ," he said. "My jaw."

"Here," I said. "Let me help you."

Frank scooted away from my hand. "Get the hell away from me. I mean it."

"Okay," I said. "All right. It's not like I'm not sorry." *I tried to help him*, I thought. *At least I tried.*

Frank didn't come home that night. The next day, while heading for the library, I passed the Boar's Head and stopped at the spot where I had punched Frank. Dried blood dotted the sidewalk. A little ways away I saw a tooth. Frank's tooth. I picked it up, tucked it into my pocket, and continued on to the library.

I used to see Phebe around the coffeeshops and bookstores, but then I started bumping into her everywhere I went. The post office. The pedestrian mall. The video store.

"You again," Phebe said and smiled. She was wearing a black skirt with a black tank top. She always wore black.

I leaned in close and whispered, "Are you stalking me?"

"I was thinking it was the other way around," she said. "I attract stalkers, you know. I'm a stalker magnet."

"Maybe I'm stalking you and not even realizing it," I said.

"Could be."

Frank, of course, had told Phebe the story about me punching him, but I could tell that she was the sort of girl who invited a certain amount of danger into her life, that danger was, in fact, the only thing that made her feel truly alive. I've known more than one writer drawn to the dark side, as it were. The truth, of course, is that they're attracted to *fake* danger. Drop them off at, say, Cabrini Green in Chicago or a crack house in the Bronx, and *then* let's see how long their interest in danger lasts. *Real* danger would scare the living shit out of them, but this sort of danger—one writer punching another— gives them a charge, a jolt. It's just enough danger to make them pleasantly light-headed.

Phebe and I hooked up that afternoon—we went straight from the video store back to her place—and for the next week we were inseparable. Instead of talking dirty in iambic pentameter, Phebe would lie awake after sex and talk about death. Anything having to do with death captivated her. She had an encyclopedic memory for the strange ways that various people had died. A man retrieving linen gets trapped inside a spinning dryer and dies. An old woman gets her arm stuck in a sofa bed and, unable to reach her phone for days, dies. A bald man, after applying glue to a toupee while inside his car, lights a cigarette; the glue fumes instantly ignite, the entire car becomes engulfed in flames, and the bald man, well, he dies. Phebe's stories were endless. She would talk about death for hours and hours until I'd fallen sound asleep, but later in the night, haunted by everything she'd said, I'd wake up screaming. It's what I imagined it would be like shacking up with Kübler-Ross—albeit a young and sexy Kübler-Ross, what Kübler-Ross might have been like if she'd shacked up with Masters and Johnson.

Phebe split up with Frank over the phone, and although I hadn't officially said anything to Carrie one way or the other about breaking up, I hadn't gone out of my way to get together with her, either. Phebe and I both agreed that it would be a good idea to keep our little fling, or whatever it was, to ourselves.

"I don't want to hurt Frank," she said.

"Me neither," I said. "I like the guy."

"Then why did you punch him?"

"I don't know," I said. "I guess I don't like him *that*

much."

One night, after Phebe and I had smoked all of Frank's pot that I had taken from his desk drawer, Phebe turned to me and said, "When did you first become interested in me?"

"When you stuck your tongue out at me," I said.

"When was that?"

"The night I punched Frank."

"Oh, yeah. I remember now." She thought for a moment, her eyelids dope-heavy. "Really? When I stuck my tongue out at you?"

"Absolutely," I said. "It's a very sexual thing to do, you know, sticking your tongue out at somebody. It's probably the most erotic thing one person can do to another person, especially if they don't know each other."

Staring intensely into my eyes, Phebe stuck her tongue out at me.

"Jesus," I said and pinned her to the bed. She laughed but kept her tongue out. "You're killing me," I said. "You know that, don't you? You're frickin' killing me."

I hope I'm not going on too long here—I know there's a word limit on these contributors' notes—but I should probably tell you a little about my past. My father was a carnie. He worked all the games. Ring a Bottle. Balloon Water Race. Skee Ball. He helped assemble and then operate the rides, too—the Zipper, Pharaoh's Fury, the Hurricane. "NOT FOR THE WEAK OF STOMACH!" my father would yell at anyone who walked by. "NOT FOR THE FAINT OF HEART!" After my mother died, when I was five years old, I started traveling with my dad from city to city, state to state, living off a steady diet of Sno-Cones, fried dough with butter, and Italian sausage sandwiches. We had a dog, too. Rosco. Rosco never barked. He'd sit next to my father and chew gum all day long. I swear, my father'd spit out a wad of Dentyne and the dog would pick it up and start chewing. He even moved it from one side of his mouth to the other, the way my dad did, and he'd watch my father unwrap a new stick and start chewing it. And sometimes I'd sit in a lawn chair and chew gum and watch Rosco chewing gum watching my father chew gum, and I'd start thinking all kinds of crazy things, like how maybe I was a figment of somebody's imagination, and how I had no will of my own, that whatever they wanted me to do, I'd do. But whose imagination? And why me? Some days, sitting at the precise center of the midway, I'd drive myself nuts thinking about stuff like that. Sometimes it made me feel like weeping, I swear to Christ, but other times it made me feel like I could do anything I wanted, since it wasn't really me doing any of those things. If I was no more than a figment of somebody else's imagination, then the repercussions would be figments, too, right?

I don't know why any of this is important—it's probably not—but I guess I wanted to put it here so that people could see how different I was from someone like Frank or Carrie or Phebe. In terms of the Workshop, I was an anomaly. I didn't go to the Ivy Leagues. I didn't go to prep school. After being homeschooled, I went to junior college. After ju-co, I went to state. Not the big state school, either. One of the satellite schools. I didn't take any creative writing courses. I hold a degree from the Department of Mortuary Science and Funeral Service. Funeral Studies, I called it. The way I figured, not every town has its own funeral home, and yet we live in a country that has exponential population growth. I'd have opened up my own funeral home, too, except that I didn't have the money and couldn't get a loan. Bank after bank turned me down. *Why should we loan you any money?* they asked. *Why should we assume all the risk for someone with no collateral and no job history?* This is what happens when you're the son of a carnie, and this is why the very sight of Frank was like having a dagger rammed through my head—in one ear, out the other.

It wasn't that Frank owned so much shit. He *did* own a lot of shit, but I didn't care about that. What irked me was that Frank wrote heaps of meaningless crap, one steaming page after another, and that this same crap would garner awards, money, jobs, maybe even fame. He was clever, and he was being patted on the back for being clever, but there was a hollowness at the core of every word he wrote. His stories were all surface, all technique. A lot of fireworks. A lot of sleight of hand. But in the end, what were his stories about? Nothing. Page after page of diddly-squat.

Maybe this is why I started dating Phebe. I wanted to deprive Frank of what little substance filled his otherwise shallow life. I wanted him to earn it. But I have to confess, I fell for Phebe. I fell hard, too. All her talk about death sent me reeling back to those lazy undergraduate days of sitting in my Funeral classes, gorgeous fall afternoons with orange leaves blowing past the windows, the professor's macabre lectures lulling me to sleep. And now, however many years later, I fell asleep thinking about me and Phebe living together in some sleepy rural town. I would be Funeral Home Director, and Phebe would be my haunted poet wife, writing morbid villanelles about the dead men and women who passed through our halls. I wanted to tell her about this fantasy, but I couldn't ever muster the courage. I was afraid she'd laugh at me. I should have risked the humiliation, but I didn't. I couldn't.

"When I die," Phebe said one night, "I want to be aware of the moment. I want to be cognizant. I want someone there with me so that I can describe it. I want to take them right up to the point where I cross the line from life to death. I want to describe it without embellishment. I want to be accurate and objective yet vivid. Is it possible to be accurate and objective and vivid all at once? Probably not. Still, I think one should *try*. I think it's possible to come *close*." Into my ear she whispered, "I want that to be my final poem." She licked my earlobe, then began to nibble on it. I don't think I'd ever been happier than at that very moment. I was about to roll her over onto her back, maybe chew on her ear, when someone knocked on her door. It was two in the morning.

"Oh, shit," she said. "Who's that?"

"Want me to get it?" I asked.

Phebe shook her head. She creaked off the bed and tip-toed to the door. She didn't have a peephole. She didn't have a safety chain. Her apartment was a burglar's dream. She opened the door. I couldn't see anything, but Phebe's voice was surprisingly loud, and I knew that this was for my benefit. I appreciated her concern.

"Frank?" she said. "What are you doing here? It's two in the morning."

Frank said something, but I couldn't hear what.

"I'm really tired," Phebe said. "Can't we talk tomor-row?"

And then I heard him: "Is that John's coat?"

"What?"

"John. Is he here?" He called out my name: "John! Are you here? John, you son of a bitch."

"Go away," I yelled.

"Don't," Phebe said.

I could hear Frank's footsteps; he was heading my way. I was naked and not in the mood to deal with the situation at hand.

"I've got a crowbar," I said. "I'll knock out the rest of your teeth if you come in here." He stopped walking. "I'm serious," I said. The footsteps retreated. Frank and Phebe whispered something, and then the door shut. When Phebe returned, I could tell she'd been crying.

"At least he's gone," I said. "The nerve!" I sighed. I shook my head. "What did he look like when I told him I had a crow-bar? What was the look on his face? Jesus, at least I didn't have to get out of bed. I mean, I'm *naked*. Could you imagine? And what the hell time is it, anyway?"

"I think you should go," she said.

"What? Are you serious?"

Phebe nodded. "I'm not ready for this. I'm sorry."

"Ready for what? Two minutes ago you were ready for *death*. What's this compared to death?"

Phebe stood silent, waiting for me to get off her bed and put my clothes back on.

"Oh, for Christ's sake. Okay, okay," I said. "I'll go." But there was no place to go. I didn't want to return to my apartment and find Frank sitting there in his ridiculous penny loafers, waiting for me. And I couldn't pop in on Carrie, not after avoiding her calls. I walked to Liberty Park and found a bench. I fell asleep. At some point in the night, a cop poked me in the ribs with a billy club.

"Up, up," he said. "The park's closed." When I stood, he said, "This time you get a warning. Next time you'll get a ticket for vagrancy. Do we understand each other?"

I stood. I rubbed the sleep-glue from my eyes. "Perfectly," I said.

Two days after the incident with Frank at Phebe's apartment, I bumped into a classmate who told me that the director of the Workshop wanted to talk to me. Since I'd never spoken to the director, and since I was pretty sure he hadn't, until recently, even known my name, I knew his wanting to see me wasn't a good sign.

I wish I could say that I had always wanted to be a writer, but this isn't true. I had wanted to be an astronaut, too. I had wanted to be a sharpshooter. I had wanted to be a physicist, a bounty hunter, and a zookeeper. Nearly everything interested me as much as anything else. But now that the director of the Workshop wanted to talk to me, I suddenly wanted nothing more in life than to be a writer. I wanted to win the PEN/ Faulkner. I wanted a Guggenheim, an NEA. I wanted to hang out with the Southern mafia—Barry Hannah, Harry Crews, and the rest of those ass-kickers. I wanted to shoot the shit with these guys. Who cared that I didn't have a drop of Southern blood in me? What did it matter? I wanted to give readings at City Lights, Tattered Cover, Square Books. I wanted everything that came with being a writer, and I wanted it so much, my heart literally hurt to think about it.

The director, slouched in his chair when I arrived at his office, had my application materials spread before him on his desk. Also on his desk was a copy of the book from which I had pilfered the story—the story I had used to gain admittance into the Workshop.

"McNally," he said. "You know what this means, don't you?" He was in his fifties but had a boyish face, and I thought maybe we could work this out, that I could show him some things I'd actually written as proof that I did indeed deserve a spot in the Workshop. I wanted to make a case that by plagiarizing I was actually doing this long-neglected author a favor. No one had paid attention to this man's work for twenty years, and by using his all-but-unknown story to get into the famous Writers' Workshop, I was saying, "Look, here's a writer who's just as good as any of these new punks who think they're hot shit!" Before I could say anything, the director said, "Your writing career is over. You fucked up. Big time. This is serious."

"You want me out of the Workshop?" I asked.

"No," he said. "I want you out of this town."

"Out of *town?* Are you *serious?* Can you *do* that?"

That night, in protest, I set up a makeshift tent in the director's backyard until he called the police. The police officers weren't interested in hearing my side of the story, but they didn't want to go through the hassle of arresting me, either.

"What do you do in town?" the short cop asked me.

"I'm in the Writers' Workshop," I said.

"Oh," the other cop said. "One of *them.*" He cleared his

throat, then spat on a tree.

The short cop said, "Okay. Run along now, John Grisham."
The other cop tried holding back his snicker but couldn't.

Later that same night I set up a tent in the backyard of
the visiting writer. The visiting writer was a brooding, tortured
man who had a reputation for nailing anything that moved,
and so I thought maybe he wouldn't be quite so judgmental,
but when he saw me hammering in posts, he came bolting out
of his house with a stun gun and told me he was going to beat
the living shit out of me if I didn't pack up and get the hell off
his property. This, I might add, from a National Book Award
winner!

I didn't really see that what I had done was so terrible,
certainly not terrible enough to justify getting chased out of
town, but with no place left to go I didn't have much of a
choice. My car had quit working shortly after moving to town,
so early the next morning I hitched a ride east. In little over an
hour, we were in another state. As fast as that, one phase of my
life was over, and a new one had begun.

Four years went by without any news of Frank, and then,
in a single month, his work appeared in *Zoetrope, McSweeney's,*
and *GQ*. Not much later I read in *Publishers Weekly* that he
had landed a six-figure advance from FSG based on half of
what sounded like the worst novel ever to be written. It was
described as what the Warren Commission Report would read
like if Richard Brautigan had written it. Could you *imagine?*
Who'd *want* to read the Warren Commission Report written by
Richard Brautigan? But there you have it—New York publishing in a nutshell. They'll give Frank six figures, the book will
sell ten copies, and everyone will wonder what the hell just
happened. Or maybe the book will sell 100,000 copies, and for
the next two years we'll suffer a string of copycat books, some-

thing along the lines of the Starr Report written by Jhumpa La-
hiri or the 9/11 Commission Report by David Foster Wallace.
And so, against everyone's better judgment, Frank Mason was
on his way up. The son of a bitch had made it.

I never really gave up the notion of becoming a writer,
even though the whole episode at the Workshop had soured
me on the politics of it all. What I did was wrong. I'll admit
that. I used poor judgment, and I deserved the boot. Still,
something about the way things happened, about the way it
all shook down, rubbed me the wrong way. I was having a difficult time putting my finger on it until I saw a publicity photo
of Frank—a headshot. In it, Frank is smiling, damned glad to
have landed his big-ass book deal, but if you look closely, you
can see the missing tooth, the one I had knocked out. Here's
a guy who could afford to get the tooth replaced but didn't.
He was showing it off. Someone told me that pirates pierced
an ear every time they survived a storm at sea, and I couldn't
help wondering if this was how Frank saw himself, as some
kind of literary equivalent to the pirate, his gap serving as
proof that he was a survivor. And then it came to me, what
it was that had rubbed me the wrong way about the Workshop: *Frank*. Frank and his god-awful writing. Frank and how
everyone had been duped into believing he was some kind
of genius, always cleverly turning a phrase, punning his way
down the page, footnoting, those vile footnotes, and how his
stories had no story, his characters no heart, no brains of their
own. Frank. I was *glad* I had knocked his tooth out, but now he
was out there parading the gap, the bastard. Seeing his picture
made me want to punch him all over again. I'd be lying if I
said otherwise.

I went through a long period of not really knowing what
to do with myself. A few summers ago, I bought a junk car, a
real beater, for about a hundred bucks. It was really a piece of

shit. It wobbled when I drove it, and bouquets of foam periodically exploded from the seats. I spray-painted the car about
a million different colors, and then I gave it a name—*Purple
America*—the title of one of Rick Moody's awful books. I took
the car to a literary festival where Rick Moody was teaching,
parked it in the parking lot of an out-of-business gas station
just before you entered the festival grounds, and I charged
people five bucks to hit it with a sledgehammer. Five bucks,
five whacks. By the end of the festival, the car was entirely
flat. I'm not kidding. Mostly it was punk kids paying the five
bucks, kids who'd heard about it from other punk kids, kids
who didn't know Rick Moody from a wingback chair, but a
few conference participants eventually wandered out, paid
their money, and took their whacks at the car. One kid was
a Richard Yates fan; his name was Michael, and I shook his
hand. "Good man," I said, slapping him on the back before
he knocked the sideview mirrors off the car and punched a
hole through the roof with his remaining three whacks. I kept
hoping someone from *Poets & Writers* would catch wind of
what I was doing and write a piece about it, but this didn't
happen. I considered pulling this stunt again at another conference, getting a Pinto wagon and naming it *Infinite Jest* or *The
Corrections*, but I didn't have the energy or the money or the
desire to travel across the country. My will, I'm sad to say, was
almost gone.

It's no secret: I went through a bad depression. I had
trouble holding down jobs. I moved from city to city, picking
up work wherever I could find it, whatever would get me by. I
worked as a lumberjack, a short-order cook, a carnival barker.
Nothing steady. Nothing lucrative. Nothing particularly grati-
fying in any meaningful way.

Most recently, I worked as a groundskeeper at a resort
in Vermont. Occasionally, businessmen would bulldoze into
our sleepy little town for a two-day huddle, or a congrega-
tion of Bible thumpers would descend upon us for a weekend

retreat. I didn't mind. I like meeting new people. I like seeing
the world through the eyes of someone who's not the least bit
like me. But then a writers' conference set up camp for an entire week, and wannabe writers came pouring in from all over
the country. Oh, they came with their laptops and precious
manuscripts and dog-eared copies of the most recent *Novel
and Short Story Writer's Market*. Agents and editors were arriving, too, and every last amateur writer thought that a book
contract was headed their way. They carried their book-length
manuscripts to their chests as if transporting bombs about to
be detonated. The faculty stayed together in the main lodge,
the same men and women of American letters you'll see at
every conference, year after year. Conference whores, every
last one. It makes you admire a guy like Delillo all the more.
You may not care for what the man writes, but at least he's not
twirling a baton at every parade.

Disgusted, I was all but ready to take the week off from
work when I saw in the distance my old friend Frank Mason.
Old Frankie boy. He'd put on a little weight—okay, a *lot* of
weight—and every time I saw him he was wearing a sport
jacket over whatever else he was wearing—T-shirt, oxford
button-down, Hawaiian shirt. It was so Frank. Frank to a goddamned tee. And watching him, day after day, made all those
old feelings bubble back to the surface, until I was feeling how
I'd felt that night we stepped out of the Boar's Head and I had
popped him in the mouth.

One morning I was sitting outside and smoking a cigarette and thinking about Phebe. Phebe was my biggest regret.
You meet someone like Phebe only once, if you're lucky, and
I should have tried harder to stay with her. But I didn't. And
so I smoked my cigarette and imagined myself dying some
pointless yet bizarre death, and then I imagined Phebe in bed
telling her latest lover about it: *Writer, on his way to the post
office to mail the final draft of his first novel to his publisher, stops
to pack a snowball for the first time in years. An icicle breaks loose*

five stories above, stabs the writer through the head, and kills him. I was trying to picture the nearly blank expression on Phebe's face as she tells the story to the man beside her, when I heard someone calling my name. I knew it was him before I even turned around.

"Frank!" I said, and I must have sounded and looked genuinely glad to see him, because he smiled at the sound of his own name. "How the hell are you?" I asked.

"Good, good. It's, well, it's sort of ironic seeing you here."

"Really?" I said. "Why's that?"

Frank looked down at his shoes, as if the answers were written on the tips. "It's just that I've been putting the final touches on a story about that time in my life." He paused, then added, "*Our* life."

"Oh, really?"

Frank frowned. "Listen. About that business back at the Workshop. I feel rotten about it. I really do. I mean, what you did was wrong, you shouldn't have used someone else's story to get in, but I should have handled it differently. We should have talked about it first. I should have given you a chance to turn yourself in. I mean, I think they'd have gone easier on you. I heard what happened."

"What happened?"

"About the blacklist."

"What blacklist?"

Frank stared at me, as if to see if I was for real or not. "All right. Let's forget it, okay? It's just good to see you. I've been wanting to apologize all these years now, but I had no idea where you were."

"You know my motto," I said. "'No apologies.'"

Frank grimaced. He nodded. "Well, I should go. I'm teaching a workshop in about, oh"—he looked at his Rolex—"two minutes."

We shook hands, and then I was alone again. What I

didn't tell Frank was that I still had his tooth. I'd been carrying it around for so long, there was a nub in my wallet where
I kept it tucked, and my driver's license looked like somebody
had bitten it.

What happened next is the sort of thing I probably
shouldn't admit. In fact, when I began writing this little piece,
I'd had no intention of admitting what really happened, but
you know how it is—sometimes the only way to get real satisfaction out of what you've done is to tell someone. Otherwise,
what's the point?

While Frank taught his workshop, delivering piercing
insights to the starry-eyed masses, I keyed into his room for
a peek around. It was here that I found his story. I sat on the
edge of his bed and started reading it. By the end of the second
page, my hands were shaking. I couldn't stop shaking, either.
The story was about me, about *us*, me and Frank, and about
how I had gotten booted out of the Workshop. He'd written
the story from my point of view—*my* point of view!—cleverly
speculating on why I had done what I had done by inserting a
brief section about my carnie past, and though I wanted to hate
it—in the abstract, the story epitomized every stinking thing
that I hated about Frank's writing—I fell, against my will, into
the story's grasp. It kills me to admit, but Frank had brilliantly
captured the way I saw the world and, in particular, why I
hated him so much. To Frank's credit, no one came off looking particularly good, not even Frank himself, who, through
my eyes, was a sad clown, a buffoon of pretense. Frank had
even captured my vocabulary, my diction, the cadence of my
speech. I had to give it to the old boy. He'd brought me fully
alive on the page. He'd pumped blood into my veins, and the
result was downright scary. I was more alive on the page than
I'd ever been in life. And when I read the part about punching Frank outside the Boar's Head, the hair on my arms rose.
I read that passage a half-dozen times. As soon as I'd finish it,
I'd start back at the top and read it again:

```
After last call, long after Phebe and
Carrie had helped each other home, Frank
and I burst out of the Boar's Head front
door and stumbled down the stairs. I
turned to Frank and said, "Rick Moody is
a terrible writer," and I punched him as
hard as I could in the mouth, dropping
him to the ground. I had no idea what
had come over me, and I immediately
regretted punching him. "I'm sorry, I'm
sorry," I said.
```

Each time I read it, I laughed out loud. But it had another effect on me, too: my pulse sped up, and an artery in my neck began to throb. I *felt* it. I could have been standing outside the Boar's Head with Frank right then and there; that's how real it felt. There wasn't a false note. *Beautiful*, I thought. *Perfect*.

I folded the story and tucked it into my shirt. After a few more minutes of searching, I found a set of disks for his novel. I recognized the title from the article about him in *Publishers Weekly*. I slipped the disks into my back pocket. I walked from the main lodge straight to my car, and once I drove out of the resort, I never returned.

I don't feel guilty taking Frank's story because his story is, after all, my story, and someone like Frank needs to learn that you can pluck away at someone else's life only so long before the one getting plucked rears up and attacks.

I'm even contemplating filing a lawsuit. I'd file it against Frank for stealing my novel. I'm the one with the disks, after all. I'm the one with solid proof of all my hard work. I know, I know. It'd be a rotten thing to do. And, yes, there are times I wonder if I've already gone too far. But what else are my options? Do I keep taking one shitty job after another? How long can one live this kind of piecemeal life?

And so I spend my days now trying to figure out where my writing should go from here. What next? And when I'm not thinking about writing, I'm thinking about Phebe. I saw recently a review of Phebe's first volume of poetry. "Hauntingly refreshing," the review called it. "Sylvia Plath on acid," it concluded—whatever *that's* supposed to mean. It could have been sweet, me and Phebe together. It could have been a really sweet life. Every time I see her name in print, I feel the breath leave my lungs, and a weightlessness settles into my chest. What, I wonder, will become of me now? Who am I? Some mornings I wake up and listen for the sound of my own beating heart. Only then do I know that I am alive. Then and only then do I know for sure that I am not a figment of someone else's wild imagination.

for Frank Mason

NOTES ON THE STORIES

While the vast majority of the stories in this book are purely the product of my imagination, a few of the stories (notably the ones based on actual people) were inspired by snippets of anecdotes from other sources. I have tried to remember where most of these anecdotes originated, but it's entirely possible that my memory, weak as it is, has failed me in a few instances.

"The Goose": The anecdote about Frazier Thomas taking the bus to and from work came from *The Golden Age of Chicago Children's Television* by Ted Okuda and Jack Mulqueen, an infinitely fascinating book for anyone who grew up in Chicago in the 1960s or 1970s.

"At the Chateau Marmont, Bungalow 5": I first read about John Belushi picking "Rantoul rag" many years ago in the controversial Belushi biography *Wired* by Bob Woodward. The story stayed with me in large part because I spent three years in the 1980s driving past the Rantoul, Illinois, exit on my way back and forth from Chicago to Carbondale, where I attended college. Recently, I looked for other sources to confirm that this anecdote was in fact true (not that it made much of a difference for my purposes, but I was curious), and I found essentially the same story in a book titled *Belushi* by John's widow, Judith Belushi Pisano, and Tanner Colby.

"The Something Something": I discovered the following quote about Gene Siskel in an entry for him on The Internet Movie Datebase (www.imdb.com): "Hated nothing worse than trying to watch a movie while a baby in the theatre is crying. Hates any mother who would bring an infant to a movie theatre and is willing to pay $10 to any usher who would chuck the baby out of the theatre along with its negligent mother." Where this information originally came from, I can't say.

"Samsonite": For an account of the Democratic National Convention of 1968, I read John Schultz's fascinating book *No One Was Killed.*

"Ascension": There are numerous accounts of George Pullman's involvement in the raising of Chicago. The actual year that Tremont House was raised, however, varies depending upon the source.

"The End is Nothing, the Road is All": I read numerous books about Nelson Algren, Simone de Beauvoir, and Jean-Paul Sartre, but the two books that were the most useful for this story were *A Transatlantic Love Affair: Letters to Nelson Algren* by Simone de Beauvoir and *Nelson Algren: A Life on the Wild Side* by Bettina Drew.

As for some of the other details...the host of the children's show in "I See Johnny" is entirely fictional; I doubt that Roger Ebert and Gene Siskel ever engaged in a public fight of the kind found in "The Something Something"; I don't know of any road trip ever taken by Walter Payton and William Perry; I found very little written about Richard J. Daley's childhood; and although Nelson Algren purportedly spoke to the homeless, Jimmy is my own creation.

ABOUT THE COVER

While I was teaching at Columbia College Chicago in the spring of 2007, the college website's homepage featured photography by their students, along with links to portfolios of the photographers' work. It was here that I found this wonderful and eerie photo of a decrepit and abandoned building. I was nearing completion of my book, and though I had not designed any of my previous books' covers, I began to wonder what the cover of *Ghosts of Chicago* might look like. I really can't articulate why, but this particular photo captured for me the mood I was searching for: colorful rooms, full of decay. Before contacting the photographer, I started tinkering with the photo: cropping it, superimposing text onto it – in short, turning it into the cover of my book. It was a presumptuous act, and I would have been deeply disappointed if I hadn't been able to secure permission to use the photograph (especially since I reworked the cover numerous times over a several month period), but the photographer proved to be both supportive and generous. Her name is Mary Farmilant, and I urge you to check out her work.

Mary Farmilant, a Chicago-based artist, received her MFA in Photography from Columbia College Chicago. Farmilant's work has garnered many awards, including the 2007 Illinois Artists Fellowship Award, the Follett Fellowship, and a Ragdale Artist Residency, among others. She currently teaches photography at Columbia College Chicago and Gallery 37 for the Arts. Her website is www.maryfarmilant.com.

ABOUT THE AUTHOR

John McNally is the author of two novels, *America's Report Card* and *The Book of Ralph*. His previous story collection, *Troublemakers*, won the John Simmons Short Fiction Award and the Nebraska Book Award, and was a Book Sense 76 selection. His short story "The Immortals" was a 2005 National Magazine Award finalist, and his story "Creature Features" received a citation in *Best American Short Stories*, 2007. A native of Chicago's southwest side and a former Visiting Writer at Columbia College Chicago, John is presently Associate Professor of English at Wake Forest University in Winston-Salem, North Carolina, where he lives with his wife, Amy, and their many animals. Visit his website: www.bookofralph.com